WHITE HEAT

[AN ACID VANILLA THRILLER]

ANNIHILATION PEST CONTROL
BOOK 1

MATTHEW HATTERSLEY

BOOM BOOM PRESS

GET YOUR FREE BOOK

Discover how Acid Vanilla transformed from a typical London teenager into the world's deadliest female assassin.

Get the Acid Vanilla Prequel Novel:
Making a Killer available FREE at:

www.matthewhattersley.com/mak

CHAPTER 1

Zelenograd is a city thirty-seven kilometres northwest of central Moscow, along the Leningradskoye Shosse highway. It is a quiet and pleasant city, in the main. Unassuming, many would say. The inhabitants are regular people. They go about their day – working and playing, striving and praying – all the while unaware that two hundred metres below street level is a huge secret enclave, built around the end of the Cold War. For many years this underground lair lay unused and dormant, until sometime in the early 90s when it was rediscovered and repurposed by one of the most shadowy and feared gangsters of the Russian mob. Artem 'Mad Dog' Perchetka.

Unlike many criminal bosses who rapidly accumulated wealth in the 1990s via the Russian privatisations that followed the dissolution of the Soviet Union, Perchetka chose to remain a dissident rather than become an oligarch. He'd always relished his status as someone who lived below the law. Below the surface, even. Besides, you couldn't 'go legit' in the eyes of society and still chop your enemy's limbs off when the mood took you – or take a group of old friends (now oligarchs) out to the Kara Sea and dump their decapitated bodies into the briny deep. The name Mad Dog wasn't an ironic or whimsical pet name. He was given it for a reason.

In his large office in the epicentre of his subterranean stronghold, Perchetka sat back in his large leather-backed chair and sipped on an ice-cold can of Pepsi.

The Choice of a New Generation.

He had it flown in especially from the US, and the large refrigerator humming gently in the corner was stocked full of the stuff. God help the man responsible if he ever went to take a can and found his stock depleted. Artem Perchetka loved Pepsi. He loved it. Most criminal bosses might have had a tasty glass of chilled vodka and puffed on an expensive cigar as an outward display of their wealth and status, but for Perchetka it was Pepsi. And Michael Jackson memorabilia. The Mad Dog loved Michael Jackson almost as much as he loved torturing to death those who wronged him. Not only had the pop sensation produced the finest music known to humanity, and in *Thriller* and *Bad* the two best albums of all time, but, like Pepsi, he was a symbol of American culture and capitalism. To own pieces of him was to own America itself. That's how Perchetka saw it, at least. And you disagreed with him at your peril.

For the last ten years, he'd been buying any Jacko memorabilia he could get his hands on – clothing, tour passes, white label vinyl. His collection was extensive and displayed proudly on the walls of his office and along the corridors leading to it. Today, in 2003, the collection was valued at around six million US dollars. But he would never sell it. These were his status symbols. His way of showing the world he'd arrived. Screw those pompous oligarchs with their mansions and their yachts; this was how true crime lords should live. Underground, surrounded by the trappings of other kings, sipping from the brown nectar of freedom.

He placed his fresh can of Pepsi down on his black-lacquered desktop. He'd heard footsteps in the corridor outside. Heavy boots on concrete. Sitting up, he adjusted himself into a thoughtful pose and gazed off into the middle distance as loud knocking emanated through the steel door of his office.

He gave it a few seconds, nodding sagely to himself to get further into character. Then, "Enter."

The door creaked open to reveal two thickset men who looked as though they'd already seen far too much of life. Grigor Lebedev and Gilal Ivanov were their names (Perchetka made sure he knew the name of every man who worked for him); they were new recruits, hired for their experience in the Felix Group in the late 1990s. The group – named after the founder of the Soviet secret police, Felix Dzerzhinsky, and more of a death squad, some said – was comprised of former operatives of the KGB and other state security agencies. It functioned to liquidate corrupt Russian government officials, and its members were deadly and uncompromising. Two traits Perchetka demanded in all his men. Those, and total adherence to his orders.

"What is it?" he asked, still staring at a point on the wall, not completely acknowledging either of the men. When no answer came, he looked over to see them both staring at Michael Jackson's white crystal-studded glove hanging in a glass case to the right of the door. The one the King of Pop had worn for his unforgettable performance of *Billie Jean* on Motown's 25th anniversary TV special. The glove was Perchetka's favourite part of his collection, so he couldn't blame them for staring. This was their first time visiting his office since they'd started working for him, and it was a lot to take in. There were such wonders here.

As he cleared his throat, the two men snapped their attention away from the memorabilia.

"What is it?" he asked again.

Lebedev held up a silver platter, on top of which was a mobile phone. "We have him on the line, sir. As you requested."

Perchetka leaned forward and placed his hands on the desk in front of him. "He's on the phone right now?" he whispered. When Lebedev nodded, Perchetka straightened his spine and lowered his voice as he continued. "Excellent. Bring it here. I shall speak to him."

Lebedev walked up to the front of the desk and lowered the platter, presenting the mobile phone to his boss with the confident air of a wine waiter in an expensive restaurant. Not that Perchetka liked eating in expensive restaurants. Or wine waiters, for that matter.

Giving Lebedev a solemn nod, he picked up the phone and held it to his ear. "This is Artem Perchetka," he said. "I trust you know who I am?"

The line was silent for a moment, and then a man's voice spoke. "Of course. Everyone worth their salt knows The Mad Dog of Moscow."

Perchetka wrinkled his nose. "Excellent. And I trust this is a secure line?"

"You don't have to worry about that."

"Good. Then I have some work for you. An ex-friend and ex-colleague of mine, Boris Bakov, has recently defected to the United States. I believe he is meeting with the CIA in return for a safe haven. I cannot let this happen. He knows too much. About me and my associates here in Russia."

The man on the line made a low growling noise. "We both know you're a man of means. Why aren't you dealing with it in-house?"

Perchetka sat back and stretched out his wide chest, delighting a little as Lebedev's eyes fell on the *Bad* tour shirt he was wearing under his silk bomber jacket. He'd bought the shirt in Munich in 1988, on the second leg of Michael's first solo world tour. "For the past ten years, I have operated away from the light," he said. "I am well known – and feared – in certain circles, and nothing but a rumour in others. I hope to change this in the coming years, but for now I cannot risk killing a Russian national on US soil, especially one seeking sanctuary there. If Bakov's death is linked to me in any way, it would be unfortunate. Which is why we are having this conversation. I was told your organisation was the best in the world."

The man's growl turned into a gruff laugh. "You were told correctly. We're the best. Second to none."

"Excellent. And if you do know who I am, then I don't need to tell you whatever I ask of you must be carried out to my exacting standards. For once, I am not trying to send a message or exact any type of hideous revenge – although I would very much enjoy that, and that disgusting man deserves it. Simply, I need him silenced and without fuss. Thus, I want Bakov's death to look like an accident. Do you understand?"

"Of course."

"I also need the work done promptly. In the next ten days."

"Also not a problem. And in terms of our fee...?"

Perchetka smiled to himself. "I got your message. And I agree with the terms. Two hundred thousand US dollars, to be paid on proof of the job being carried out to my instructions. Once I know there is no link to me or my associates and the CIA has put the matter to bed, you will get another hundred thousand. This is fair, yes?"

"Sounds more than fair, old boy. I'll get my best people on it straight away. You won't hear from me now until I have proof of completion."

Perchetka beckoned Lebedev closer, narrowing his eyes as he finished the call. "Thank you, Mr Caesar. I know I can rely on you to get this done."

"Count on it. This is our bread and butter, old boy. We won't let you down."

"I hope not." He winked at Lebedev. "Goodbye, Mr Caesar."

He hung up the call and placed it back on the offered platter.

"Is all good?" Lebedev asked.

"Oh yes," Perchetka said. "All good. Now the fun begins."

CHAPTER 2

Spitfire Creosote rocked his weight onto his back foot, grounding himself in a defensive stance. In front of him, the young assassin steadied herself, but he could tell from the tension in the muscles around her eyes and at the edge of her jaw that she was preparing to attack.

He raised his chin and smiled, counting on a display of conceit not only intimidating her but also riling her into making a mistake.

"Come on, girl. What are you waiting for?"

She didn't respond but raised her fists higher; one to guard her face, the other poised to strike. She didn't blink as Spitfire stared into her eyes.

Acid Vanilla.

She was certainly a fiery young thing. Having only turned twenty a month earlier, she was already making a big impression in the ranks of Annihilation Pest Control. She was focused, intelligent, eager to learn, and with an uncommon way of approaching situations that often gave her a supreme edge. In an instant, she could switch from being cold, calculating and cruel to someone who knew exactly how to employ her personality, wit and looks to her advantage. These were the perfect traits for a high-class assassin, and it was clear she was destined for big things. But she wasn't there yet. She was also impetuous, needy, and far too excitable. Plus, she only had two hits under her belt and had yet to be sent on any big assignments.

Caesar had plucked her out of a home for psychologically dangerous girls and, once more, Spitfire was impressed with the boss's ability to spot talent in unusual places. Even though he was the better athlete and fighter – and was about to prove it – there was certainly something remarkable about Acid Vanilla. And it wasn't just her looks or the enigmatic way she viewed the world. She was special. Dangerous. Yet whilst innate skills and personality had gotten her feet under the table at Annihilation, some aspects of the job could only be learnt by rote and experience.

She let out a grunt as she lunged at him, her tight fist swishing through the air towards his face. But he'd seen this coming two moves ago and dodged the blow with a graceful side-step. With her fist arcing through the air, the momentum left her unbalanced and, as she moved past him, he grabbed her wrist and shoved her arm up her back.

"Shit!" she spat, but the way her voice faltered as he twisted her elbow joint delighted him. "Get off me."

As she struggled to get free, he kicked her legs out from under her. Still gripping her wrist, he followed her to the mat before jamming a sharp knee into the small of her back.

"Think that's you finished, Acid." He released her wrist and pushed down on the back of her head, grinding her face into the plastic mat.

"Piss off," she hissed. "I'll kill you."

"Now, now, darling. That's not going to happen, is it? You need to tap out. We're done."

The young woman snarled and spat, squirming to get him off her, but it was useless. She was going nowhere.

"Tap out," Spitfire told her, grinding his kneecap against her spine. "There's no point prolonging it."

"Fuck! Fine!" She slapped the mat with the palm of her hand and he got up. Normally – if he was sparring with Davros Ratpack or Barabbas Stamp, say – he might have dug his knee in harder as he got to his feet, just to show them who was boss. The fact he didn't with Acid confused him. He didn't think it was a concession to her gender or age. But maybe it was.

"Here." He held his hand out to her as she rolled over, but she stared at it for a second before jumping to her feet unaided. "I was only trying to help."

"I don't need your help."

"Clearly not."

She stood in front of him with her hands on her hips while she caught her breath. She'd tied her thick, dark hair in a ponytail and, even as red and sweaty as she was, he couldn't help but appreciate her looks. Those full lips, ever pursed in a sharp pout. And her exotic eyes, one blue, one brown. Intense and catlike even without make-up.

"What are you staring at?"

He shrugged. "I wasn't staring."

He held her gaze. She wanted him. Clearly. But he assumed most women he encountered wanted him. It was no doubt true – he was rather irresistible, after all – but he also had a theory that thinking this way became a self-fulfilling prophecy. Assuming attraction from someone made you act differently around them. You exuded attractive energy, which they then picked up on. It also helped if you were blond, six-three, tanned, and a damn fine specimen of a man in every regard.

"You did well today," he told her. "You're getting better. But try to stay focused and don't let your anger get the better of you.

Also, keep your limbs looser. Like I told you – if you're tensed up, you can't react as well from moment to moment."

Acid nodded. "Yes. I get it."

"Good." He tilted his head to one side. "What are your plans now?"

She sniffed. "Going to have a shower. Then go home."

"Or, we could go for something to eat?" The words were out of his mouth before he'd considered what he was saying. Caesar didn't mind his operatives hanging around together in their downtime, but it wasn't the done thing. Plus, what did he expect would happen? What was the endgame to this invitation?

"I can't tonight," Acid said, looking away. "I've got some reading I want to catch up on."

"Anything interesting?"

"Not really. A book on modern European history that Caesar lent me. He said it'd do me good to expand my knowledge."

It was funny. At times, Acid's accent was plummy, almost aristocratic, but then she'd slip back into the dropped Hs and glottal stops of her original East London drawl. In a lot of ways, she sounded like a female version of Beowulf Caesar himself, affected and upper class in the main, but always with a hint of their cockney roots. It was like in the late sixties, when all the working-class musicians affected posh accents. To be fair, Spitfire's accent was similar, but though he'd grown up in Tower Hamlets he'd always been careful how he spoke. For him, it was about proving to the world you didn't have to be tied to, or defined by, where you came from. It was where you were heading that mattered. That was why he loved working at Annihilation Pest Control. Caesar valued knowledge and culture in his operatives just as much as ruthlessness and guile. His dream was to create an organisation of elite killers, not thugs.

"Well, keep up the studies," he told her. "It's an important part of your training."

"Is it?" she asked. "How is knowing about the Portuguese revolution going to help me assassinate the head of a Mexican cartel?"

Spitfire grinned. "You never know what solutions that knowledge might inspire out in the field. No one ever wished they knew less about the world. You'll thank Caesar in the long run. Everything has its place."

"I've got nothing better to do, anyway."

"Some other time, then?" he said. "To get some food, I mean. Or a drink."

"Maybe."

As they continued staring at each other, a cool silence fell between them. Spitfire remained still, not wanting to look away first. It said a lot about a man if he could hold an attractive woman's gaze. From somewhere, music could be heard. A muffled, trebly version of The Jam's *Eton Rifles*. It took him a moment to realise it was the ringtone on his mobile phone.

"Do you want to get that?" Acid asked, a flicker of amusement on her face now.

Spitfire tore his eyes away from her and walked across the room to where his kit bag was lying against the wall. Kneeling, he unzipped the side compartment and picked out his phone. The caller ID showed 'Home', meaning it was Raaz Terabyte calling, head of communications at Annihilation Pest Control. He was still getting to grips with her being able to reach him at any time, day or night. But he understood that the appropriation of new tech was imperative for the industry.

"Spitfire Creosote," he said, on answering. Across the room, he thought he heard Acid snickering to herself, but he ignored her.

"Where are you?" Raaz asked. She was always like this. There was never any 'hello' or 'how are you?' For someone who was so obviously infatuated with him, she hardly ever showed it.

"I'm at the warehouse," he told her. "Just finished a sparring session with the new recruit."

"Oh. I see."

"Come along, Raaz," he said, lowering his voice. "Jealousy is very unbecoming."

"I'm not jealous," she snapped back. "I just don't see what everyone else sees in her. She's reckless and cocky, if you ask me."

"Don't let the big man hear you say that. She's his new protégé. He loves her."

"Maybe so. But I've told him what I think and he agrees with me. She needs more focus. Anyway, he wants to see both of you at HQ. Now. That's why I'm calling."

Spitfire glanced over at Acid, who was gathering up her things on the other side of the room. She saw him looking, so he raised his hand for her to wait.

"Fine," he told Raaz. "We'll get changed and I'll drive us over. We'll be there in thirty minutes."

"I'll let him know."

She hung up. Spitfire turned his ringtone to silent and chucked the phone on top of his kitbag.

"What is it?" Acid asked.

"Not sure," he replied. "But the Portuguese revolution is going to have to wait, I'm afraid. The boss wants to see us."

CHAPTER 3

Caesar leaned back in his immense red-leather chair and cracked his knuckles. "Look, mate, all I'm asking is, can it be done?"

The man standing on the other side of the desk swallowed, his Adam's apple rising and falling visibly. It gave him the look of a cartoon animal that had come face to face with a much bigger, scarier creature.

"I mean... yes. I can certainly build a spring door in the floor that is operated via a remote device."

"Such as a button on the underside of my desk, for instance?"

The man nodded. "I don't see why not."

"And you could make it so this... door was all but invisible until opened?"

"With the right materials and some airtight strips, it could be flush with the original floor." The man grimaced. "But it'd be a health and safety nightmare. And against building regs. If someone fell through it, they could break their neck."

"They'd wish it was that quick," Caesar muttered to himself. He was losing patience with this guy. "But it is doable. Thank you. That's all I wanted to know at this stage. And how much do you think it'd put me back for something like that? Ideally, I'd like it to self-close once opened. I'm thinking some kind of spring mechanism."

The man puffed out his cheeks. "Anything is possible with the right engineering. Cost-wise, though, you'd be looking at a few thousand with something that bespoke."

"A few thousand? Is that all?"

The man nodded. "But I can't do it, I'm afraid. Not with the way the world is these days. If someone hurt themselves, I might be liable."

"Yes, you've already voiced your concerns." Caesar sighed, imagining opening a trap door right now and sending the simpering fool to his demise. What would he put down there? Sharks? (No, too done.) Spikes? (Same.) It was a tricky one, and something he'd need to give more thought to if he was to go through with these renovations.

He was pondering whether he should let the diminutive handyman leave, or if he might be better silenced, when there was a knock on the door.

"Well, thank you for coming in," he said, getting to his feet and moving around to the front of the desk. "I have a meeting now, but I appreciate your thoughts." He loomed over the smaller man.

"Y-Yes. Great. I'll see myself out, shall I?"

"My associate will show you to the exit."

Placing one of his large bejewelled hands on the man's back, he guided him over to the door, opening it to reveal Raaz Terabyte. She was wearing a purple and teal tracksuit and had a Day-Glo pink scarf around her head.

"Ah, there you are," Caesar said. "This fellow was just leaving. Can you see him out?"

Raaz darted her gaze from Caesar to the man and then back again.

"See him... *out*?" she enquired, meaning should she see him out or see to it that he was taken out?

"He can go," Caesar told her. "He won't tell anyone about our little meeting today. Will you, old chap?"

The man looked up at him, his face like a deer in the headlights. "No. Of course not. Client confidentiality is my utmost concern."

"Wonderful. That and health and safety, hey? I like it. A good, solid, belts-and-braces approach to work. You can't beat it. It's what this great country was founded on." He shoved the man out into the corridor before shifting his attention to Raaz. "Are they here?"

"Yes, I'll send them straight in."

"Good girl."

He shut the door and walked the short distance back to his desk. Once there, he straightened his tie and smoothed down his red three-piece suit. It was a recent addition to his closet, and he was still unsure whether it complemented his large frame. It looked good on the hanger but, being made of silk, it didn't fall right. And, boy, was it hot.

Sitting down, he leaned back and took in his office, wondering again what he needed to do to give it a new lease of life. It was a large square room with dark mahogany wood panelling on the walls and ceiling and a plush carpet the colour of blood. The overall feel was that of a cigar lounge in an old-fashioned gentleman's club, the look he'd wanted when he'd bought the building a few years earlier. Yet one's taste changed, and over the last few months he'd grown tired of it. Being in Soho, and so close to the action, had been useful in the early days, but as the organisation branched out and its client base became more elite and international, this was less and less important. He'd give it another few years, perhaps, and then look for something grander, perhaps somewhere out in the country. An estate.

Hell, he could afford it now.

Business was good. Very good. Since he'd started Annihilation Pest Control over a decade earlier, with just himself and Davros Ratpack as the main operatives, it had grown exponentially. He now had nine operatives working exclusively for him and was looking to expand further in the next couple of years. Not just that, but they were fast becoming the go-to organisation for those in the highest echelons of society who had a pest they needed disposing of. These days, he had princes, politicians and movie producers on his client list, as well as cartel bosses and mobsters.

He took a moment to compose himself at the sound of another knock on the door, before calling for them to enter. The door was opened by Spitfire Creosote. He stepped aside to let Acid Vanilla enter before him.

"Ever the gentleman, old boy," Caesar bellowed, as Spitfire entered the room after her. He was wearing a tight-fitting navy suit and matching tie, and looked dapper as buggery, as per usual. "And how are you, my dear?" he asked Acid. "I hear you've been training hard."

"Yes. I have," she replied, waiting by the door as Spitfire closed it, then following him over to Caesar's desk.

"We've just finished sparring," Spitfire said. "She almost beat me. She's becoming a genuine force to be reckoned with."

"That's good to hear. And you're still enjoying yourself here, Acid?"

"Absolutely. I can't wait to get out there and do some real work."

Caesar ran his tongue over his gold-capped canine tooth as he considered his new recruit. She was wearing that awful leather jacket she'd acquired on her first job, matched with a pair of black jeans. But she looked good. If you liked that sort of thing.

"All in good time, sweetie," he said. "Let's not try to run before we can walk. But I do have a job for you. For both of you."

Spitfire raised his chin. "Both of us? The same job?"

"That's right, dear boy. Not a problem, is it?"

"What's the job?" Acid asked. "Where?"

"I think you're going to like this," he said, pausing for dramatic effect. "You're going to New York City."

"Are you serious?" she squealed. "New York?"

"That's right," Caesar replied. "But this is an important job and I need you to focus. Do you understand? No more messing around. This is the big leagues and I'm trusting you to get the job done without fuss. Don't let me down."

Acid nodded. "I promise. Thank you." She glanced up and met Spitfire's eye. "And we're going together?"

"Correct. I need both of you on this. Like I say, it's an important job."

"What do we have to do?" she asked, her eyes widening. "Where are we staying?"

"Pissing well calm down, will you?" Caesar barked. "It's a job. You're not going on holiday."

Her expression fell as she realised her mistake. Shoving her shoulders back, she looked him dead in the eyes. "Sorry, Caesar. I get it. I am calm. But I'm also eager to make my mark in the industry. Eager to impress you."

He wagged a finger at her. "I understand, sweetie. But it's that sort of eagerness that gets a person killed out in the field."

He sat back, taking the young woman in. It was true he'd never met anyone quite like Acid Vanilla, and he stood by his decision to hire her, to train her, to mentor her. But she was only twenty years old, and with that came all the trappings of youth –

inexperience and overzealousness two of the main ones. Whilst he got off on her enthusiasm and desire to learn all she could about the murder-for-hire business, she wasn't as good as she thought she was. Yet. She needed to appreciate that, if she was to make it to the next level.

"You'll be shadowing Spitfire on this job," he told her, holding a hand up in anticipation of her reaction. She opened her mouth, but he glared at her until she shut it again. "I know you're going to tell me you're ready for a lone assignment. But I'm telling you, I want Spitfire running lead. So please, keep that in mind. Understand?"

Acid chewed on her lip.

"Acid! Tell me you understand."

"Yes. I understand."

"Good girl."

He drew in a deep breath and sat back, steepling his fingers under his sizeable chin as he shifted his gaze from Acid to Spitfire, who was now staring straight ahead with a stern expression tightening his perfectly symmetrical features. He knew what was expected of him. Or, at least, he thought he did.

"When are we going?" Acid asked.

"The next few days. But remember, at all times you should be ready to fly across the world at the drop of a hat. Are you?"

"Yes. I'm always ready." She lifted her chin and clicked her heels together.

Jesus pissing Jones.

There was nothing like over-egging it. But Acid's reaction to the news of her first overseas assignment was exactly why he'd called them both in to see him. He was a master tactician. A chess player on a grand global scale. And, as such, he needed his pieces to do exactly what they should do. No exceptions.

"Good. Then that will be all," he told her. "Raaz will contact you the usual way with the details."

Acid furrowed her brow, ready once more to say something – to ask another bloody question.

He dropped his hands onto the table with a loud thud. "That will be all, Acid!"

She bowed her head. "Yes. Thank you, Caesar."

She turned and walked to the door. As she did, Spitfire broke his stance as if he was about to follow her.

"Not you, Spitfire," Caesar told him. "I need a word. In private."

Spitfire frowned. "Yes, boss. Of course."

"Good man," he said. "Acid - Raaz will call you car." He watched as she opened the door. Before she left, she looked back at Spitfire. And, at that moment, there was a hint of something in her eyes. It wasn't love, or even lust. But it was something.

Caesar smiled to himself as she exited the room, and waited until he'd heard her Dr Martens boots clumping down the corridor before speaking again.

"All right, sit down, Spit," he said, gesturing to one of the two matching chairs on the opposite side of his desk. "There's something you need to do for me. And I'll warn you from the off, you aren't going to like it."

CHAPTER 4

Spitfire stared at Caesar, studying the boss's face for tells. Except for the few beads of sweat that were usually present atop his bald cranium, there was nothing.

But why would there be?

Caesar was smart and uncompromising. He was the boss for a reason. If he didn't want to give anything away, he wouldn't.

"You know, I was thinking of getting a trapdoor built into the floor," he said, grinning. "Right where you're sitting."

Spitfire shifted in his chair as a sliver of adrenaline shot down his spine. "Do you want to get rid of me?"

He laughed. "Not at all, dear boy. You're one of my best operatives. You know that." He sighed dramatically. "I would like a trapdoor, but it's probably too much of a cliché. Too... Bond villain. Although I expect you'd like that."

It annoyed Spitfire somewhat, the constant James Bond comparisons. But it was good-natured and there were worse people one could be likened to. He always thought he was more Moore than Connery. Sophisticated and arch rather than thuggish. That was the persona he liked to project. These days, at least. There had been a time in his youth when being a thug was all he knew. But those days were long behind him.

"What would be underneath this trap door?" he asked. "A pool of sharks?"

He'd meant it as a joke, but from the way his boss twisted his mouth to one side, it seemed he was considering it.

"Hmm. It's too much, isn't it?" Caesar coughed out a breath. "Anyway, back to business. This New York job..."

Spitfire crossed one leg over the other and brushed a speck of lint off his knee. "Why the mystery? Why call us in?" Normally Raaz sent new jobs to his flat by a special courier, hidden in the data on a run-of-the-mill music CD.

"It's not actually that big a job," Caesar said. "In fact, you could do this in your sleep. You've heard of Artem 'Mad Dog' Perchetka?"

Spitfire nodded. "The Russian gangster."

"That's the fellow. Well, he's having a bit of bother with one of his men going rogue. A fellow called Boris Bakov. Perchetka believes Bakov is defecting to the USA and is ready to share secrets with the good old CIA in exchange for sanctuary. Obviously, our friend Mad Dog doesn't want these secrets getting out. He wants the guy hit before he has a chance to blab."

"Why doesn't he do it himself? He's got people. Why outsource it?"

"He doesn't want to operate on US soil, just in case," Caesar said. "Either that or he's just lazy. But a part of me wonders if this is more of a rehearsal for us and that he wants to utilise our services in the future. Which is a good thing, obviously. And if he's got the money, I'm not pissing well complaining."

"Fair enough," Spitfire replied. "But it's not a two-man job, is it?"

Caesar clicked his teeth. "Not exactly."

Spitfire leaned back. "What is it, boss?"

"Perchetka wants the hit to look like an accident. If Bakov is arranging to talk to the CIA, it's going to look suspicious if he dies in any mysterious circumstances, so we need it to be clean and concise and with no comeback to Russia. I mean, the Americans will put two and two together, of course they will. But with no evidence, and with them being so cloak and dagger anyway, it'll be swept under the carpet if you do it right."

"Not a problem. It sounds straightforward."

"It is. A three-day job, max. But I want you to take five. You see, old boy, when the job arose, I had an idea." He cricked his neck to one side, then the other. Usually, Spitfire enjoyed the boss's histrionics, but at times like this, when he was weary and eager for him to get to the point, it became tiresome. Caesar smirked as if reading his mind. "I'm sure you're aware, as I am, that Acid Vanilla is a tremendous addition to the organisation. But she's young and flighty and her focus is all over the place. I need her reined in."

Spitfire uncrossed his legs and shifted forward in his seat. "She is rather excitable."

"Exactly. And I don't know if she's taking matters as seriously as she should be. Everything is a game to her, presently. She's wild and unyielding. I need her broken in. It might sound counterproductive but if I destroy her spirit somewhat, I believe it will solidify her place in the organisation. As well as making her more powerful. I need her cynical rather than cocky. Do you get where I'm coming from?"

"I do. So... what? You want me to carry on training her whilst we're away?"

"In a sense," Caesar replied. "I want you to make her fall for you."

Spitfire rocked forward. "Fall for me? What do you mean?"

"She's too wide-eyed, too volatile. Yes, she's had plenty of hardships in her life and she can be ruthless when she wants to be. But in terms of how she sees the world, she's like a kid in a sweet shop. She can't be like that if she's going to survive in this industry. So, you're going to make her love you, and then you're going to break her heart."

Spitfire didn't respond right away. He was doing all he could to keep his trademark coolness in place. What Caesar was asking of him was ridiculous. He was Spitfire Creosote. Mr Sensational. The Flash Boy Assassin. He didn't do feelings. Ever. And yes, he found Acid incredibly attractive and would love to bed her. But he'd assumed that was going to happen anyway, eventually. Having her fall in love with him? That was a completely different matter. How did one even start with something like that?

"I'm not sure this is a good idea," he said. "As you say, she's volatile and hot-headed. If she finds out that we've planned this, it could send her over the edge."

Caesar cleared his throat. "I wasn't asking for your opinion, Spitfire. I'm telling you – this is how it will go down. Think of this mission as killing two birds with one stone. You'll take out Bakov and use the rest of the time away to work your charm on Ms Vanilla. I don't care how you do it. But if anyone can capture her heart, then it's you, you smooth bastard." He let out a loud guffaw that made his entire face shake, before stopping abruptly and eyeing Spitfire with one beady eye. "Now get to work, you dirty sod, and I'll see you in a couple of weeks. Any questions about the assignment, Raaz is your point of contact from here on in."

Spitfire gripped the arms of the chair. He had plenty of questions about many things, but when Caesar was like this it was pointless to go there. He got up and buttoned his suit jacket.

"No problem," he said. "I'll see you when I get back. When *we* get back."

CHAPTER 5

Spitfire had parked his car (a mint-condition 1967 Jaguar Mk2, in pale blue to match his eyes) a few streets away from Annihilation HQ, on Denmark Street. It being late in the day, he'd assumed parking fares would have ended. But when he rounded the corner at the end of the street, he saw the unmistakable yellow and black square of a parking ticket tucked under his windscreen wiper blade.

"Bastard, shitting, fuck," he snarled as he got up to his prized car. Snatching the ticket from the wiper's clutches, he stuffed it into his jacket pocket and opened the door. "Stupid bloody..."

He caught himself and sucked in a deep breath, regaining his composure before climbing into the driver's seat. These days he had more money than he could spend. It wasn't the ticket that was making him angry. Closing the door, he gripped the steering wheel tightly and closed his eyes, working through the hot rage firing through his system.

Come on, son.
Keep it together.

He wasn't a babysitter or a fucking gigolo, and he certainly wasn't boyfriend material. But he did understand why Caesar was asking this of him. Acid Vanilla had so much potential, but she was young and capricious. If this was the way to make her more jaded and temperate, then who was he to argue? Plus, it would be nice to get away for a week and he did like New York. The last time he'd visited it was winter then, too, and the snow on the ground gave the city an air of timeless beauty. Who knows; it could be fun.

Some parts of it most definitely would be.

He started the engine and took a right, putting his foot down as he pulled onto Tottenham Court Road. He'd recently bought a new flat over in Islington, but he felt too worked up to go home just now. Instead, he carried on through Hampstead until he reached Camden High Street and then took a right down the side of St Martin's Gardens. A minute later, he pulled up in front of Berry Gold's Boxing Gym and switched off the engine.

Standing on the corner of George Street, opposite the canal, the old gym was a North London stalwart for people like Spitfire, who liked their workout regimes to be basic but brutal. He'd been coming to this gym ever since he was a teenager, and some of the older guys (Berry Gold included) still knew him as Stephen Carter. Thankfully, most of those that knew him by his real name were getting on a bit and rarely attended the gym these days. To the younger members, he introduced himself as Rufus Andrews, which was the main alias he used when in civilian mode.

He grabbed his kit bag from the back seat and headed up the flight of stone steps to the gym's side door, buzzing the intercom at the top. As he waited, he rolled his head around, stretching his neck and shuffling his shoulders, limbering up for the session. On days like today, when he suspected the tension across his upper back was down to something other than muscle strain, coming to the gym always helped. Pumping iron or taking his irritation out on the bags left him feeling centred and calm.

"Who's there?" a voice crackled over the intercom.

Spitfire moved closer to the microphone. "Sonny? You all right, pal? It's Rufus Andrews. Can I come in?"

The intercom went quiet before a buzzer sounded, followed by a click, denoting the door had been unlocked. Spitfire pushed on through and ran up the stairwell to the first floor.

Down a short corridor and into the main space, he headed for the changing rooms on the far side, nodding to a few familiar faces as he crossed through the weights area and then past the bags. There was an old ring in the centre of the room, but no one was sparring tonight. A long time ago, the young Stephen Carter had fancied his chances as a tasty middleweight, but life and other things had conspired against that particular plan. Then he'd met Caesar.

A quick change into his workout gear and he was back out into the gym. He bench-pressed 90kg for four reps of ten and deadlifted 150kg for one rep of five, but despite these weights being in his top range, he wasn't feeling the burn and his heart wasn't in it. Leaving the free weights, he moved onto the bags, slamming his fists into a heavy hanger for five minutes before switching to a speed bag and pummelling it for all his worth for another ten. Normally, time at the bags sorted out all his problems, but tonight his knuckles were red and sore before he'd received even a modicum of relief.

What the hell was going on?

As a last resort, he grabbed one of the old ropes from off the wall and went to work skipping, employing the classic boxer's step-jump, shifting his weight from one foot to the other. By the time he'd finished, he was sweating and out of breath but felt no more settled. If anything, he was tenser than when he'd walked in. Maybe it was best to call it a day. Go home. Get some rest.

Whilst drying himself in the changing rooms after his third shower of the day, he overheard a group of men on the other side of the room arranging to go for a drink in the pub around the corner. He knew a couple of their faces, and they were about his age. For a moment he wondered about asking them if he could tag along, but it was too risky. Whilst he was skilled at coming up with extensive backstories for himself on the fly, it was exhausting remembering what he'd told to whom. Experience had taught him it was best to stick with your own kind in this life. People who understood who you were. And what you were.

As the men laughed and jeered at something one of them had said, he felt a pang of something like regret but pushed it down immediately. Fuck those guys. He didn't need them. He took some time at the mirror, combing his hair into a neat side-parting, before walking past them out of the changing room and down the stairs to his car.

As he drove home, his mind drifted to thoughts of Acid and what Caesar wanted him to do. There was no doubt in his mind that under most circumstances he could woo Acid into bed. But making her fall in love with him – that was a big ask. He'd slept with a lot of women in his thirty-five years, but had never once been in love. Not even close. He had no idea what it felt like, and that's the way he preferred it. He'd seen what loving the wrong person could do to someone. His mum had loved his dad more than life itself; she'd stayed with him when all her friends told her he was a bad man, that he'd hurt her one day. Why? Because she loved him. She loved him right up until the point the old sod came home drunk one night and pushed her down the stairs.

People said she'd broken her neck and died instantly. That she'd felt no pain. But Spitfire knew different. He was eight at the time and in bed, but he'd heard everything. She'd been making a low groaning noise for a good twenty minutes before she fell silent. His old man, being an ex-copper, was able to cover it up with the help of his mates on the force, and his poor mum's demise was ruled as death by misadventure. The old bastard even cried at her funeral. Spitfire hated him for that.

So, yes, he knew all about love.

He knew it wasn't for him.

Back at his flat he headed straight for the stereo and pressed play on the CD player, pleased when the opening notes of The Who's *Baba O'Riley* burst out of the speakers. Something loud and heavy was just what he needed to get him out of his head. He side-stepped over to the drinks cabinet next to the stereo and poured himself a large scotch from a bottle of Glenmorangie single malt. He took the drink over to the couch and sat, crossing one leg over the other and stretching one arm across the backrest. The fact he held himself in a refined poise even when alone told him how far he'd come in his life. He couldn't pinpoint exactly when it happened, but somewhere along the way he'd fully stepped into the well-crafted persona he'd created for himself. Stephen Carter was no more. These days he *was* Spitfire Creosote. Sophisticated, intelligent, debonair, unfazed by anything life could throw at him.

But that didn't mean he didn't feel fucked up and fucked off on occasion. Like now.

He sipped at his drink and closed his eyes, putting all his attention into his hearing, trying to lose himself in Roger Daltrey's raw baritone. But it was no good. Thoughts of Acid and their imminent trip plagued him.

He loved going away on overseas jobs almost as much as he loved sleeping with new women – especially twenty-year-olds that looked like Acid. Yet he couldn't shake the notion that Caesar was making a massive mistake. Acid was an unknown quantity. If they pushed her too hard and messed with her head too much, it could be disastrous. He sighed and opened his eyes, not sure exactly what he was looking for as he glanced around his flat. A distraction, perhaps? The answer to all life's mysteries? All he got was a room tastefully decorated with expensive sixties furniture and beautifully polished original oak flooring.

"It's too much," he whispered to himself. "She won't go for it."

And was that the crux of it? Was he worried he didn't have it in him to make someone love him?

Who the hell cares?

Love was messy and complicated. It was for normal people. Civilians. Not for people like him.

"Pull yourself together," he muttered to himself. "It's a job. You're playing a part. Like you always do when you're in the field."

Because regardless that he thought this was a bad idea, it was what the boss wanted. He might be a suave and sophisticated man about town, but he was also a soldier, a weapon. He took orders. That was who he was.

He gulped back the scotch and was about to get himself another when he felt a quivering sensation in his chest. For a second, he thought he was having a heart attack, before he realised he'd put his mobile phone in his jacket pocket at the gym. He was still getting used to the vibration function. He took it out and answered.

"Why do you always take so long to pick up?" Raaz hissed down the line.

Spitfire composed himself. He could feel the last gulp of scotch burning its way into his stomach. "Good evening to you too, Raaz. What can I do for you?"

"Where are you?"

He smirked, imagining the gesture would articulate itself in his tone. "Why do you always want to know where I am? Do you worry I'm out with other women?"

The line buzzed as Raaz sighed. "Stop it. This isn't professional. And we don't have that sort of relationship."

"Oh, come on, Razzy. Just a bit of fun. Light relief."

"Don't call me that. It's not my name."

It was his turn to sigh. He couldn't catch a break tonight. "Why *are* you calling?"

"Ten minutes ago, a man called Letvin Gurkin landed at JFK airport. That's the alias Boris Bakov is using. He's in New York. So we need you in the field sooner than expected."

"I see."

"Problem?"

He screwed up his eyes to think. He had his go-bag under his bed – a suitcase containing three suits, shirts, underwear and toiletries, as well as a thousand in dollars and euros. "No. It's fine."

"Good. Because you need to get over there. Now. Return air tickets are waiting for the two of you at Heathrow. You'll need your Dr Charles Summers passport and papers, and Acid is going under her Dr Miriam Morgan alias. There's a science conference at the Metropolitan Pavilion this week on atmospheric pressure. That's your cover, but don't worry, we don't expect you to attend."

Spitfire was about to say something witty but thought better of it. "Is Acid aware of these new developments?"

"No. You need to pick her up on your way to the airport. You can tell her then. Make sure she hurries. Your flight is at 4 a.m."

Spitfire looked at his watch. It was a few minutes after ten. It was enough time. "Can you ring her and give her the heads up whilst I sort myself here?"

"No, Spitfire. I have other work to be getting on with. You know how this works. From now on, you're in play. You're the lead operative. Good luck."

She hung up and Spitfire glared at the phone for a moment before flinging it onto the couch beside him. "Buggering hell."

He was tired. He didn't need this right now. But there it was. He was in play. It was time for Spitfire Creosote to do what he did best.

It was certainly going to be an interesting week.

CHAPTER 6

Acid was in her bedroom when she thought she heard the doorbell chime. She had her music turned up so loud (Black Sabbath; it had to be loud) that, at first, she wasn't sure if she'd heard correctly or if the buzzing noise was part of the backing track. Walking into the front room, she turned down the volume on her new CD player and listened. The doorbell went again.

Buzz - buzz - buuuuuuuuzz.

Whoever it was, they were impatient.

She placed her glass of white wine on the stereo unit and strode over to the intercom. It was new. She'd only used it a few times, so was still tentative as she pressed the button and spoke into the microphone.

"Hello? Who is it?"

"It's me," a man's voice said. "Spitfire."

Acid's head spiralled. She hadn't had anyone over to her new place since she'd moved in. Least of all someone from work. Least of all... him. She glanced around, seeing now the dirty plates and glasses, the clothes and CD cases strewn about the place.

"Oh, hey," she called out, wondering how she might gather up the mess with her finger still pressed on the intercom button. "What do you want?"

"I want to come in! I have news. About the job."

Acid grimaced. "Oh? What is it?"

"Acid, let me in! For Christ's sake!"

"Yes. Sorry." She buzzed him in and spun to face the room. It would take about thirty seconds for him to reach the door to her flat. She ran around, stacking the plates on top of each other and throwing them into the sink. Some had food stuck to them from weeks ago. She really needed to start looking after herself properly. Like an adult. Like a real human being.

Coming back into the front room, she gathered the CD cases into a neat pile on the edge of the unit before doing a final circuit and kicking clothes that were lying around – mainly old t-shirts and discarded bras – under the couch out of sight.

Just in time. The sound of knocking startled her. She hurried over to the mirror next to her bookcase to check her make-up and smooth her hair, before unlocking the door and easing it open.

"Don't worry, I've got all day," Spitfire said, stepping past her into the room.

She closed the door but remained in front of it. "Is everything okay?"

"No. It's not. Do you have a go-bag packed and ready?"

She frowned. "Yes. Of course. Caesar told me I should have one ready at all times and—"

"Get it. Now. We have to get to the airport. We're leaving for New York in three hours."

Acid tensed, working hard on not showing her glee. "We're going tonight?"

"The mark has just landed at JFK, so it's game on." He glared at her. "Go on then, get your stuff together."

"I'll need to get changed," she said, glancing down at her outfit, an oversized David Bowie shirt from the Glass Spider Tour and a pair of black leggings.

Spitfire raised his eyebrows, before seemingly catching himself and shifting his expression into a forced smile. "Fine. Be quick as you can."

"No problem."

She hurried into her bedroom and over to the dressing table. Except for the bed and the closet, it was the only piece of furniture in the room. Even with the huge Ramones poster above her bed, the place looked sparse and unlived in. Having never lived on her own before, she wasn't sure what she should buy to make it look more like a home. She'd gone straight from living with her mum to Crest Hill, to Caesar moving her into Honeysuckle House, where she'd undergone her training.

She peered up at the poster and grinned. It was a photo from the band's shoot for their first album, the four of them resplendent in leather jackets standing outside CBGB's, the infamous music club in New York's Bowery. Joey and the gang stared back at her, stoic behind dark shades and sneers. The epitome of New York cool.

"I'm coming to see you," she whispered to the poster.

Turning back to her desk, she pulled her make-up box in front of her and flipped the lid, hastily applying mascara, eyeliner and dark eyeshadow, before grabbing up her favourite new lipstick – *Rouge Triomphal* by Chanel – and applying it liberally. The colour was bright red. Bold and chic. Two traits she intended to carry with her as Acid Vanilla. But she wasn't there yet. She craned her neck towards the front room as the stereo grew in volume. Spitfire must have turned it up, and she wondered if he liked the same sort of music she did. She didn't think so. He was too well presented, too suave and classically good-looking. Not her usual type. At all.

Yet there was something about him…

She got up from the chair and moved over to her closet, swerving that particular thought before it had time to develop. She was doing well, currently. Her moods were stable and the bats were quiet. Hopefully it would stay that way. She pulled her suitcase out from the bottom of her closet and unzipped it. Inside she'd assembled a week's worth of clothing like Caesar had instructed her to. There were jeans, t-shirts, underwear, a red-and-black striped mohair jumper and a fresh pair of Converse. She smiled to herself as she zipped the case up. Her first assignment abroad and she was going to New York. This was truly the jet-set lifestyle they'd promised her. Who cared if she'd had to lose a large part of herself to get it?

A lot had happened in the last eighteen months. A hell of a lot. She'd killed two people in that time. Three, if you counted Alice Vandella – the young girl from Dagenham she'd been before she met Beowulf Caesar and her life took an unexpected turn. Not that she was complaining about seeing the back of her old life. She missed her mum, but she was putting things in place to remedy that, and it was better for them both if she stayed away from her for now. Her old life was over. She was part of something much bigger and more important. And, god, it felt good. She was made for this world. Killing people for her was just part of the job. And they deserved it. Caesar had told her no one got a hit put out on them unless they were a bad person (a shit of the highest order, was how he put it), so why feel bad? If anything, she was making the world a better place. Plus, she'd earned more money in such a short time than she'd ever known.

She slipped off her leggings and pulled on the tight black jeans that had lain in a heap next to her bed. Finally, she replaced the Bowie t-shirt with a black-and-white striped top that was tight-fitting and made her tits look big. It was just a coincidence it was close at hand, she told herself, as she grabbed her leather jacket and slid her case off the bed.

Spitfire was standing with his back to her when she walked into the front room. Seeing her new apartment through his eyes, she suddenly realised how much work she had to do with the place. As it was in her bedroom, the décor here was minimal and due to a lack of inspiration rather than by choice. Apart from her stereo, which she'd spent a small fortune on, her furniture was basic and functional and her style unclear.

"Ready," she said, holding her case up as Spitfire turned around.

He looked her up and down, and when his mouth twitched at the corners, she was glad she'd worn the top.

"Very nice," he said. "You'll need a warm jacket, though. It's cold in New York in January. They've forecast snow while we're there." He was wearing a long, dark navy overcoat over his suit.

"I've only got my leather jacket," she said, holding it up. "I've got jumpers though, and—"

"We'll get you something over there," he butted in, eyeing her jacket. "You might need something a little less... street, anyway."

Acid's heart sank. For her, New York was all about leather jackets. It was about the Ramones and the Velvet Underground and punk. Not to mention CBGB's. She hoped there'd be time to visit while they were there. If not, she'd make time. She had to. She'd dreamed of going ever since she could remember. A smile formed, but she stopped it. For some reason she felt self-conscious. Spitfire staring at her like he was didn't help.

"I'm just keen to get there and start the job," she said, but Spitfire looked away and shook his head. When he huffed out a sigh, Acid wanted to curl up into a ball. Either that or jump out the window. Failing that, a swift kick in his balls could be a satisfying third option.

"Listen," he said, holding his hands up as he turned back to her. "I know this is big for you. Your first overseas assignment. But try to keep a lid on the girly exuberance. We're elite killers, but we're not above the law. You've impressed a lot of people with your abilities and attitude, but those things are pointless if you get yourself on the authorities' radar. Remember this, Acid: from now on, you exist in the shadows."

She bit her lip and nodded. "Yes. Thanks. I get it."

"Good." He narrowed his eyes at her. "Then in that case, I think we're going to get on famously this week." He followed up with a slight smirk and a flick of the eyebrows.

Was he flirting with her?

Her cheeks warmed. She tossed her hair over her shoulder. "Yes, me too. And I won't let you down."

"No. You will not." He stretched his arms, expanding his impressive torso, before stepping forward and taking the case out of her hand. "Now we should head to the airport, my dear. We've got a date with a Russian gangster."

CHAPTER 7

Despite his new partner's palpable excitement – and the troubling extracurricular element of his assignment – Spitfire rather enjoyed the drive to the airport. Acid Vanilla might be an unknown quantity right now, but as she relaxed he found her to be good company. She was a smart girl; and funny, too, which he hadn't counted on.

"Charles Summers suits you," she said, as they left Notting Hill and entered the outskirts of Brentford. She had both their passports on her lap and held his open, comparing the photo to him in real life.

"You see me as a summery kind of guy?"

She laughed. "Maybe not summery, but the overall name is cool. Charlie Summers. Chuck Summers. Old Chucky Boy."

"All right, calm it down. Charlie will do. Or Dr Summers to you, maybe." He winked and she turned away, stifling a smile.

"I don't know why I have to be Miriam bloody Morgan," she muttered. "I sound like an old woman."

"You didn't choose the name?"

"No. It was Raaz. I don't think she likes me."

"Don't worry, she doesn't like anyone. In her opinion, she

single-handedly runs the organisation, and we all exist to piss her off."

Acid laughed again and the atmosphere shifted. She shuffled around in her seat so she was facing him. "I suppose it's not any more ridiculous than Acid Vanilla."

"You don't like that one either? That's a shame. You picked that yourself, though."

"Yeah. I don't know. I suppose I'm still getting used to it. It seems silly. I'm worried it might put people off."

"If it does, fuck those people, they clearly have no imagination," he said. "I think it suits you. It's edgy, but sexy."

She fell silent as he said this, and he made a mental note not to push the charm so heavily going forward.

"Besides," he said, "you'll have so many aliases over the years that you'll be glad of it. Think of Acid Vanilla as a placeholder. A way back home to yourself. It can fuck with your head, this life; it's good to know who you are under all the lies and fake names."

"But Acid Vanilla is a fake name."

He tilted his head and smirked. "Not anymore, darling. Not anymore."

They got to the airport a few minutes before two. Spitfire parked at the far end of the long-stay car park and jumped out of the driver's seat to walk around and open the door for her. Ever the charismatic charmer, he'd have done this regardless of his extra assignment, but now it felt forced, and he didn't like that.

Acid stared up at him with wide eyes as he opened the door, then glared suspiciously at the hand he offered her, as if no one had ever treated her so chivalrously before. The poor girl didn't know how to react.

"Come on," he said. "Let me help you."

With a giggle, she took his hand and stepped out of the car. "I could have managed."

"I know. But it's nice to be nice, isn't it?" He said it in his usual low, suggestive drawl, yet he couldn't help but cringe.

It's nice to be nice? Jesus.

He led the way into the airport and over to the check-in desk. There was a bit of a tense moment when the pretty blonde behind the counter couldn't locate their tickets, but it turned out she was looking at the wrong system. Whatever that meant. If Spitfire had been travelling alone, he'd have assumed she was doing it to prolong their encounter and would have got her number for when he returned to the UK. Today, however, with Acid loitering beside him, he let the matter pass with a polite smile.

Once the tickets were in hand, it took them another forty-five minutes to get through passport control and security. It was bloody annoying. Ever since that group of idiots flew those planes into the World Trade Centre just over a year ago, the whole aviation industry had gone crazy. The security people even had him take off his new Barker brogues, which seemed like overkill.

By the time they got through to the departure lounge, they only had time for a swift drink before boarding.

"Come on, kid," he said, placing his hand on the small of Acid's back and guiding her to the bar. "One for the road."

He rested his forearm on the bar top and squinted at the bottles on the back wall as the barman sidled over to them.

"What can I get you?"

"I'll have a Johnnie Walker Green if you have it."

The barman screwed up his face. "I think we've only got the basic one."

"Yes, of course. What *was* I thinking?" He rolled his eyes. "And what is that? Red? Black?"

"Red, I think."

"Fine. I'll have a double. No ice." He turned to Acid. "What would you like?"

She looked surprised at the question. "Whatever's good. I'll have the same as you."

He smiled and turned back to the barman. "You heard the lady. That will be all, thanks."

The man scampered away, and Spitfire turned to Acid, looking past her to a free table a few feet away. "Do you want to get those seats and I'll bring them over?"

He watched her as she walked over to the table. Maybe this assignment wasn't all bad. Playing with people's emotions – involving emotions at all – didn't sit well with him, but he didn't have to think about that. If he treated her well and made love to her well, it wouldn't be his fault if she fell for him. And if he remained grounded and didn't say anything to her he didn't mean, he might get through this week with his dignity intact.

He sometimes found it strange he had such strong views on morality, doing what he did. But many others he'd encountered in this industry, Caesar included, held a strong personal code. He supposed, being above the actual law, it was important to have such boundaries. Life laws they set for themselves to adhere to. It was what elevated their roles as elite assassins above the grunt work of a run-of-the-mill hitman or mercenary.

"Here you are, sir, two double Johnnie Walker Reds." Spitfire turned around as the barman placed the drinks down. "That will be seventeen pounds, please."

Spitfire reached into the inside pocket of his jacket and pulled out his leather wallet. Removing a twenty, he creased it between his thumb and first two fingers before offering it to the man. "Keep the change," he drawled, picking up the heavy-bottomed tumblers and joining Acid at the table.

"We'll be boarding in twenty minutes, I expect," he said, setting her whisky down in front of her. She was grinning like a bloody idiot, and as he sat opposite, she rubbed her lips together to try to stop herself. "What is it?" he asked.

She frowned. "Sorry. I know we're on an important job – and I promise I'll take it seriously and I will not let you down – but I've always wanted to go to New York. I can't believe I'll be there in a few hours."

Spitfire picked up his drink and took a long sip. It tasted like what it was – mediocre whisky. "Well, believe it, kid. It is a great city. But this is not a holiday. For anyone."

She scowled. "Yes. I am aware. I've got two kills to my name already, Spitfire."

"Hey!" he snapped, looking around. "Watch what you're saying." But no one was looking their way and the ambient noise would have covered her words. Yet this was why he was uneasy about working with her on this job. Yes, it sounded straightforward and, yes, she was well-trained and would be an asset one day. But she wasn't there yet. And he wasn't her mentor. He'd enjoyed teaching her how to shoot and fight, but she was Caesar's protégé not his. He had his own shit to deal with.

"No one heard me," she whispered. "You worry too much, you know that?"

She picked up her glass and took a large drink. The look on her face said she wasn't expecting it to be quite so strong. She rode it out, staring intently ahead as she swallowed it down, but he could tell she hated it.

"Nice?" he asked, licking his lips to cover his smirk.

"Mmm." She nodded defiantly.

Spitfire's phone vibrated in his jacket pocket. He took it out and saw he had a message from 'Home'. A text, as the kids called them. He was still getting used to being contacted this way. He'd preferred it when Raaz had to reach him via a pager, and he'd find a call box to ring the secure line. That way, he operated on his terms. Plus, there'd been occasions when he'd used the pager to woo a young female, pretending he was a surgeon on call. Now Raaz could get hold of him any time of the day or night. It was intrusive, is what it was. He knew his life belonged to Annihilation Pest Control, but one still needed some downtime away from work.

"What is it?" Acid asked, leaning over to see.

"Raaz," he replied, not looking up. "She's sent all the relevant notes on the case to a secure email address we can access when we get to New York. There's a laptop in the apartment we'll be staying in. She's going to send another text with a password to get through the encryption."

He looked up, and maybe it was the exasperated look on his face or the tetchy way he said the words 'text' and 'encryption', but Acid laughed.

"Don't worry, Grandad, you'll get to grips with the technology. I can help, if it's all too much for you."

"Piss off," he said. "And watch who you're talking to!"

But he liked the banter. He'd rather she act cocky than meek and uncertain of herself. This way, at least, she was fair game.

As a husky female voice boomed over the public address system, announcing their flight was boarding, he winked at her. "Come on, trouble. That's us."

CHAPTER 8

As the closing bars of Ralph Vaughan Williams' glorious *Five Variants of Dives and Lazarus* floated through his skull, Spitfire felt himself drifting away. It had been a long day and his mind and muscles were tired. He hoped to sleep for the rest of the journey and wake up in New York refreshed and ready for action. Taking in a deep breath, he held it in his chest before exhaling all the stress and tension he'd been carrying with him. Sleep was here. A benign emptiness where nothing mattered...

"What are you listening to?"

His eyes snapped open as his headphones were snatched from his head. Instinct had him make a fist, but as he twisted in his seat he found Acid Vanilla looking at him with a mischievous grin on her face.

What the fuck?

Ten minutes previously she'd been fast asleep with her own headphones on, muttering something about bats. Now she looked hyperalert, practically bubbling with energy.

"Can I listen?" she asked, placing his headphones over her ears.

Spitfire opened his mouth to reply, but no words came to him. He had thought she was annoyed with him. There'd been a moment at the departure gate when he'd tapped her playfully on the arse, and it hadn't gone down well. She'd not said a word to him since they'd boarded the plane. Either he'd scared her by coming on too strong, or she was acting out some silly feminist stance, but he'd assumed it was going to be radio silence all the way to New York. Not that he was bothered about that fact.

But now here she was, full of beans and sneering as she listened to his music. "Classical?" she yelled.

"All right, give." He took the headphones off her. "You're shouting."

"Is that what you're into?" she asked. "Violin music?"

"Now and again," he said, sitting upright. "I find it relaxing after a busy day. I was *trying* to sleep. I thought you were out for the count."

"Yeah. I was. But then I woke up. I'm feeling a bit manic, to be honest." She frowned and sucked air through her teeth. "Not manic. Excited. Eager to get going with the job."

Her eyes were wild, and Spitfire wondered for a second if she'd taken something. "Yes, well, like I keep telling you – it's crucial you remain focused in these situations. The most important aspect of any job you'll ever do is patience. Learning to wait for the right moment. I've been doing this job for ten years; I've spent nine of those years waiting around."

"Yes, I know. And I can do that." She lowered her head and looked at him through her lashes. "Don't misinterpret my youthfulness for naivety, Spitfire. Or my excitement for flippancy. I know I can be a little erratic sometimes, but I'm working on that. I know how lucky I am to be in this position, and for Caesar to take me in and train me as he has. I also appreciate I'm working alongside the best in the business and I'm not there yet. But I will be. I'm going to be the best assassin in the world one day. The deadliest. The most feared."

"Okay," he whispered, looking through the crack in the seats to make sure the couple in front were asleep. "How about you just work on being the quietest one for now?" He patted her on the arm. "There's a good girl."

"Patronising prick." She muttered it under her breath as she slumped back in her seat, but he heard her.

Maybe he was a little grumpy. And being condescending probably wasn't the best leverage for courtship. He needed to pull this around to have any chance of fulfilling his clandestine assignment for Caesar.

But bloody hell...

Even just the thought of this ridiculous side-mission turned his stomach. Courtship. Romance. Love. None of those concepts was familiar to him and that's the way he wanted it to stay. He eyed the cute air stewardess as she passed by, holding eye contact until she smiled shyly at him, then sending her on her way with a wink. This was his style. Brief encounters. Ships passing in the night. Wham! Bam! Thank you, ma'am!

"What else do you listen to?" Acid was back, seemingly unable to hold a grudge for long. He'd closed his eyes, but she nudged him with her elbow. "You must like other music."

"Yes, I like music. I like The Who, The Jam, Small Faces."

"Oh god," she exclaimed. "Are you a mod? Shit, of course you are. That explains it."

"I'm not a mod," he said, whispering as he glanced around at the passengers asleep on all sides, modelling to Acid that she lower her voice as well. "I just like that style. Proper music played by skilled musicians." He had owned a scooter as a teenager but, to be fair, *owned* was pushing it in terms of definition. He'd *stolen* a Lambretta from outside a club one night and had ridden it for a few months before his dad found out and sold it to one of his mates from the pub.

Acid pretended to vomit, but she did at least lower her voice when she spoke. "It's all a bit dad-rock though, isn't it, that kind of music? It's not very exciting."

"Tell me, what are the kids listening to these days?"

"I've no idea about the kids," Acid said, arching one eyebrow. "But I like punk and heavy rock. I'm a rocker through and through. Probably why we don't get on. The old Mods vs Rockers thing."

"Who says we don't get on?"

She smiled and looked away, but if she was feeling any twinge of awkwardness now, it didn't stop her gabbing. "That's why I'm so excited to be visiting New York. All the culture, all the music. That city has produced some of the best bands ever. Velvet Underground, Ramones, The New York Dolls, Talking Heads..."

She was speaking fast, without taking a breath. But rather than being irritated by her exuberance, Spitfire found it rather endearing. Wide-eyed passion was something he'd pushed down in his persona in favour of withering cynicism. The way he saw it, it helped to not expect anything of the world; after that, everything was a bonus. He considered the young woman beside him. Possibly it was this plucky aspect of Acid's character that worried Caesar the most. And why he wanted her broken in, as he'd so delicately put it.

"I'm hoping we can get the job done early and I'll have time to visit CBGB's," she whispered.

"What's that?"

"CBGB's?" she said, her voice rising. She looked him up and down like he was an alien lifeform. "You've never heard of CBGBs?"

He dropped his voice to a low growl, not enjoying her mocking tone suddenly. "Why don't you tell me what it is?"

"It's a music venue," she said with a grin. "In the East Village. It's where the punk scene began, where all these amazing bands started their careers. Television, The Dead Boys, Richard Hell, Jonathan Richman. My mum used to go there all the time when she lived in New York. She met Johnny Thunders once and—"

"Whoa! Whoa!" Spitfire said, holding his hand up. "You know the rules, Acid. We don't talk about our past lives."

"But I just meant—"

"No! I don't want to hear about your mum or what she did. You're Acid Vanilla. You don't have a mum. You don't have a past. Same as me."

He was speaking the truth – this was how Caesar wanted things done at Annihilation Pest Control – but he was also glad to nip this conversation in the bud.

Acid straightened in her seat and crossed her arms. Spitfire watched her for a moment, wondering if she was done. If he could get some sleep.

Oh for a Xanax or a Valium right now.

He adjusted his position, spreading his legs a little wider as he settled himself and finding comfort in the roll of padding on the side of the headrest. The cabin was quiet and sleep felt close once more. He closed his eyes.

"I have been thinking about the case."

He flicked one eye open to find Acid leaning into him. "Oh?"

"What you told me in the car, about this Russian gangster not wanting to step on US soil. Don't you think that sounds odd?"

"Not really. The Americans will already know Boris Bakov worked with him. They'll be expecting the Russians to make a move if he's ready to blab. So, if we slip in quietly and make it look like an accident while Perchetka and his men are all safely tucked away in Moscow, the fallout will be reduced."

"Easy as that?"

"Yes. As easy as that." He closed his eyes, praying that was the end of it.

"I just think there's something off," Acid whispered. She was leaning in so close he could feel her breath on his cheek and neck. It wasn't unpleasant. "If that's all it is, why send two of us?"

Spitfire shrugged. That was a question for Caesar. He didn't want to give credence to her enquiry by answering.

"He must have plenty of men who could hit this guy. It seems strange to involve other people and pay out a massive fee if you don't need to."

"Listen, kid," Spitfire said, opening both eyes and fixing her with a hard stare. "You're a wily young thing and you've got a good brain. That's clear to see. But don't let your imagination run riot on a job. It's easy to let it happen, but it doesn't help and sometimes it can be dangerous. Stick to the facts. Stick to what you know."

"Which is?"

"That we've been hired to do a job. Not to think. We have one job. We do it well. We go home. We get paid. Easy." He sat back in his seat.

"But I just think—"

"Go to sleep!" he snapped. "We've got a busy few days in front of us. We need rest."

"I don't."

"Well, I do. So sit back, close your eyes, and stop bloody talking. Do you hear me?"

"Fine."

"Fine!"

He shuffled around in his seat so he was facing away from her. He hoped from the frostiness coming off her, she would stay quiet now. For a while, at least. He closed his eyes and a cloak of weariness descended on him. As he drifted off to sleep, his last words to Acid replayed through his mind.

We have one job. We do it well. We go home. We get paid. Easy.
Easy?

There was nothing like tempting fate.

CHAPTER 9

The plane touched down at John F Kennedy International Airport at 7.30 a.m. local time. It felt good to be arriving there at the start of a new day, but getting through customs and security took forever. At one stage, Acid worried they were going to be questioned about their reason for travelling, but then the guard waved them through the barrier to freedom.

She'd arrived. America.

New York City.

There was already a dusting of snow on the ground as they jumped in a cab (an actual bright-yellow cab, like in the movies) and she pressed her face against the window, watching in awe as they drove through Queens and then on towards the river. The apartment where they were staying was in the Upper West Side, and she had hoped they might travel via the famous Brooklyn Bridge. It was doable that way (sort of, she'd looked it up on a map), but as they got closer it became clear the driver was going to take the Queens Midtown Tunnel to get to Manhattan. But no worries, there'd be time for sightseeing after they'd completed the job.

Caesar had a lot of faith in her, sending her to New York on only her third assignment. It was vital she didn't let him down. Or Spitfire. Not that she was happy with how eager she was to impress the man sitting across from her in the back of the cab. But despite him being surly and uncool (and most definitely NOT her type), he was her colleague and her superior. No doubt he'd be reporting back to Caesar. Which was why she was so keen to seek his favour.

The only reason.

As they emerged from the tunnel, the sun was visible over the tops of the tall buildings. This was the New York Acid had always imagined. The New York from the books and the movies. She pressed her face against the glass, gazing out the window as they drove along 3rd Avenue. When the driver turned the corner, the park was right in front of them. Central Park. *The* Central Park. And the cab driver was taking a route straight across it. She didn't know you could do that.

Spitfire, clearing his throat, got her attention. "We're here for five days," he said. "There'll be time for sightseeing once we're done. Not before."

She tore herself away from the window to look at him. "Yes. I get it. But will there?"

"With a bit of luck, there's no reason we can't box this off in the next two days. That's what I'm aiming for."

Acid could barely contain herself for the rest of the journey. By the time the driver pulled up on West 81st Street, at the address Spitfire had given him, her head was buzzing with ideas and intrigue. The bats had been quiet of late, but ever since the flight she'd felt their presence once more, scratching at the edges of her consciousness. She referred to her condition as the bats because that's what it felt like when she was in full on manic-mode – like a flock of bats were flapping their leathery wings against her psyche, nibbling at her nerve endings with their vampire teeth. But also it was a technique her former therapist, Jacqueline, had taught her. A way of viewing the more extreme aspects of her condition as something outside of her, a separate entity, rather than who she was. It helped her cope. Most of the time.

She felt a cool breeze whip around her face as Spitfire opened the car door for her. There he was again, offering his hand. This time she took it without question, feeling rather regal and dainty as he helped her out of the cab. She even smiled and thanked him. She could do serene and ladylike when she wanted to. Just watch her.

"Well, this is it," he said, walking around to the rear of the car while the driver popped the trunk. He nodded at the large three-storey building in front of them as he pulled out their cases. "Home for the next five days."

A shiver of anticipation ran down Acid's body as she took in the building. It was a classic New York City townhouse, what they called a brownstone, with steps up to the front door and the same distinct windowsills, lintels, and front stoops she recognised from a host of American movies.

"It's amazing," she said.

"Don't get too excited. We've only got the second floor. It's all apartments now."

"Of course." But it was still impressive. Still the stuff of dreams.

"Come on. I'll show you around," he said, carrying the cases up to the front door and letting them in.

She hurried after him, along a dark hallway and up two flights of stairs to the second-floor landing. There was a strange smell in the air, some kind of spice she didn't recognise, but it wasn't horrid.

"Does Caesar own this?" she asked, as she joined Spitfire at the front door of the apartment.

"The organisation does," he said, fiddling with a set of keys to find the right one. "We've got properties in most of the major cities in the world. It's where you'll stay when you're in the field. It's safer and easier this way than having to deal with hotels and booking systems. Russian gangsters aren't the only ones who prefer to operate under the authority's radar. To date, not one of Caesar's operatives is on any police department records. Anywhere in the world. He wants to keep it that way." He held up a shiny key and gave her a pointed look.

"What's that supposed to mean?"

"What do you think it means?" he said, unlocking the door and pushing it open. "It means watch yourself."

"Jesus," she muttered, as he stepped aside to let her in first. "Does every moment have to be a teaching point with you?"

Either he didn't hear, or he was ignoring her. Regardless, any annoyance she might have been carrying fell away as she stepped into the spacious, open-plan apartment. In front of her, a lounge area complete with an immense L-shaped couch looked out over the street, and next to this was a large dining table set out for eight. To their immediate right was a kitchen, decked out in white tiles with white units and a black granite worktop. There was also a huge American-style refrigerator unit propped up against the wall.

"Whoa. It's amazing."

It's all right," Spitfire replied, shuffling past her with the cases as the front door shut behind him, and nodding to a door on the adjacent wall. "There's a bathroom and two bedrooms through there. They're both a decent size, so you can have the first choice."

"Cool." She was already opening the door and striding down the short corridor. The bedroom doors were open, so she could see they'd been decorated in the same fashion; white linen bedspreads and wooden floors with a closet and a dresser.

Putting her head around the door of each room, she opted for the one closest to the bathroom. "I'll take this one," she said, as Spitfire joined her.

"Fine. That makes it easier for me."

"How so?"

He winked. "Because all the good stuff is in my room."

She frowned and, by way of explanation, he beckoned her into the next room with a curl of his finger. He walked to the far end of the bed and leaned down to lift the mattress. It was an ottoman bed, with a hydraulic arm under the metal frame, and as he opened it fully, Acid moved forward to get a better view.

"Wow!"

There were more guns and weaponry under the bed than she'd ever seen in her life. It was reminiscent of one of those photos the Feds release when they've seized some drug cartel's stash. There were machine guns and shotguns, revolvers and semi-automatic pistols of all makes and models. Some she recognised, some she didn't. Alongside these were boxes and boxes of ammo, as well as a number of knives and even a sword.

Spitfire met her eye and flicked up his eyebrows suggestively. "Not bad, hey?"

"Are we going to need all this?"

"Not this trip. But it's worth having, just in case. And if things go well this week, you'll be back again within the next year, I expect."

She nodded. Not knowing what else to say. Everything had moved so fast for her since meeting Caesar. Some days it felt like she hadn't yet come to terms with the magnitude of her new life. But she would. She'd have to. She was Acid Vanilla now.

"This is what I was after." Spitfire reached down and picked up a silver laptop and a small zip-up bag from the bottom right corner of the bed frame. He lowered the bed and placed the laptop on top of the mattress, before unzipping the bag and pulling out two identical flip-top phones. "Here you are," he said, handing one to her. "Carry this with you at all times. The only numbers stored in the contacts list is the one for my phone and Raaz's secure line. If we get split up for any reason, we contact each other using these only. Understood?"

Acid opened the phone and inspected it. "It looks like a normal mobile phone."

"It is, by and large. At least, I think it is. And there's something else. Hang on." He lifted the bag and shook it until two tiny metal boxes fell out onto the bed. Picking one up between his thumb and forefinger, he placed it in Acid's open palm. "A tracker. Keep it on you. Somewhere safe. It uses something called GPS and is synched to my phone. I'll have this other one. It means we can find each other wherever we are."

"How very James Bond," she said, and immediately regretted it. From the way his eye twitched, she didn't think he appreciated the reference.

"Yes. Quite. What will they think of next?"

She slid the phone and tracker into her jacket pocket. The technology was new to her but, after being in Crest Hill for so long, most modern technologies seemed practically space age. She never knew how mesmerised she was supposed to act when Caesar or Raaz introduced her to new equipment.

"What now?" she asked.

Spitfire looked at his watch. "It's just gone twelve. I suggest we freshen up and have a look at these documents Raaz has sent over. If we know where Bakov is staying, we can stake out the place this afternoon, get eyes on him and hopefully track his movements. Sound good?"

"Fine by me." She shuffled her feet. "Shall I...? Umm..."

"Yes. You have a shower and get changed, and once I've done the same, we'll head straight out." He looked her up and down. "Go on then. What are you waiting for?"

"Yes. Cool." She hurried out of his room and entered her own.

"There should be some towels and a robe in the closet," Spitfire shouted after her.

She smiled to herself. Spitfire might be a deadly killer, but he was also a proper gentleman. She enjoyed having someone be so attentive to her needs. She'd never experienced it before.

"Thank you," she called out, before going to the closet and selecting a large white bath towel from a stack at the bottom. It looked and felt brand new. She undressed and wrapped it around her before tentatively opening her bedroom door. Looking to her right, she saw Spitfire's door was ajar and she could see him sitting on the edge of the bed with the laptop open in front of him. He was topless, and she was shocked at how tanned and muscular he was. But she was more shocked at the white-hot shiver that ran down her body as she gazed at his naked form.

Stop that!

You're a professional now.

So bloody well act like one.

She left her room and tiptoed into the bathroom. It was a square room, with the same white tiles as the kitchen covering the walls and floor. A huge free-standing bathtub stood in the middle of the space, with a toilet and bidet next to each other on one wall and two sink units and an enormous mirror on the wall opposite. A walk-in shower cubicle, bigger than any she'd ever seen, took up the far corner. Except for the chrome taps and pipework, everything in here was white and modern. She liked that. It felt expensive and contemporary and only added to her glee that she was here in New York, on her first major assignment for Annihilation Pest Control. She could not mess this up. She'd make Caesar proud.

Walking over to the shower unit, she twisted it on before

stepping out again to allow the water to heat up. As she did, she realised she'd left the bathroom door open a few inches. If Spitfire put his head around the side of his door, he'd have a clear view of her in the shower. She was shocked once again to discover this excited her. Turning her back to the door, she slowly unhooked the towel from around her chest and let it drop to the tiled floor. As she cast a coquettish glance over her shoulder, she was half-expecting him to be standing in the doorway. She closed her eyes, imagining him pressing his toned body against hers, his hands caressing her skin, exploring the hills and valleys of her physique. The bats sang their approval, sending another electric shiver running down her spine. If he wanted her, he could have her. She'd slept with boys before, but she was young then and so were they. It had never been a passionate experience. With Spitfire she imagined it would be nothing but passionate. He was so tough, so manly and different. He was...

Jesus.

Stop it. Stop it now!

She shook the thoughts away and hurried over to the bathroom door, closing it firmly and pressing her hand against the wood as she composed herself. What the hell was she thinking? She wasn't some dippy teenager, eager to live out some ridiculous fantasy. She was an elite assassin. A trained killer. She let go of the door and walked back to the shower.

This giddiness had to stop. Right now. She had to act like Caesar expected her to. Cold. Unflinching. Clinical. That's how she became the best. That's how she took control of this new world.

And, yes, she was in New York and, yes, working with Spitfire again had stirred something inside of her. But this wasn't a movie. And even if it was, it was a thriller, not a romantic comedy.

"Pull yourself together," she muttered to herself. "You're Acid Vanilla. Remember your training. Remember who you are now."

She closed her eyes and stepped into the shower. The hot jets felt good against her naked body, and she put her head under the water to wash her hair. It was going to be okay. A little blip was to be expected. She was new to this game. But she could handle it.

She could handle anything.

CHAPTER 10

Spitfire took a sip of his coffee. Considering he'd purchased it from a hot dog vendor down the street, it was surprisingly good. He held the paper cup to his face, letting the steam warm his cheeks and nose. It was a bitterly cold day, and as they'd walked down Amsterdam Avenue there'd even been a few flakes of snow in the air. It had come to nothing, thankfully, but he was regretting not bringing gloves with him.

Next to him, Acid was huddled over her cup of Joe, looking like one of the homeless bums they'd walked past on the way here. She had her leather jacket zipped up and the cuffs pulled down over her hands, but she still looked freezing.

"Are you sure you're okay?" he asked.

She glared up at him. "Yes. I'm fine. I told you already."

"It won't go down well if you freeze to death, darling. Why don't you run along and buy yourself a winter coat? Our per diem for this job is a hundred dollars each. I bet you can get something decent for that. Something pink and pretty."

He knew he was being obnoxious with his choice of

language, but it was on purpose. He was taking her lead in the flirtation stakes and she seemed to enjoy the gentle ribbing.

"Piss off," she told him. "I'm warm enough."

This was her big problem, as he saw it. She didn't listen to reason. She might think she knew best, but the truth was she was inexperienced, not only in the world of elite assassins but as an adult human. It was understandable – having been locked up since the age of fifteen until relatively recently – that she had no proper spheres of reference. But that's why she should take heed of those who did. Hell, the silly girl didn't even know how to dress for the weather.

But let her shiver if that's what she wanted. Maybe he could warm her up later. Maybe…

Placing his attention on the matter at hand, he craned his neck to look around a passing bus as a man exited through the main doors of the hotel across the street.

Was this their guy?

The man took a left down West 73rd Street, towards Broadway. He had short greying hair like Bakov, but he looked more Middle Eastern than Slavic. It wasn't him.

"Where's the Chelsea Hotel from here?" Acid asked.

"Not sure. Why?" He didn't take his eyes off the hotel entrance.

"Why?" She scoffed. "Surely you've heard about the Chelsea Hotel."

Spitfire bit his lip.

Remember the assignment, old boy.

"I know it," he said. "It's where Sid Vicious killed his girlfriend. Right?"

More scoffing from Acid. He didn't look at her. If he did, he might elbow her in the face.

"Sid didn't kill Nancy," she informed him, in an annoying tone. "He would never have done that. He loved her."

This time Spitfire scoffed. "Love can make you do a lot of strange things. A lot of people kill those they're supposed to love."

"Yes, well. He didn't. It was a drug dealer they owed money to. But anyway, the Chelsea Hotel isn't just famous because of that. Loads of people have stayed there. Ginsberg, Kerouac. Dylan Thomas was staying there when he drank himself to death in the White Horse Tavern down the street. Shit. Is that still open?"

Spitfire shook his head. "I've no idea. But can we focus, please? Bloody hell. How many times do I have to pissing well say it?!" As he glanced down at her, he noticed she had that same wildness behind her eyes as on the plane.

"Sorry," she said. "I am focused. I am."

"Okay. Well, good." She was infuriating as hell, but he had to stay calm. On this job, she was as much his mark as Bakov was. Only in a very different way.

He watched her out of the corner of one eye as she scowled at the hotel entrance. "You know a lot of stuff for someone who's just turned twenty," he told her. "About certain things, at least."

She shrugged. "It's stuff I enjoy learning about. I read a lot of books when I was in Crest Hill. There was nothing much else to do."

Spitfire understood. It had been the same for him while he was in the army. He'd trained for a year at Sandhurst. After excelling in all fields, he was on his way to being fast-tracked to a lieutenant position when an altercation with a fellow cadet resulted in him breaking his captain's nose. It was always going to happen; he was an angry young man back then, rage never far away, and he saw his father in every authority figure he encountered. It wasn't long after they'd thrown him out of the army that Caesar found him.

"But I promise, Spitfire. I am taking this seriously." Acid's protestation snapped him back to the present. "Just let me know what you want me to do and I'll—"

"Wait!" He shushed her with a wave of his hand. Another man had just left the hotel. It was Bakov, he was sure of it. He nudged Acid. "There. See?"

Bakov was wearing a dark pea coat with the collar up, and had a red woollen beanie pulled down over his ears, but his wide nose and heavy-set brow were distinct.

"Got you, you bastard."

The Russian was speaking to someone on a mobile phone. From the stiff way he was walking and the way his eyes darted up and down the street, Spitfire assumed it wasn't a social call. Bakov walked a few feet along the sidewalk towards a newsstand, where he bought a magazine (it could have been a girlie mag, but it was hard to tell from this distance), and then turned and hurried back into the hotel.

"Shit," Acid whispered. "Now what?"

"This is fine," Spitfire replied. "We've placed him now. We know he's in there. All we need to do is wait for him to leave and follow him."

"What if he doesn't leave?"

"He will. He'll have to. Raaz thinks he's not got much to offer in terms of information. The CIA might try to turn him or make him an asset, but they won't spend any money at this stage on protection. I imagine they'll want to sound him out first, assess his value. If he is meeting with them, it'll be with a low-level operative initially, somewhere out in the open. As long as we're here when he leaves, we're golden. Then it's a matter of following him and staying open to opportunities."

Acid looked confused. "What are you thinking?"

"I'm not sure yet. But this is New York. Fatal accidents happen all day long, all over the city. Trust me, that part will show itself. We just need to be motivated and ready."

"Can't we go up to his room?" she asked. "People have accidents in hotel rooms as well." Her teeth chattered as she spoke.

"Jesus, kid. You need to get yourself a coat. Seriously." He pointed a finger at her. "That's an order, Acid. You're no use to me as a block of ice."

He almost smiled. There was a joke in there somewhere. A reference to his other assignment.

"I said I was fine," she replied. "I want to stay here. I don't want to miss anything. Please. I want to get this guy."

She glared at him with a fervour he'd not seen before. But at the same time her lips were turning blue.

"Oh, for f— Right! I'll get you a damn coat."

"What? No. I don't need you to—"

"Shh!" He held his hand up to her. The mark was back in the hotel and there was no way of knowing how long they'd be staking the place; he couldn't have the girl getting hypothermia. Plus, he wanted to get himself some gloves at the same time. "We passed a couple of clothes shops on our way here. I'll be back in ten minutes."

"No. It's fine. I don't want to be a bother. I'll go. I know what I like."

Spitfire frowned. "Yes. I can imagine you'd come back with some hideous black furry thing that makes you stand out like a sore arse. I'll get you something that's suitable."

Acid looked at the ground and dropped her shoulders. It was a sign she was finally concurring. "Thank you."

"Yes, well... whatever." He rubbed at the back of his neck. "But I need you to keep watch on the hotel while I'm gone. If you see Bakov, ring me. Immediately. Do you understand? He might have changed his clothes, so don't be complacent."

She nodded. "I won't let you down."

Spitfire shot a look across the street, then back to Acid's willing smile.

Jesus.

How was he supposed to operate in these conditions – all the time aware in the back of his mind he had to make this crazy female fall for him? One second she was cold and moody, the next she was over-enthusiastic, bordering on manic. In any other situation, he'd have already decided that getting into her panties wasn't worth the grief.

Women. He didn't understand them. Never had. That's why he never got involved with any beyond a one-night stand – maybe two nights if they were a nine or ten. It wasn't cricket, what was being asked of him. Because what if she did fall for him? The last thing he needed was some lovesick twenty-year-old cramping his style. Or going psycho on him when he let her down. He really hoped Caesar knew what he was doing.

Drawing in a cool breath, he addressed Acid.

"Right, then. Pay attention. I'll be back soon." And without waiting for a reply, he turned and strode away up the street.

CHAPTER 11

Acid bounced from foot to foot, rubbing her hands together and blowing on them. She didn't know how she felt about what just happened. Part of her was angry Spitfire had resorted to treating her like a silly child who couldn't dress herself. But another part of her rather liked that he was taking care of her. No one had ever shown that much interest in her comfort before. Regardless of how infuriated he'd appeared, Spitfire had taken note of her size and shape and was now buying her a coat to keep her warm. She couldn't remember the last time anyone had bought her clothes. It certainly hadn't happened since she was a very young girl. Her mum loved her and provided for her as best she could growing up, but most of the time Louisa had too many of her own problems to notice what was going on with her daughter.

This was why Acid felt so drawn to her new life at Annihilation Pest Control. Caesar was supportive and open and genuinely seemed to want to help her become the best person she could be. Finally, she felt part of a family. A nefarious, dangerous and fucked-up family. But a family all the same.

She blew out a long breath, marvelling at the icy cloud that formed in the air before it dissipated into the atmosphere.

A family...

And who was Spitfire in this scenario? Her older brother? If that was the case, she shouldn't be looking at him the way she was. The memory of how she'd behaved earlier, hoping to lure him into the bathroom, made her stomach churn.

What the hell had she hoped would happen?

And what if they had screwed? What then?

Caesar would be furious. That much, she was sure. She knew her mentor wasn't into women in *that* way, but he had a soft spot for her. She'd even heard Raaz complaining that *bloody Acid Vanilla* was the boss's new favourite. Why that was, she wasn't entirely sure. But she liked the idea of being someone's favourite. She didn't want to ruin it.

Bugger.

It was all so confusing. Is that what being an adult was like? Did office workers have to deal with such interpersonal strife and bullshit?

"Come on, Acid. Focus."

She said it to herself out loud; but rather than feeling silly, it sharpened her resolve. She found it helped to talk to herself like this. It snapped her out of her spiralling thoughts and reminded her who she was now and how far she'd come. If it wasn't for Caesar, she might still be rotting in Crest Hill. Or worse, working a dead-end job for a pitiful wage with no end in sight. She sure as hell wouldn't be in New York. The best city in the world. The home of punk and the Beats, of Warhol and the Factory. There was so much she wanted to see and do whilst she was here. The Empire State Building, the Statue of Liberty, the Museum of Modern Art. A rush of impatience washed over her. It was frustrating being so close to everything but unable to experience it. She yearned to get this job over and done with as soon as possible, yet at the same time she wanted to do it to the absolute best of her abilities. It was another damn dichotomy. Sometimes it felt as if her entire life was one big dichotomy.

She rolled her shoulders back, stretching out the tension across her chest where she'd been twisted up tight because of the cold.

"Keep it together," she muttered to herself.

When her moods were high, her thoughts were super creative and she could see the truth in matters more clearly. Often this was a blessing rather than a curse, yet at the same time she'd act reckless and impulsive. Like stripping naked with the door open in the hope her colleague might burst in and ravish her. This irresponsible aspect of her condition was one thing she was trying to hone. If she could get a better handle on the bats, she suspected this volatile aspect of her persona could be valuable. Many times, when the bats were in flight, she was so sharp-witted and full of energy she felt invincible.

Something at the corner of her eye caught her attention. She cast her gaze across the street and saw Boris Bakov standing in the doorway of his hotel. The hat was gone, revealing a head of long grey hair combed back from his face, but it was him all right. He was still wearing the grey pea coat with the collar turned up, and she recognised his face from the photo Spitfire had shown her this morning. That was another useful aspect of her condition. She only had to see something once and she had an almost photographic recall.

He looked both ways down the street, then straight at her.

"Shit!" She froze, whispering through gritted teeth. "What do I do now?"

But if Bakov had seen her standing there, she hadn't spooked him. He looked away, before hunching his shoulders and taking a right out of the hotel, walking at a casual pace. As Acid watched on, he took the next right down the side of a bakery and was gone.

Bloody hell.

She shot her attention up and down the avenue, standing on her toes to peer over people's heads, hoping she'd see Spitfire on his way back. But he was nowhere to be seen.

"Shit, shit, shit."

If she crossed the street and followed Bakov she'd be able to catch up with him, but another thirty seconds or a minute and he'd be long gone. She pulled the mobile phone out of her pocket. But what was the point in calling him if he wasn't close by? Bakov was alone, heading for what could be a secluded part of town. Secluded for New York, at least. If she pursued him, she might get the hit. They could have the job signed off by dinner. Caesar and the client would be happy and she'd have ample time to explore the city.

She clicked her teeth, trying to decide what to do. Reason told her to wait. This was only her third job and Spitfire had been adamant she call him rather than take matters into her own hands. But he wasn't the boss, was he? And the bats were becoming more unbending in their tenacity. They screeched across her consciousness, telling her how powerful she was.

She glanced both ways down the street and, when she still didn't see Spitfire, crossed the avenue and headed down the side of the bakery after Bakov.

She was doing this her way.

She was Acid Vanilla.

It was what she did.

CHAPTER 12

Boris Bakov was walking with purpose, but every so often he'd stop and look back the way he'd come. Each time, Acid ducked into a doorway or behind a group of pedestrians so he didn't see her. She was fast and elusive. Like a shadow. Like Caesar and Spitfire had trained her to be. At the end of the next block, he took a right and then the next left, as if moving in a zigzag formation. Acid slowed her pace.

Had he seen her?

Was this him trying to throw her off?

As she followed him onto the next street, she hung back in case he looked around, but he continued his journey, weaving in and out of people on the busy pavement towards the park at the far end. Looking up, Acid felt as though she recognised the building on the corner, and as she passed it she peered up at the impressive structure. Of course. It was The Dakota building. Home to so many famous people over the years. Judy Garland. Roberta Flack. Mark David Chapman shot John Lennon four times in the back and shoulder as he entered the building through the main archway to her left. The irony that she was here to assassinate someone wasn't lost on her. But as she considered the matter, she felt an affiliation only with Lennon, not his killer. Like Lennon, she was a rebel and an underdog, railing against a world she saw as immoral and broken. Her mark was a Russian thug, a killer himself. He deserved what was coming to him. She was nothing like Chapman.

Up ahead, Bakov took a left at the end of the street and disappeared from view. Shit. He was getting away from her. Quickening her step, she barged through a group of old folk who were milling around on the corner and found herself on a long street with four lanes of traffic. A row of bony winter trees stood on the outskirts of Central Park across the other side of the carriageway, and there was an old-fashioned newsstand by the roadside fifty feet down to the left. But the mark was nowhere in sight.

"Bugger," she cried out. "Where have you gone?"

She skipped down the street, darting her attention up, down and around, not caring that she was getting bustled and shoved by people walking in the other direction. Some of them might have even said something to her but she didn't hear them. Where the hell had he gone?

Panic bubbled in her stomach as she walked down as far as the newsstand. Spitfire had been vigorous in his instructions that she call him the second she got sight of the mark. Why hadn't she listened to him?

She'd fucked up. She'd let the bats get the better of her. She'd... Maybe not.

On the next corner she noticed the sign for the 72nd Street subway station and a flight of steps leading down. Racing over to them, she took the steps two at a time, entering a wide, beige-tiled corridor on the lower level with a barrier between her and another set of steps. Putting her head down, she ran at the barrier and vaulted the turnstile, not stopping when someone shouted after her. The stairwell beyond led to the platforms for both north and southbound trains. She leaned into the metal handrail as she ran down the steps, jumping the last few and not stopping as she reached the bottom. The station was quiet and she saw Bakov straight away. He was standing at the far end of the northbound platform, staring at the tracks with a stern expression on his face. She shifted behind a metal advertisement board where she could watch him without being seen. He seemed pensive. But why wouldn't he be? Even if he was unaware she was following him, he'd have to know Perchetka would do everything in his power to silence him.

The air trembled and a high-pitched whistling sound told her the next train was imminent. Leaving her position, she crept along the platform, staying close to the back wall and out of Bakov's line of sight. She felt a rush of cool air as the train pulled into the station beside her. She waited to see what the mark would do, and when he got on, she did the same, selecting the compartment one along from his but in the same carriage. This way she stayed out of sight but had access to him if needed.

Bakov perched on a bench seat near the door. She remained standing, facing away, but at such an angle she could see him in her peripheral vision. As the train lurched forward, she gripped the overhead rail to steady herself, riding the movement of the carriage as it gathered speed.

The train was busy with passengers, but they looked to be locals rather than tourists. It was evident in their detached expressions and lack of eye contact, and the fact most of them were lone travellers. More than that, though, she just sensed it. She was good at reading people – who they were, what they were thinking. It was another innate skill of hers that was useful for this line of work. She might not have much experience yet as an in-field assassin, but there was a reason Caesar had hired her.

As the train emerged from a dark tunnel, she found her

eyeline blocked by another passenger. A man. He was tall and broad-shouldered and had a bushy blond beard that covered most of his face and all of his neck. As she focused in on him, she realised he was looking right at her. She tensed. Because he wasn't just *looking* at her. Glaring would be more accurate a description. As their eyes met he didn't look away, like most people in polite society would have done. If anything, his stare intensified. His too-close-together eyes were like black pinpricks, devoid of any empathy or compassion, beady and cruel under white-blond eyebrows as bushy as his beard. He was wearing grey canvas trousers and a dark green corduroy jacket. Underneath this, was the hint of a grey threadbare cardigan and a creased white shirt. All his clothes were creased and she wondered if he was a homeless person, riding the subway to keep warm. If so, the years of living rough might explain the mad, almost psychotic way he was staring at her. She shifted over to the other side of the carriage to escape his glare and so she could get eyes on the mark. But as she did, the big man stepped into her line of sight once again.

What the hell was going on?

Cursing the big brute under her breath, she perched on one of the bench seats so she could see around the side of him. Bakov was still there, but the train was slowing and he looked as if he was readying himself to disembark. She drew in a long breath and held it in her chest, working on slowing her pounding heart rate as Spitfire had shown her.

All at once she felt lost and unsure of herself. What was she doing here? Spitfire would have returned to their stake-out point by now and would be furious she'd disobeyed him. This would be exacerbated by the fact there was no signal down in the subway and he couldn't call her.

Stay strong.
You can do this.

As long as she kept Bakov in her sights, an opportunity to take him out would show itself. It had to. That way, if she carried out the hit before Spitfire caught up with her, all would be forgiven. She smiled to herself at the thought of taking out the mark alone. It would solidify her position once and for all as a force to be reckoned with in the organisation. Caesar would love her for it.

As they pulled into the next station, Bakov got up from his seat and moved in front of the nearest set of doors. She was now only a few feet away from him and saw his eyes were the palest blue she'd ever seen and, when the train slowed, they darted fretfully through the window, taking in the platform beyond. This station was a lot busier than the last one and there were a sea of people waiting to board. That was good for her. A busy train station was more helpful than a quiet one. It had to look like an accident. But as Spitfire said, lethal accidents were two a penny in a city like New York. You simply had to stay open to opportunities.

Getting to her feet, she side-stepped closer to the doors, preparing herself to exit when the train came to a stop. She could sense the big, bearded man was still staring at her, but she didn't look at him. He was probably imagining himself following her down a dark alley and raping her. Well, let him try it. He wasn't the first weirdo to attempt to make her feel uncomfortable on public transport, and he wouldn't be the last.

The train jolted to a stop and the doors slid open. Acid stepped out onto the platform behind the mark, but as she was making to follow him, the surge of people trying to get on the train bustled him away from her. She fought for her position, elbowing her way through the bodies. Bakov was still in sight, hurrying along the platform towards the stairs. She pushed through and followed him up, reaching the next level a few seconds after him. The scene in front of her took her breath away. The concourse was a bustling mass of bodies and a sign overheard read *59 St – Columbus Circle Station*. It had to be one of the busiest subway stations in the world. This city was so much bigger than she'd ever imagined.

She moved over to where a kiosk was selling pretzels and donuts. Stepping up on the ledge that ran underneath the counter, she could see over people's heads. The pressure in her chest was extreme, as if she needed to scream or hit something to release it. But then she saw him, the mark, making his way up the escalator on the far side.

"Got you."

She stepped down from the ledge and ran after him, pushing past people and twisting around others. She was light on her feet and shoved her way through the barrier behind a tall man in a suit, getting to the escalator before Bakov reached the top. Taking the right-hand lane, she raced up the moving staircase. Bakov was moving faster now, weaving around people on his way to the exit. A sign hanging from the ceiling told Acid the next stairwell led up to street level and 8th Avenue. She knew this was a major road through Manhattan with multiple rows of fast-moving traffic. Fast-moving for New York City, at least. Fast enough that if someone got pushed in front of a bus or truck, they'd be lucky to survive. And if the person doing the pushing carried out the hit without being seen, then the death would be ruled as misadventure. A tragic accident.

Motivated by her new plan, she hurried along the concourse towards the exit. Bakov was already on the stairs, but she kept him in sight. She had this. She was going to make—

Shit!

Something large and heavy barged into her. She yelled out as she slammed against the wall and stumbled over onto one knee. Looking up, she saw the homeless man from the train. He grinned at her, his mouth barely visible through his thick rusty beard.

"What the fuck?" she spat. "Leave me alone."

She placed her hands on the cold tiled floor and went to push herself up, but a heavy knee ploughed into her side, knocking her to the ground.

"Go to hell," she gasped, fighting to breathe. It felt as if her ribs had been crushed. Peering about her, she tried to catch someone's eye, hoping a passer-by might step in and help. But everyone was hurrying past as if she was invisible.

She glanced up the stairs. Bakov was getting away.

"I swear to god you've picked the wrong girl," she snarled at the man, scrambling to her feet. "Get out of my way."

She pushed off the wall and launched herself at him. He shifted away, but she grabbed his arm and used the support to knee him in the groin. He let out a dull groan and doubled over, lashing out as he did and smacking her around the side of the head with his fist. The world spun as a deep pain spread through her skull, and for a few seconds she didn't know which way was up.

Bastard...

The screeches from the bats filled her head as a red mist washed over her. It was the same all-encompassing rage she'd experienced many times before: when she'd walked in on Oscar Duke, standing over her mum's bleeding body; when she'd found out Big Ella had killed her only friend at Crest Hill; when she'd discovered her therapist, Jacqueline, had been lying to her. All those times had ended badly for those involved.

She got to her feet and wiped her hand across her mouth. This guy was going down. He might have been twice her size, but at times like this, when the bats were in charge, she wouldn't stop until one of them was dead. She rounded on him, claws out, but before she could pounce he backed away. She tensed, readying herself for a counterattack. The man looked her up and down, then turned and lumbered away towards the exit.

"Hey!" she yelled after him. "Get back here! Fucking prick!"

With the red mist blinkering her vision and the bat chorus spurring her on, she ran after him. Up the steps to the street she went, head down and with such ferocity driving her that even tough, world-weary New Yorkers jumped out of her way. Once outside, she paused to get her bearings. In front of her was a traffic circle with a stone monument in the centre, similar in design to Nelson's Column in London but not as tall. As the underground station was Columbus Circle, she presumed it was Columbus standing on top.

Shifting her focus to the other side of the street, she saw her attacker running away from her down 8th Avenue. She raced after him, with her teeth grinding together and only vengeance on her mind. Despite his size, the man was fast. Her sides burned with a stitch as she pursued him across an intersection and down the next street. The traffic here was sporadic, and she moved into the road to avoid having to slow down around passing civilians. At the next intersection, the man turned and roared at her like some wild animal, before veering right down a side strip.

If he was trying to intimidate her, to make her back off, it didn't work. It had the opposite effect. Quickening her pace, she took the corner, catching sight of him as he headed down a ramp into an underground parking lot. Now she had him. The fucker would rue the day he ever picked a fight with her.

She crossed the street and ran down the ramp, slowing as she reached the lower level. The air was icy and smelt of gasoline. There was also no one else down here and the juxtaposition with the busy street was stark. She was startled as laughter echoed through the underground car lot. That prick. He was mocking her. Over to her left, the concrete sloped down to another level below the one she was on. That's where the laughter was coming from. With a blinding fury sweeping across her awareness, she headed for the ramp, face twisted in a cruel pout and fists balled up in readiness. At the bottom was a long passageway that disappeared around to the right. She could still hear the man's booming laughter bouncing off the walls.

The scruffy bastard had no idea who he was dealing with. She wasn't some twink he could intimidate by leering at her or knocking her over. She was Beowulf Caesar's star pupil. She was fast, strong and highly skilled. She was Acid Vanilla. She was...

Ah, shit....

She was screwed!

She'd presumed the passageway would bring her out into another section of the parking lot. But as she turned the corner, she found herself in a concrete box room about fifteen feet square and with no windows. Rage morphed into regret and then panic as she spun around to see the man standing in the doorway behind her. His huge shoulders were rising and falling with each breath, but the look on his face was one of unadulterated glee.

Bugger.

He hadn't been running away from her. He'd been luring her here. And once again she'd let her anger get the better of her. As the giant man stepped towards her with his arms out, it appeared this time she was going to pay the ultimate price.

"Okay, you ugly bastard," she said, raising her fists. "Let's see what you've got."

CHAPTER 13

Spitfire got to the end of the street and had almost reached the first clothing store before he realised what he was doing. When it hit him, he stopped walking and did an almost comedy double-take. He was going to buy clothes. For a woman. Because he was concerned she might be cold.

What in the name of bloody hell was going on?

It was only because she was young and inexperienced, he told himself as he continued onwards to the store. It had to be. If she was a male recruit, he'd be doing the same. He was a gentleman, after all. A proper grown-up. This was the sort of thing you did for those in your charge.

In the store, he made a beeline for the winter coats and grabbed the first suitable thing he could find that would fit her (the fact he knew her exact size and shape didn't concern him too much). It was a red overcoat made of thick, stiff material, with a belt around the waist and long enough to keep her warm. She could even wear it over that damned leather jacket if she wanted to. A good choice, he thought. Although why he cared so much about her wellbeing was another matter, and one that plagued him as he approached the counter. He handed the coat to the perky young assistant and didn't even flirt with her as she rang it through the till.

It was too much. Caesar was asking too much of him for this job. He knew he was a charming son of a bitch, but bedding a pretty young airhead and making someone like Acid Vanilla fall in love with him were very different undertakings. It was too difficult. The variables were too unknown. At the same time, his mind was doing mental gymnastics rather than focusing on the one thing it should be – taking out the mark.

That was why he was here.

It was what Spitfire Creosote did best.

Love? Not for him.

He handed the brunette his credit card, and the fact that he now felt the familiar ripple of sexual energy shoot through him as their eyes met empowered him further. Yes. He'd tell Caesar he'd tried his best with Acid but it wasn't happening. The boss might be annoyed for a while, but he'd be a damn sight angrier if Bakov got away. And that was looking more and more likely while his mind was on other things.

As he marched out of the store with the new coat, he was resolute. On the walk back to the hotel he even considered Acid's plan.

Only, when he got there, she was nowhere to be seen.

Fucking hell.

That bloody girl!

Cursing the day he'd ever met the foolish cow, he marched to the end of the block and back again, all the time with one eye on the hotel opposite. But neither Bakov nor his wayward partner was anywhere to be seen. He pulled out his phone and called her, but got an out-of-service tone. That meant she either had it switched off or was out of range, possibly on the subway. He pocketed the phone and shot his attention back over to the hotel, stroking the short layer of stubble on his chin as he considered the options. His instructions couldn't have been clearer. She was to call him the moment she saw Bakov leave the hotel. But to someone like Acid – hot-headed, impulsive, naïve in the ways of fieldwork – instructions were probably viewed as mere suggestions. There was every possibility Bakov had appeared and she'd followed him. She was so desperate to show Caesar what she could do, he wouldn't put it past her to want sole credit for the hit.

"Bloody shitting hell."

He grabbed hold of the signet ring on his right hand, breathing slowly through his nose as he twisted it around.

"Buggering bastard fuck!"

Once in control of the rage that flooded his system, he remembered he had a better tool at his disposal. Technology. Namely, the tracking system Raaz had developed. He pulled out his phone once again and scrolled through the options on the screen until he found the maps software. A screen flashed up showing a basic layout of the surrounding area, and using the keypad he could zoom in and out. As he did so, he saw a small red dot at the right-hand corner, flashing on and off.

"There you are," he whispered to himself.

Raaz Terabyte might have been a sour-faced cow most of the time, but she was also a bona fide genius. He zoomed in on the red dot. It showed Acid's location as Columbus Circle, on the edge of Hell's Kitchen.

He set off, his wide, pissed-off strides turning into a determined run as he headed for the subway on the corner of the next block. There was no one waiting at the ticket counter when he got down to the first level, and he threw a note at the bespectacled man behind the glass, requesting two seven-day passes before grabbing them and racing down to the platform.

A train was already waiting as he got there and he jumped on as the doors slid shut, choosing to stand rather than sit. As the train trundled out of the station and picked up speed, he perused the Manhattan underground map on the carriage wall. Columbus Circle was the next stop, but he traced the route to the end of the line, counting the stations as he went. Anything to preserve his composure until he knew what he was dealing with.

Five minutes later and the train pulled into the station. The second the doors opened, he leapt out onto the platform, moving through the station like a sidewinder after its prey. As he ran up the final set of steps leading to the street, he flipped open his phone, holding it in the air to speed up the connection. Acid had moved since the last time he looked, but the red dot was now stationary. He zoomed in and saw she was in a multi-storey parking garage two blocks away. Shoving the phone into his pocket, he set off.

A part of him now hoped Acid had followed Bakov and was taking care of the hit. Hell, he'd even congratulate her and allow her to take full credit for the job. But the closer he got, the more his instincts told him that wasn't the case. Something didn't feel right.

He pressed on. The roads here were covered in a smattering of dirty slush from the recent snowfall and he almost slipped over as he weaved around a group of civilians walking in the other direction. At the next corner he checked his phone. The red dot hadn't moved. Acid was still in the parking lot on the other side of the street.

He crossed over and ran down the first ramp, calling her name.

"Acid! It's me. Are you here?" On the next level he stopped to listen. "Acid?"

From the level below, he could hear grunting and the sound of something being dragged across the concrete floor. It didn't sound good. Moving swiftly but silently, he made his way down the ramp. The sounds of a struggle were more pronounced now and he followed the grunts and groans along a wide corridor before it opened out into a larger room. A single security bulb buzzed intermittently on the wall but provided minimal light. As his eyes grew accustomed to the gloom, he saw a blond-haired giant kneeling on the ground on the far side of the room. Acid was underneath him, struggling to get free.

Spitfire grabbed hold of the doorway, using this split-second pause to assess the situation. Acid's attacker was huge in both stature and frame. The element of surprise was required if he stood half a chance of taking him down.

With the assessment done, instincts took over and he ran at the man, smashing a flying knee into the side of his face. It was a heavy assault administered in textbook fashion and Spitfire had counted on it doing more damage. But as he leapt back, he saw it had only knocked the big bastard off balance.

Blondie released Acid – leaving her rolling on the floor gasping for air – and got to his feet. He rubbed at his cheek where Spitfire had kneed him, but an evil grin was present under his rusty beard.

"Who are you?" Spitfire asked. "What do you want?"

In way of response, the brute hunched over in a fighting stance. Spitfire did the same, his senses tingling with readiness. He stared at him, searching for a tell, something in his face that might alert him to his next move.

With a growl, Blondie sprang forward, but Spitfire saw him coming and side-stepped away, punching him in the kidneys as he passed by.

Jesus Christ!

His body was thick and firm. He wasn't just huge, he was muscular with it. Spitfire stepped back, dancing from foot to foot and keeping his limbs loose and ready. Both his experience and training told him it was stupid to trade blows with a man of Blondie's size. But whilst he might not defeat him with brute force, there were other ways to win a fight. When Blondie circled to his left, Spitfire answered him with a left hook to the chest. Blondie countered, circling to the right, but Spitfire countered this with a right hook to the jaw. He was confusing the big man, baiting him into the response he wanted. But regardless of his superior tactics, his punches were having little effect.

"I kill you," Blondie snarled in a thick accent. He powered towards Spitfire, who side-stepped him once more. But it was one move too many. The big man was expecting it and, at the last second, he twisted round and smashed his elbow into Spitfire's forehead. The room spun. Flashing lights invaded his eyes. He staggered backwards, putting as much space between him and his foe as possible while he regained his focus.

Bollocks. That hurt. But he was still standing. He dodged out of the way as Blondie's enormous fist blurred through the air. It caught him on the shoulder, knocking him against the wall and winding him. He coughed, fought for air. Blondie lunged forward and punched him in the solar plexus, knocking the rest of the air out of him.

The big man laughed as Spitfire stumbled forward onto one knee. "You think you can fight me and win? You can't fight me. You can't win."

Spitfire looked over at Acid. She was on all fours, coughing her guts up. She looked wrecked, but she was alive. Whether either of them remained that way depended on what he did next.

"Come on, tough guy," Blondie said, beckoning Spitfire forward as he got to his feet. "Let's go."

With a grunt, Spitfire pushed off from the wall towards him, but at the last second stepped over to his right. Bewildered by the shift, Blondie swung his arm wide. At the same time, Spitfire launched himself into the air and stomped on the side of the man's knee. He felt the joint buckle beneath his weight, but it didn't snap. Blondie roared and staggered over to one side, clutching at his leg. Seizing the opportunity, Spitfire grabbed his immense head and ran him forward, smashing his skull against the wall. The impact of bone against concrete made a dull thud and his body went limp. Spitfire let him tumble to the ground before finishing him with a sharp kick to the face, which opened up his snout like a crimson rose.

"Well, what do you know, *tough guy*?" he said. "Looks like I won after all."

As his body relaxed and his lizard brain gave way to reason, Spitfire saw Acid across the other side of the room. She was leaning against the wall and looked like she'd seen a ghost. As their eyes met, she nodded.

"That was amazing," she gasped.

"It wasn't," he replied. "But we need to get out of here. Come on."

Looking around, he picked up the new coat from where he'd dropped it and flung it at her.

She caught it and wrinkled her nose. "Red? Really?"

Spitfire shot her a stern look. "Put it on," he growled. "Now!"

CHAPTER 14

Spitfire dabbed at his face as he walked along, checking his fingers for blood. He appeared to have got away with just a dull ache in his head and a few bruised ribs, but as he looked down at his hands his anger swelled.

Bugger.

He'd forgotten to buy gloves at the store. Which meant, so far today, Acid had lost the mark, almost got them both killed, and was occupying his thoughts so completely he was forgetting things.

This wasn't on. At all.

But at least it solidified his stance regarding Caesar's ridiculous request. There was no way in heaven or hell he could make this crazy bitch love him, even if he wanted to. She might be full of potential, but so far she'd been nothing but a liability.

"Hey," she said, sidling up and nudging him as they walked along Broadway back to the apartment. "I'm sorry about that."

"Oh, you're sorry, are you? Fuck me!" He kept his head up. "I told you to call me if you saw Bakov leave the hotel. That was your only order."

She sniffed. "But if I'd done that, we'd have lost him. And

yes, I know we lost him anyway, but that wasn't my fault. I had him in my sights. I was ready to take him out. If it hadn't been for that fucking prick, I'd have—"

"Jesus, Acid!" He stopped and faced her. "What do you think would have happened if I hadn't shown up? You'd be dead right now. I'd be scraping whatever was left of you off the floor of that parking garage."

She chewed her top lip as she gazed up at him. He couldn't make out whether she was holding back tears or anger.

"I'm sorry I got in a mess, but I wasn't expecting that guy to jump me."

"But he did! And that's what you're dealing with when you're out in the field – unexpected eventualities. You've got to be prepared for anything to happen, and you weren't. It sounds to me like you were so damned focused on getting the hit, you overlooked dangers and weren't thinking clearly."

He paused in the hope his words might sink in. Though, he didn't know why he was trying to help her. As far as he was concerned, she deserved to get choked out by that big bastard.

"Maybe it's a good thing," he said. "Maybe you need to understand what happens when you go off-book. You swan around like you're the fucking Queen of Sheba, but you're nothing but an amateur. I know Caesar has a lot riding on you, kid, but you aren't living up to your potential yet. And if you think you are, it's only going to go badly for you."

He set off walking before she could respond, but made sure he could hear her footsteps following him before crossing onto Amsterdam Avenue. His plan now was to get back to the apartment and call Caesar. He should make him aware of how unruly his beloved protégé had acted today.

At the next intersection he waited for her to catch up. When she did, he noticed a deep scowl creasing her features. It made her look kind of cute, but he shook that thought straight from his head.

Nope. Not a chance.

This one was far more trouble than she was worth.

"Who do you think that guy was?" she asked.

"Blondie? I've no idea," he replied, eyes on the walk sign. As it changed, he set off again, not looking around but sensing her skipping along beside him. "Probably he was some sex-crazed chancer who liked the look of you." When Acid didn't respond, he turned to check her out. The scowl was still there. "What are you thinking?"

"I thought the same as you. At first. But now I wonder if there's more to it. What if he was following Bakov and that's why he attacked me in the station? He wanted to stop me from getting to him."

Spitfire rolled the idea around in his head. "Why would he want to stop you?"

"Maybe he's a rival assassin. He wants the hit. Wants the contract on Bakov."

"No, that doesn't make sense."

"Doesn't it? He seemed pretty tasty from what I saw. And he said something while we were fighting before you showed up. Something about me not getting what I wanted. I thought at the time it was odd. But it was like he expected me to be there. Or was ready for me? Or something. I don't know."

Spitfire ran his tongue across his top teeth. She was speaking fast and frantic, as if her thoughts were hitting her mouth before she had a chance to process them. But he agreed with her. It was a strange thing for the stranger to say, given the circumstances.

"He can't be a rival," he said. "The job isn't an open contract. It was a private agreement between Caesar and the client. No one else in the industry would be privy to it."

"Yeah," she replied. "It's weird, though."

Spitfire widened his step. They were getting close to the apartment. Another few minutes of walking. "Let's get back to the digs. We can rest up an hour and take stock." He pulled one of the seven-day subway passes out of his pocket. "Here, I got you this. Use it. We don't want to alert the authorities to our presence here."

She took the pass without comment and neither of them spoke again for the rest of the journey. Small mercies.

Back inside the apartment, Spitfire hung up his coat and walked through into his bedroom. Slipping out of his suit jacket, he took a hanger from the closet and placed the jacket carefully on the rail. He was still furious with Acid, but there was no reason to take it out on his clothes.

After unbuttoning his cuffs and collar, he went back out into the main space and over to the large steel refrigerator, which was stocked with bottles of water. Grabbing one, he twisted off the top and drank most of it down in one go. As he lowered it, he saw Acid leaning against the doorframe that led to her bedroom. She'd been watching him.

"What is it?"

She shrugged. "Nothing. I just don't think you need to be so nasty. I was trying my best."

He sighed. *Fucking women.*

This was why he didn't do relationships. Why he didn't do partnerships of any kind if he could help it. He finished the water and placed the empty bottle on the worktop.

"I need to ring the boss," he said, walking past her to his room and slamming the door. As soon as he did, he was annoyed with himself. He hardly ever lost his cool these days. It was her. She had that effect on him.

Taking a moment to compose himself, he went to his suitcase and unzipped the inside compartment, taking out his regular mobile phone and switching it on. Once it had settled, he scrolled down to 'Home' and tapped the call button. It was 5.30 p.m. New York time, making it 10.30 p.m. in London.

Raaz picked up the call after a few rings. "Do you have news for me?" she asked.

"Hello to you too, my dear."

Raaz sighed. "Oh, piss off, Spitfire. This is not a Bond-Moneypenny relationship, so stop trying to make it one."

He swallowed, a little thrown by the outburst. "Is everything all right?"

"Yes. Fine. But I've got four operatives in play at opposite ends of the world and none of you seems to be doing what you're paid for. Please tell me you're about to send me the photographic proof of your job being completed."

"Not yet. But soon." He sat on the edge of the bed and eyed himself in the large mirror above the dresser. "I was hoping to speak to the big man. Is he around?"

Raaz made a sound like an irate snake. "One second. I'll check."

The phone went silent. Spitfire leaned into the mirror and moved his head from left to right, checking for any injuries. The old boat race was as handsome and unblemished as ever. He could do with a shave, however. He straightened up at the sound of a click on the line and then a booming voice.

"What is it, old boy? I was just about to head out."

"Is this Russian job definitely a private contract?" he asked.

"Yes. It is. Why? What's happened?"

Spitfire paused, wondering how best to broach the subject. "Long story short, we were in pursuit of the mark when this big guy jumped us. And I mean big. The fucker must have been about six feet five, built like a rugby prop. But he had skills, too. He was fast and he was tough. It's probably nothing, but it got me thinking he might be a freelancer going after our contract."

Caesar scoffed. "And what happened to this fellow when you met him?"

"We fought. I overpowered him. Introduced his skull to a concrete wall."

"And...? Is that the end of him?"

Spitfire rolled his head back. *Shit.* Why the hell hadn't he killed him when he had the chance? He stared up at the ceiling, but it provided no answer.

"No, I don't think so," he said. "I assumed at the time he was an opportunist mugger, not worth bothering with. It was only once I'd left the scene I started wondering if there was more to it."

He glanced at the door, aware he was relaying Acid's hypothesis; the one he'd played down only half an hour earlier. But if this came to anything, it was only fair he got the credit. He was the lead operative, after all.

Caesar made a low, grumbling sound like he always did when he was thinking.

"You really think he's a freelancer, trying to take our business?"

"It happens. You know it does. Especially now a lot of the jobs are appearing on the blasted internet." It was still a bone of contention for Spitfire. People said the information superhighway was going to revolutionise the industry, but so far all he could see was a lot of problems. "Or is it possible Perchetka has sent someone else to take out the mark?"

"No. That's not how this works. He knows that. He might be Russian, but he's not stupid. No assassin organisation would ever work for him again if he broke the code so blatantly."

Spitfire got up off the bed. "That's what I thought. But is it worth Raaz searching the forums and databases?" The internet had some useful features, he supposed. "He was about six-five, three hundred and fifty pounds. Distinguishing features – thick blond hair and a huge strawberry-blond beard. I'd place his country of origin as Germany or Austria from the accent."

"Okay, Spit. You were right to be concerned. We can't have some lone wolf taking our business. It makes us look bad. If you see the fucker again, make sure you eradicate him. I'll pass on the description to Raaz and see if she can get an ID on him. She'll call you. Meanwhile, there's the minor matter of the hit on Bakov. Can we please box this off soon? If this big German fellow is trying to steal our thunder, the best attack is to get to the Russian first before he has a chance. To be honest with you, when Raaz put your call through, I was expecting you to tell me it was done."

Spitfire returned to the mirror and stared into the eyes of his reflection. "It will be done. Tomorrow." For the first time, he noticed fine lines at the corners of his eyes. He didn't like that.

"Good man," Caesar said. "And while you're on the line – what about the other little task I set you?"

He turned from the mirror. "That's in hand."

"Is it now? You dirty sod!"

Spitfire closed his eyes. He was in no mood for Caesar's bawdy humour. "I mean, I'm working on it. It's not easy though, Caesar. I want to manage your expectations here. I can't promise that I'll—"

"Just get it done," came the reply. "Kill the mark. Get the girl. Save the universe. Isn't that how it goes? Something like that, anyway."

Spitfire exhaled slowly through pursed lips. "Fine. I won't let you down."

"I know you won't. But for now I must dash. Toodle-pip." He hung up before Spitfire could respond.

Damn it.

He'd been ready to tell him he couldn't follow through with the Acid situation, but now, with Blondie in the mix complicating matters, he didn't want to sound like a complete incompetent. He'd kill Bakov, then tell him.

He placed his phone back in his suitcase and headed for the door. There was a bottle of Four Roses Bourbon next to the fridge and he felt like he deserved a glass or two. Okay, so today had been a write-off, but it happened, put it down to jetlag. Tomorrow he'd get serious again. No more messing around buying coats or worrying about silly things like emotions. He would find his mark, and he would kill him. Because that was what he did best.

He opened his bedroom door and was met with Acid Vanilla standing in the corridor outside.

"Oh, hello," he said. "What do you want?"

She'd tied her hair back in a ponytail and had changed into fresh jeans and a white vest top. From her stance, he surmised she'd been waiting for him to come out for some time, but she didn't look pleased to see him. Her face was twisted in an angry snarl.

"You conniving bastard," she spat. "I'm going to fucking kill you!"

CHAPTER 15

Spitfire moved past Acid into the living space, but she followed him.

"I heard you just now, telling Caesar you thought that guy might be a freelancer," she said, her voice rising a few octaves. "That was my theory, and you pretty much told me it was a load of crap. That's really shitty, you know that? You make out I'm naïve to think that way, but then present it to the boss as if you came up with it."

"I was doing you a favour," he replied, turning to face her once he'd put some distance between them. That was for her benefit, too. When he got mad, he didn't trust himself to act so gentlemanly.

"Oh, you were doing me a favour? Thank you so much. Whatever can I do to repay you, kind sir?"

"Don't push it, Acid. It was better coming from me. Do you want Caesar to know about the shit you pulled today? Not only did you jeopardise the mission, but you almost got us both killed."

"What do you mean?" Her eyes burned with intensity. He'd never seen her look so ferocious. "What do you mean, *jeopardise the mission?"*

Spitfire held his ground. He wasn't going to be intimidated by some kid. By a woman. "What if the mark saw you? I told you to call me the second he stepped out of the hotel. That was your only order. But, no. You chase after him like some hot-headed fool, trying to get all the glory for yourself. It doesn't work that way, kid. You need to pay your dues, do what you're told."

Acid scoffed. "Jesus, who do you think you are?"

"I know who I am. Can you say the same? Because right now you're acting like a petulant bitch." He gritted his teeth. "Bloody hell. I knew this was a bad idea. I told them as much. I don't need a fucking sidekick. Especially one who hasn't the first clue how to conduct herself in day-to-day life, never mind whilst working in the field."

He meant his words to be weapons, and they seemed to do the trick. Acid had been staring open-mouthed, readying herself to reply, but these last few statements made her close it again. Spitfire held her gaze, his face hard with indignation, not backing down one iota.

"It... was... my... theory," she hissed.

"There is no such thing as *you*. There's *only* the organisation. Coming from me, Caesar has taken the new information seriously. That's what's important." He placed his hands on the side of the kitchen unit and looked down. His knuckles were covered in grazes and dried blood. "Go to bed, Acid. Get some rest. We'll both feel better after some sleep."

"I don't need sleep. I need you to respect me. I need you to listen to me and not treat me like a kid."

"Then stop acting like one."

He looked up at her. And at that moment, any belief he might have harboured that the matter was settled fell away. Acid approached with a look in her eyes he'd never seen before. It wasn't anger or hurt, but something far more primal. For a split-second, it made him forget who he was.

"I am not a kid," she repeated, but her voice was softer. "I am Acid Vanilla. I am a killer. I was doing my job today. I could have finished it."

"But you didn't." He pulled in a deep breath as he turned to face her. They were standing just a few feet apart. He exhaled, slowing his system. "But no harm done. We can go out again first thing. I'm sure no one saw you, and if you listen to me this time, then—"

"Ah, piss off. You're just like every other stupid man I've ever met." She grabbed up the empty water bottle from the side and flung it at him. It bounced off his chest and onto the floor. "I don't need you telling me what to do."

The impact of the bottle hardly registered, but the fact she'd done it sent an army of rage marching through his system. He stepped forward and grabbed her by the wrists.

"Get off me!" She writhed and wriggled as he walked her across the room, gnashing her teeth and snarling as she tried to get free. But he was a lot stronger than her. He hustled her down the corridor to her bedroom and stopped outside. With his hands still tight around her wrists, he straightened his arms and looked her in the eyes.

"You need to calm down. Do you hear me? We both do. Now get in there and get to sleep."

"Piss off, old man. Let me go. You're hurting me."

"Acid. Settle down."

"What? You're sending me to my room? I'm not a damn kid. I'm a trained killer. I'll kill you."

"Is that right?" He released his grip and shoved her away. She stumbled backwards into her room and, as the bed frame hit the back of her knees, sat abruptly on the bed. It was sort of comical, but neither of them laughed.

"Now stay there," Spitfire yelled. "I mean it. For both our sakes."

He grabbed the handle and slammed the door shut. When he was certain she wasn't going to burst out of the room and claw his eyes out, he wandered back into the kitchen. The muscles in his forearms and across his shoulders burned with tension.

"Stupid, bloody…"

He grasped the neck of the bottle of Four Roses and dragged it across the counter. Screwing off the top, he was about to take a swig straight from the bottle but he stopped himself. Despite his recent outburst, these days he was a man of refinement. Drinking bourbon from the bottle was the behaviour of a cheap thug. He opened the unit on the wall in front of him and took down a glass tumbler, pouring himself a large measure and gulping it down in one. He poured himself another and placed the bottle down next to the glass.

Over the years he'd learnt how to calm himself at times of heightened stress – it was vital in this game that you remained grounded and didn't let your emotions get the better of you – but some things just needed time to settle.

He lifted the glass and took a gentle sip of the bourbon, tasting it properly now. It was floral and smooth and he could pick up hints of apple and honey. Closing his eyes, he finished the glass, holding the liquid in his mouth before swallowing it. He could feel himself calming with every second that ticked by, but his system was still in fight mode. It takes time for the adrenaline to be absorbed by the body. Which is why it was important to remove himself – or rather her – from the equation just now.

Walking back to his room, he retrieved his cigarette case and lighter from his jacket. Flipping open the case, he slid a Marlborough Red from beneath the metal arm and screwed it between his lips. He lit it as he walked back through into the kitchen, sucking back a long drag and blowing a plume of thick smoke into the room.

"Acid bloody Vanilla," he muttered to himself. But there was a wry smile on his face.

She certainly was a fiery one. Infuriating and intriguing in equal measures. But he liked that she didn't take any shit. Even if she was a royal pain in the arse most of the time.

He took another drag of his cigarette, closing his eyes as the nicotine hit his bloodstream.

She was damn sexy, too. He couldn't deny it. There was something about the way her hair had whipped across her face as she screeched at him just now that turned him on a great deal. She was a wild thing, a little unhinged, but who wasn't in this life? And he did appreciate a challenge.

With his cigarette dangling from his lips, he took down another glass from the wall unit and placed it next to his own. Filling both glasses with bourbon, he walked them over to Acid's bedroom door and tapped his signet ring on the wood.

"Hey, you awake?" he asked, cigarette dancing with the movement of his lips.

There was no answer. No sound at all. Balancing the two glasses in his left palm, he raised his right hand to remove the cigarette from his mouth.

"Listen, kid, we've both had a busy day. Why don't we put that little blow-up down to experience and move on? What do you say?"

Still nothing.

"I've got you a drink out here if you want it. Bourbon."

He heard a sound from inside the room. The bed springs, clanging. A second later, the door opened a crack to reveal Acid. Her hair was covering most of her face, but he could see her eye make-up was smudged. A slender arm snaked through the gap in the door and took the drink from him before it retracted back into the room and she shut the door in his face.

"Charming." He pulled on his cigarette and blew the smoke against the door. "We've still got a job to do, Acid. You want to show Caesar you're up to the task, right? First thing in the morning, we'll return to the hotel and stake it out until Bakov shows up. Then we'll take care of him. Nice and quick. After that, we can celebrate. Do some sightseeing, or whatever it is you want to get out of this little trip."

No answer.

He raised his fist to knock on the door, but brought it to his mouth instead, biting down hard on his forefinger. He wasn't going to say sorry. Not a chance. Spitfire Creosote never apologised.

He stepped back as the door opened, and was about to say more when she shoved the empty glass at him. As he stared at it, she shook it.

"You want another?" He couldn't help smiling as she shook it again in response. "Fine. There's plenty. But why don't you come out and we can have a drink together? Clear the air."

He pushed at the door and, getting no resistance, opened it fully. She was still dressed in the vest top and jeans, but had taken off her boots and socks. Her toenails were painted black. No surprise there.

"Are you coming out?"

He walked back into the kitchen, scooping the bottle of Four Roses off the kitchen counter and taking it over to the dining table. Acid joined him there as he pulled out two chairs and sat on one of them.

"I'm not your sidekick."

He leant back. "I'm sorry?"

"You said I was your sidekick. I'm not. I'm no one's sidekick. I never will be." She skidded her empty glass across the table at him and slumped onto the chair opposite. Not the one he'd pulled out for her.

"Did I say that?" He chuckled as he poured her another bourbon. "That is a bit harsh." He slid the glass over to her. "But you were acting like a little brat."

She made a sound halfway between a snort and a scoff, but accepted the drink all the same. "If I was your sidekick – which I'm not – I'd have expected better treatment from you than I've had so far."

"Is that so?"

"Absolutely. If I had a sidekick, I'd be a lot nicer to them."

"Do you think?"

"I know. And regardless, this is only my third job. My first one overseas. You could afford me a little leeway. It was only eighteen months ago you were training me. I'd say I've excelled since then. I thought I was doing the right thing today, following Bakov. If it wasn't for that guy... you know..."

She trailed off and Spitfire decided not to reiterate his thoughts on the matter. There was little use going over it again. She'd fucked up, they'd both said their piece, and they were now moving past it. He took time finishing his cigarette, stubbing it out on the amber glass ashtray in the middle of the table.

"You need to control that temper," he told her, wafting away a plume of rising smoke. "It's going to get you into bother."

Acid didn't look up as she took a long sip of her drink. "I can control it. And it's not a temper. Not really. It's weird and hard to explain. Sometimes I get these urges and feelings that take me over. I think they help. Most of the time."

Spitfire sat forward. "What sort of urges and feelings?"

"Umm... It's like I have a force driving me. My brain feels super sharp and I can see things more clearly. Sometimes, it's as if I'm moving one step ahead of the rest of the world. It's like I'm full of electricity and static noise. Like bats chattering and screeching." She met his gaze and her cheeks flushed as she looked away. "I told you it was weird."

"Well, whatever it is, you need to get a handle on it. Whilst we're here *working alongside each other,* I can't have you running off again. Do you understand, Acid?"

She nodded. Reluctantly, perhaps, but it was concurrence all the same. Maybe they weren't too dissimilar after all. Two hot-blooded souls, raging at the world and their past lives in equal measure. He'd thrown the word volatile around a lot recently when considering Acid, but he was just as bad. The difference was he'd learned to control his darker urges over the years. Some of them, at least. She would, too, given time. Sitting here now, he even wondered whether he might be the one to help her do it. He had enjoyed training her.

"You'll get there," he said, and when she looked up again he winked. "Caesar wants you to succeed. We all do."

She grinned mischievously. "Careful there, Spitfire. You'll have me all teared up."

"Oh, do piss off." He grabbed up his drink and slung it back. "You make me laugh; you know that?"

"Really? Do you want to tell your face?"

He actually did laugh at that one. "Seriously, though, kid. We've got this. Tomorrow we get Bakov and we box this job off. It shouldn't be hard."

Acid rolled her now empty glass along the tabletop. "So... tonight... maybe we could do something fun?"

Something other than adrenaline fired in Spitfire's system. "What did you have in mind?"

She grinned. "Go out. Explore the city. There are so many places I want to see and we've only got a few days. I know you want to get the job done first, but I thought if we could—"

"Whoa there, darling." He held his hand up. "I meant what I said earlier. We could both benefit from an early night. This job might be straightforward, but we need to stay sharp. We'll go out and celebrate once Bakov is dead and we've got proof for the client." He looked at her, forcing his eyes not to wander lower than her face, lest he change his mind.

Come on, old boy.

You're a professional.

There'll be plenty of time for that, too, when the Russian was on a slab in the city morgue. Or splattered under the wheels of a taxi. For now, he needed to heed his own advice and get some rest.

Scraping back his chair, he got to his feet. "I'll see you in the morning."

He didn't look at Acid again as he walked past her to his bedroom.

CHAPTER 16

In her room, two hours later, Acid lay on top of the bed, staring at the ceiling.

It was no use.

She couldn't sleep.

After Spitfire had turned in for the night, she'd helped herself to another glass of Four Roses before using the bathroom and then retiring to her room. She'd had every intention of sleeping like he wanted her to. She'd even got undressed down to her knickers and climbed under the covers, but her mind was racing with thoughts and ideas and her nerve endings tingled with expectation. The same way they always did when she was in one of her manic phases.

Accepting defeat, she threw off the covers and got up. Checking her mobile phone, she saw it was almost ten-thirty. Still early for New York. She walked over to her suitcase where she'd flung her balled-up jeans. She pulled them on and selected a new top from out of her case, a black t-shirt with the sleeves cut off. On top of this, she put on a black hooded sweatshirt and finished the look with her leather jacket. For all of one second, she thought about putting on the red overcoat Spitfire had bought her, but the thought made her shudder.

Not a bleeding chance. Not where she was going.

She moved over to the mirror and inspected her make-up, spitting on her finger and rubbing at the mascara and eyeshadow around her eyes until most of the smears were gone and what remained looked as if it was meant to be that way. Leaning closer to her reflection, she saw her pupils were huge, but that was also normal when she felt this way.

Reaching for the make-up bag, she applied a fresh smear of lipstick and stepped back to inspect the result. She looked good. Like a real New Yorker. She didn't know how long she'd been lying in bed, but it was long enough that Spitfire was hopefully asleep by now. He'd be furious if he knew she was sneaking out, but as long as she was back before he woke there'd be no issue.

Did he really expect her to be in New York and not want to go out on the town? There were places to see. Drinks to be drunk. After being anti-alcohol for most of her life, she'd now got a real taste for it and enjoyed the release it provided. With a couple of drinks inside her, she felt even more invincible than she already did, yet at the same time it seemed to mellow the sharper edges of her personality. She picked up her phone and the card purse containing a stack of twenty-dollar bills Spitfire had given her for taxis and meals when in the field (yeah right, whatever!), and stuffed them in the inside pocket of her jacket. She could hardly contain her excitement as she eased open her bedroom door and tiptoed out. New York City was calling. And if she was going out drinking, then there was only one place to go.

———

CBGB's. It sounded busy as she stood in front of the famous awning thirty minutes later.

She was here.

She was actually here.

She gazed up at the iconic sign, mouthing the letters *C-B-G-B* to herself. As a die-hard fan of the scene that arose from this small music venue in Manhattan's East Village, she knew the letters stood for *Country, Bluegrass and Blues*, and the *OMFUG* acronym below *Other Music For Uplifting Gormandizers*.

Gormandizers.

She liked that word. It meant someone who devoured ravenously, and that was exactly what she wanted to do with every experience available to her inside these hallowed walls. At the entrance, she paused to appreciate the moment, then pulled the door open and stepped inside. The room in front of her was hot and stuffy after the biting chill outside. Rather than use the underground, she'd travelled here by taxi and had felt like rock royalty as she'd given the driver the name of her destination in her part-aristocratic, part-cockney accent. But now, as she looked through the curtain into the main room, she was dismayed to see the clientele was not as she'd imagined it would be. At all.

Where were the punks and the freaks? The artists and the drag queens? Debbie Harry and Nico once graced this room, along with Johnny Thunders and Iggy Pop. Stiv Bators, Richard Hell, Poison Ivy. Messed-up, ugly-beautiful souls from the dark side of the street. People just like her. Tonight all she saw were old guys in plaid shirts and faded band t-shirts. Dropping her shoulders, she shuffled over to the desk next to the entrance, where a man wearing thick glasses and a baseball cap was sitting in front of a yellowing computer.

"Y'alright there?" he said.

She nodded. "Are there bands playing tonight?"

"Sure are. A cool girl band from Japan called Raging Insides. It's Screamcore stuff. Pretty good."

Acid puffed out her cheeks. "Okay. Fine. Just me then, please."

"Do you have ID?"

"Oh. Yes. Somewhere." She pulled the card purse out of her inside pocket and unzipped it, rifling through the twenty-dollar bills until she found what she was looking for. "Here you are." She handed the ID card to the man.

As he inspected it, she peered through into the room beyond. There were a few people close to her age hanging around the bar, but they were wearing Green Day and NOFX shirts. Not the sort of people she thought she'd find here. But what did she expect? This was a working venue, not a time capsule.

She so wished it was a time capsule.

"Miriam Morgan," the doorman read. "Cool name."

"Oh? Yes. Thanks."

"What's your date of birth, Miriam?"

Shit.

She knew Caesar had made all her aliases twenty-one so she could get into bars and clubs anywhere in the world if required. But the exact date? *Bugger.* She closed her eyes and pictured the ID card in her mind. She'd only glimpsed at it when Spitfire had given it to her in the airport.

"Twentieth of November," she said. "Nineteen eighty-one."

The man looked her up and down and then handed her the card back. "Cool. I have to check. You look young."

"I am young," she told him, taking back the ID card. "But I'm old enough to be here."

"No worries. That'll be five dollars."

She gave him a twenty and told him to keep the change, as she was feeling on the back foot and needed to regain the elation and excitement she'd felt in the cab ride over. The man looked stunned at the heavy tipper, but she headed through to the bar before he could say anything.

At least the venue looked like she'd imagined. The bar and stage – along with the seating area to the left of the bar and all the walls – were covered in stickers and graffiti. Like in every photo she'd ever seen of the place. Down in the depths of the venue, people were milling around, waiting for the band to start. Up on stage at the far end, a tiny Japanese girl with pigtails and a low-slung Les Paul was sound-checking her vocals.

Acid leaned her forearms on the sticky bar top and raised her chin at the nearest server, a woman a few years her senior.

"What can I get ya?" she asked in the most perfect Brooklyn drawl.

Acid pursed her lips. "I'll have a beer," she said. "A Bud is fine."

The woman nodded and grabbed a bottle from the fridge behind her, opening it with a bottle opener attached to her belt.

"That'll be four dollars."

Acid slipped her a twenty but waited for the change this time. As her gaze drifted back towards the stage, she saw three men sitting on high stools a few feet away along the bar. They'd set their stools out in a triangular formation, so she could see all three were staring at her.

"Hey," one of them said, as she met his eye. "Wassup?"

Acid shrugged. "Just getting a drink."

"Whoa, English. Cool accent." The men nudged each other and snickered. "What are you doing so far from home, hot stuff?"

She turned as the server appeared in her peripheral vision, giving Acid her change along with a vague smile of solidarity, but saying nothing. Acid tipped her three dollars and pocketed the rest of the change before heading for the stage. The band was about to start.

"Hey. I was talking to you!" One of the three boys slipped off his stool and blocked her as she tried to pass. "You rude?"

Acid stopped, clutching the bottle of Budweiser to her chest. The man was at least a foot taller than her and, although not particularly well-built, had a ruggedness to his demeanour she found disturbing. His hair was thick and black and he had a smattering of pimples across his cheeks and chin. He was wearing a dirty white t-shirt with a picture of a pin-up girl on the front. His friends, who were also both slipping off their stools, were around the same height as him, their hair shorter and brushed forward.

"What's the rush?" Pimples asked, as she tried to step around him. "Sit with us. I'm only trying to be friendly. You all alone?"

"No," she replied, but her voice sounded hoarse, and it had no breath behind it. She tried again. "No! I'm here with my friend. My boyfriend."

"Ah shoot, she's got a boyfriend," he said, slapping his buddies on their chests. "Best we back off then, guys. Only, I don't see anyone with you."

"Yeah," one of the others said, looming over her. "I say you take a seat. And we'll have some fun."

CHAPTER 17

Acid glanced at the three young men in turn. They were nasty and sneery and bristled with conceit. She didn't want to spend another minute in their presence. She certainly didn't want to have 'fun' with any of them.

"I'm here to watch the band," she said, making to walk away. But Pimples seized her shoulders.

"Bobby said sit down!"

He shoved her and her lower back hit the top of the stool, but there was something else there too. A hand. Bobby's hand. He grasped her arse and squeezed it.

"Get the fuck off me," she yelled, jumping forward, but right into Pimples. He barged into her and she felt another hand grab her between the legs, fingers pressing against the seam of her jeans. A sharp rush of panic overcame her, followed by one of rage.

"You like that?" Pimples growled, his hot breath on her cheek as he groped at her. "You want to take this out back?"

"Piss off." She pushed him away from her with all her strength. As he stepped back, he laughed.

"Fucking bitch."

She glared at the three of them as they brayed nastily in her face. They were horrible, dumb jocks playing at being alternative. Exactly the sort of person she hated. This wasn't their world. This wasn't their bar. CBGB's was supposed to be a haven for the broken and chaotic, those on the edges of society. She darted her attention around the room, to the woman behind the bar, to the older men drinking at the tables. No one was looking her way. No one was coming to help her.

Pimples held his hands up. "Why don't we calm down, huh? I was just being friendly. Just relax and we can have some f—"

"Stay away from me," Acid snarled, as a fresh and more constructive surge of rage consumed her. She held up the bottle of Bud. "I mean it. Bugger off."

"Bugger orf! Bugger orf!" The men all repeated, mocking her accent, before Pimples stepped forward and all the humour dropped from his face.

"You're a fucking prick tease, you know that? You know what happens to girls like you?" He went to grab her, but she moved back. Every one of her nerve endings was alive with distress and indignation. Behind her, the band had kicked off their set. The music was loud and fast, but she hardly heard it over the cacophony in her head. She gripped the bottle, seeing herself smashing it off the nearest surface and into this prick's throat. It would shock his buddies enough she could get away before they jumped in. But as she cast her attention down the room, she saw a large group of people in front of the exit. They could be a problem if she needed to make a swift exit.

But the bats wanted blood.

Kill him, they said.

Kill them all.

She was motionless, unable to think straight. What did she do? What would Spitfire do now? Or Caesar?

The answer, of course, was that neither of them would be in

this situation. They were both men. Nasty little boys like this didn't pick on men, just women they thought they had power over.

Smash the bottle.

Slice the fucker's throat open.

She stepped back, readying herself, remembering her training. But the last step, striking out with the bottle, she couldn't do it. It was three against one, and the way they were staring at her made her stomach turn. For the first time in years she felt vulnerable. Alone. Holding her breath, and with her head down, she ran, leading with her shoulder and barging between two of the men. One of them said something as she pushed past, but she wasn't listening. She was concentrating only on the exit. Barging through the crowds, she left the bottle of beer on a table and burst through the door and into the street.

"Bastards!" she yelled into the cool night air. "Rotten pricks!"

But her anger was directed at herself as much as those men. She'd let herself down. Shame and frustration washed over her in equal measure as she prowled up and down.

Should she go back inside?

Her pride wanted her to. The bats did, too. But even with insane amounts of adrenaline filling her system, her instincts held her back. Those pricks weren't worth getting arrested over.

"Stupid rotten place," she yelled at the building, before shoving her hands into the pockets of her jacket and walking away.

Her head was spinning as she wandered down the Bowery. She had a vague notion of where she was going but didn't know how long it would take her on foot. She needed to find a cab. There were none in sight. As she walked, she heard men's voices behind her. They were shouting and jeering, but she didn't stop or turn around to see if it was the men from the bar. Quickening her pace, she covered two more blocks before the avenue forked in front of a small patch of grass with a low railing around its perimeter.

Opting for the left-hand option, she pressed on. Behind her she could hear heavy footsteps. It sounded as if they were matching her own, step for step.

Shit.

Breaking into a run, she crossed two intersections, finding herself alongside an old church. The avenue here was busy with traffic and she could have hailed a cab if she waited, but she didn't want to stop in case the men caught up with her. Her pulse throbbed in her neck and inner thigh as she raced down the side of the church and through a small garden on the other side. Taking a left, she ran down the next block until a sign informed her she was on Broadway. That was good. If she stayed on this road she'd eventually reach the apartment. She kept her running pace up for as long as possible, before the pressure in her chest and pain in her sides became too much and she slowed to a walk as she reached a small park.

A dome-topped building was visible over on the far side and a sign read *Union Square Subway*. She risked a furtive glance over her shoulder. A group of guys stood on the corner surrounded by cigarette smoke, and on the other side of the street a man and woman were strolling arm in arm. But no sign of the three men who'd assaulted her.

Cursing them – and herself for overreacting – she hurried across the park and down the steps into the subway. Glad of the pass Spitfire had given her, she swiped herself through the barrier and ran down to the platform where a train was waiting. She boarded and stood near the doors, peering up at a peeling subway map overhead. She'd have to change at Times Square to get to her destination. Not ideal, but at least she was on her way home.

As the doors slid shut and the train set off, she shuffled over to the nearest seat. Her heart was still beating fast as she sat. Tonight was a wake-up call. Not only had she put herself in danger, but she'd allowed fear to get the better of her. She was supposed to be a deadly assassin, for heaven's sake! A killer! How was she supposed to deal with mercenaries and cartel militia when she lost her arse confronted by three spotty kids?

"Idiot," she whispered to herself. "Stupid bloody idiot."

The train trundled on and she put her head in her hands, fighting the deluge of pitiful emotions bubbling inside her. Times Square was the fourth stop, and as the train slowed she got to her feet, jumping out onto the platform as soon as the doors opened. Swerving around the other passengers getting off, she headed for the platform opposite where she could continue her journey to 79th Street. From there, it was only a few minutes walk back to the apartment. Only there was no train. She checked her mobile phone. The display showed the time as 00:51.

Did the trains stop at night?

And why was it so damn hot down here? It was the middle of winter, for Christ's sake.

She rubbed her sweaty palms on the side of her jeans as she peered down the platform into the empty tunnel beyond. As she shifted her attention the other way, she noticed sudden movement out of the corner of her eye as a figure disappeared into the tunnel leading between the two platforms.

She sucked in a sharp breath. Was it one of the men? Had they followed her here?

Goose bumps prickled her arms and up the back of her neck as she forced herself to keep looking. She felt exposed. As if she was being watched. Her breathing had become shallow. Raising her head, she looked back at the tunnel, but there was no one there. No one watching her.

"Stupid cow," she scolded herself under her breath. She

knew not to let her mind run away with her. It was jetlag. It had to be.

Relief came in the form of the subway train, and she jumped on board, choosing to stand by the doors and holding onto the upright handrail as it set off. On the way, she sucked in deep breaths and held each one for a count of five before releasing a deep sigh. Spitfire had taught her the process. It was supposed to slow the heart rate, but she wasn't sure if she was doing it right. Nevertheless, by the time the train pulled up at the 79th Street station eight minutes later, she was calmer and the chaos in her head had subsided. Although, she was no less annoyed at herself for how tonight had gone.

Maybe she wasn't cut out for this life, after all.

The train doors slid open and she jumped out onto the platform, immediately breaking into a jog through the station and running up the stairs to the street. It was icy cold as she got outside, and she danced on the spot to keep warm as she read the street signs. There was a church on the corner and beyond this was West 80th. Their apartment was on the next block.

She ran up the avenue, not stopping or looking back until she reached the front door of their building. As she stopped to get her key out of her pocket, she thought she heard heavy footsteps behind her. Fumbling the key in the lock, she finally got inside on the third attempt, falling into the relative warmth of the building, slamming and locking the door behind her then leaning her back against it, panting for air.

She was home. She was safe. But she was also crushingly aware that she wasn't as smart or as invincible as she'd thought.

Pushing off from the door, she headed upstairs. From now on there'd be no more fooling around.

She was an elite assassin.

It was time to start acting like one.

CHAPTER 18

Spitfire had been drifting in and out of sleep ever since climbing into bed. Jetlag. He had hoped the bourbon might have eased the transition from Greenwich Mean to Eastern Standard time, but it wasn't to be. He'd heard Acid leave her room and tiptoe across the apartment, and had even got out of bed when he heard the front door open and then close. But he was damned if he was going to get dressed and stop her. She was a grown woman, after all, and he wasn't a damn babysitter. If she wanted to act recklessly and jeopardise her standing with Caesar, so be it. Plus, he had the tracker and could see where she was heading (that silly punk rock bar she couldn't stop nattering about, by the look of it). He'd got up and poured himself another glass of Four Roses before returning to bed, muttering to himself about how he didn't need this hassle.

He hadn't expected to fall asleep but he must have done, because the sound of a key in the lock woke him. Rolling over, he grabbed his gold Rolex off the nightstand. It was a few minutes after one. He remained still, listening to the sounds coming from the main space. The footsteps were soft and moved swiftly across the tiled floor. He could tell it was Acid by her breathing. At least she was back. Tomorrow he'd speak to her about her actions, but wouldn't be too harsh on her. Since deciding not to get involved in Caesar's twisted mind games, he found her a lot easier to stomach.

As the door to her bedroom clicked shut, he wondered if he should go see her. She was awake. So was he. And whilst he was now resolute in his position regarding romance, that didn't mean they couldn't do other things. He often wondered what she looked like naked. He closed his eyes, imagining her above him, wild hair whipping across her face and breasts—

Aaaand enough...

He screwed up his eyes to dissipate the imagery. It was a nice thought. But it was unprofessional, and if he was to chastise her about her actions tonight, he needed to play it with a straight bat. First things first, get the hit. After that, they'd see about having some fun.

He pulled the sheets over his head, trying to ignore the sounds coming from her room, trying to pretend she wasn't just a few feet away, separated by a mere stud wall and plasterboard.

To help him get back to sleep, he concentrated on his body, relaxing each area in turn. The muscles in his face, then his limbs, imagining his torso sinking into the mattress. It was an old army trick, a way of falling asleep quickly even in a noisy barracks or out on manoeuvres. It usually worked well for him, but not when there was one muscle in particular that refused to relax.

Stop thinking about her.

Go to sleep.

Sleep...

Sleep...

He repeated the word to himself as if it was some hippy

mantra for the emotionally bereft, and after a few minutes all thoughts of Acid's naked form had drifted from his mind. A blanket of warm repose crept over him and he drifted into the benign valley of half-sleep, bordering on the cusp of nothingness. His breathing fell heavy and slow. The pillow under his head was so soft and warm, the air still and quiet, until... a sound! It was the quietest of creaks, the squeak of bending rubber, perhaps, but his highly trained senses picked up on it. As the needle in his alertness level shot into the red, he was aware of a presence in his room and something close to his face.

Shit.

His eyes snapped open and he intuitively grabbed for the suppressor muzzle a few inches from his head, twisting it away as it fired. The sonic crack was still loud enough to knock out his hearing and he let go of the hot muzzle as he flipped out of bed, launching himself at the shadowy figure standing over him. It was the man from the parking lot, all six-foot-five of him. A blond version of Bluto from the Popeye cartoons he'd watched as a kid.

Spitfire caught him with an elbow to the neck, grabbing for the pistol with his other hand. They grappled and Blondie barked something in German before slamming his fist into Spitfire's cranium, knocking all thoughts from his head. The room went dark and then far too bright, but he held on, twisting at the man's arm and chopping at his neck with the blade of his hand. As long as the gun was pointing away from him, he had a fighting chance. A knee to the brute's upper thigh jarred his muscle and, as he stumbled over, Spitfire was able to attack the pressure points on his wrist. He pressed down hard, grinding his thumbs against gristle and bone until, finally, with a grunt, Blondie released his grip. As the pistol tumbled away, Spitfire shoved off from the man's torso and into a fighting stance. He realised at this point he was naked, but that only filled him with more fire. He was a feral gladiator. A wild man. Crying out, he leapt forward, catching the big man with a left-handed uppercut and following up with a sharp knee to the groin.

Yes! Come on!

He bloody well had this.

It was all over

He dodged out of the way as Blondie lunged at him, appearing to have lost his balance. Spitfire raised his fist, ready for the knockout blow, when the goon swung back at him. There was a blur and a thud and a heavy pain bloomed inside Spitfire's skull.

Fuck...

The room turned to confetti and light as he did a full pirouette on the spot, wondering what had happened to his legs. Before he could answer that question, a thick python snaked around his neck and yanked him off his feet.

"Now you die."

A fresh surge of adrenaline brought the room back into sharp focus. He grabbed at the arm around his throat, legs flailing as he kicked against the bed frame. It was no use. Blondie was strong and immovable. He gasped for air as he struggled to free himself. He knew if the carotid artery at the side of his neck got blocked, he only had seconds before the lack of blood to his brain shut down his system. After that, he imagined he'd receive a single shot to the head from the fallen pistol and it would be goodnight Vienna.

He kicked out, stamping his heels down on Blondie's calves whilst digging his fingernails into his forearms. Nothing helped. He was fading away. He was done. He managed to get both feet up onto the bed, and was preparing for one last push, when he heard an ungodly screech then the dull thud of something hard connecting with bone. The man groaned and loosened his grip on Spitfire's neck. As he fell forward on the bed, Spitfire twisted around so he was facing upright and locked his arms, keeping the big fucker away from him as he stumbled over. Blood was pouring from a large gash on the side of his head and his eyes had rolled back in his head.

"Give it here," Spitfire yelled to Acid, who was standing in the doorway with the glass ashtray clutched in her fist.

She chucked the ashtray onto the bed beside him. As Blondie groaned, showing signs of coming round, Spitfire grabbed it, smashing the blunt object into the side of the big man's head. The same spot where Acid had hit him a few seconds earlier. He felt the man's muscles release and he pushed him over, quick to get out from underneath him as he slumped face down on the bed.

Acid helped Spitfire up onto his feet, and he noticed now she was wearing only a pair of black knickers and the white vest top from earlier.

"It's the guy from the parking lot," she said. "He must have... He must have followed me here?"

Spitfire tilted his head to one side. "Do you think so?"

Leaving the sarcastic comment hanging in the air, he shoved past her and bent down to pick up the gun from the side of the bed. As he got to his feet, he saw her staring. He was still naked and, looking down, he was pleased to see the fight-or-flight response hadn't been too unkind in its shifting of blood from unwarranted areas during the attack.

"Seen something you like?"

Acid looked down and away from him. "Sorry."

"What for? Ogling? Or bringing this big fucker to our door?"

She didn't look up. "Everything."

"Yes, well. We'll talk about that later. Here, take hold of this. Keep it pointed at him."

He handed her the pistol and walked over to his suitcase,

selecting a fresh pair of white boxer shorts from the pile. After stepping into them, he moved over to the closet and removed a small leather case from the top shelf. The house Q&A kit. Zipping open the side pocket, he found a selection of black plastic cable ties and removed three of them. As he bound Blondie's arms behind his back, he noticed the wound on the side of his head was still gushing with blood. He placed two fingers against his neck, but his pulse was strong.

Satisfied the big man's hands were secure, he rolled him off the bed and onto the floor. "Help me get him through into the kitchen," he told Acid. "The lighting's better through there. It'll help the ID process for Raaz."

Together they dragged him through into the main space and propped him up against the fridge.

"All right, wait here." He strode back into his room and came back a few seconds later with his spy camera, Blondie's gun and the Q&A kit. Handing the gun to Acid, he placed the leather case on the kitchen counter and knelt in front of the unconscious man, holding the camera. It still amazed him to this day that the tiny device took useable photos. It was the length of a matchbox with a tiny lens on one side; to take a photo, you squeezed the ends together until you felt a silent click, which is what Spitfire did now.

"That should do it," he said, getting to his feet. He saw the confusion on Acid's face and held it up. "Spy camera," he said. "*Very* James Bond." He winked at her, but it might as well have been a slap. She turned away with flushed cheeks. It was almost endearing to him, but he had no desire or time to process what that meant.

"Right then. Let's get to the bottom of this."

Acid raised her head and frowned. "Are you going to kill him?"

"Eventually." He walked over to the counter and unzipped

the leather case's main compartment, flipping over the central leaves to reveal the goods. Held in place by thick elastic loops, like in his men's grooming kit, were a selection of scalpels, gouging rods and spike wheels. All gold-plated and shiny. He tilted the case so Acid could get a better look.

"This is what we call the Q&A kit," he told her. "For obvious reasons. We ask questions and these items help us get the answers we need. You see, this unpleasant individual *is* going to die tonight, but first I want to find out who he is and what he's doing in New York. If he is linked to the mark, then I want to know how. Because it's poor form on the Russian's part if we haven't been told."

He removed a scalpel and held it so it glimmered in the light.

"Do we need to put something down on the floor?" Acid asked. "For the mess?"

"No. We have a clean-up team here that we can call on. They're not nearly as dedicated as Ethel and Doris, or as quaint, but they do a good job for the price. They'll sort it."

The big man on the floor made a moaning sound. Spitfire placed the scalpel on the counter and faced Acid.

"As soon as he comes around, we'll start. In the meantime, keep that gun pointed at him. I mean it. Don't take your eyes off him. If he wakes up, shout for me. If he tries anything, shoot him in the knees."

"Where are you going?" she asked.

He picked up the camera. "I have to plug this into my laptop and email the photos over to Raaz. If he won't talk, she might be able to ID him with her new software. Either way, HQ needs to know what we're dealing with." He glanced down. "And I might put some more clothes on. If that's all the same with you."

Acid swallowed, but this time she looked like she wanted to slap him. "Fine."

"Cracking." He pointed to the gun in her hand and then to

Blondie. "I'm serious. If he moves, tell him to stop or you'll shoot him. If he carries on moving... shoot him!" With that, he strode into his room and shut the door.

Well, what do you know?

He was going to have some fun tonight, after all.

CHAPTER 19

The second Spitfire's door closed, the big man's groans became more regular. Acid gripped the gun with both hands and shifted her position into a shooting stance.

Considering she'd brought danger to their door and almost got him killed, Spitfire seemed relatively composed. But this was him in work mode. Cool, calm, calculating. She imagined once he'd finished with the Q&A kit, he might have more to say on the matter.

But fair enough.

The big goon must have been waiting around the vicinity of the mark's hotel, perhaps hoping to catch sight of them. And she'd led him straight to their apartment.

That was not cool.

Not cool at all.

She shouldn't have gone out in the first place. It wasn't like it was even worth it. She'd had a rotten time. As the big man's groans morphed into slurred words, she raised the gun.

"Don't fucking move," she hissed as his eyelids flickered. "I'll kill you."

His eyes snapped open, and as he struggled to free his hands, she stepped forward and shoved the gun in his face.

"Please," she said. "Give me one excuse to pull this trigger. Just one."

He lowered his head. "Fuck you."

"Is that all you've got? Or do you feel like talking?" Spitfire had said to call him when he woke up, but he'd be back soon enough. There was no reason she couldn't start the Q & A. "What's your name?" she asked.

He bared his teeth; they were bright pink, framed by his blood-splattered moustache and beard. "Mickey Mouse."

The response angered her more than it should have done. Prickly heat spread down the back of her head. "Really? And who do you work for, Mickey?"

"I don't work for anyone. I'm a figment of your imagination."

"Yeah?" She stabbed the end of the suppressor nozzle into the bleeding gash on his head. He winced and his breathing quickened. She ground it in deeper, receiving a rush of excitement as he fought the pain. "I know I have a rather fucked-up imagination, but even I wouldn't conjure up something as ugly as you. Now tell me. Who are you? Who sent you?"

Standing over this huge thug of a man, and him cowering in pain, she felt invincible once more. If she got the information out of him, it would be a step towards fixing the mess she'd made up to now. Spitfire would be pleased. Caesar, too.

"Name," she growled, leaning in. "Or I'll make this a lot worse for you."

The man whimpered. "No. Please."

"My friend is currently sending your mugshot to our best tech people," she went on. "When he's done, things are going to get nastier and more unpleasant for you. But I can make it easier. A lot easier. Tell me what I want to know." She stepped away, removing the suppressor from his head and pointing it at his abdomen.

"What do you want?" the man asked.

"Who are you? Where did you come from?"

The man lowered his gaze. "They'll kill me."

"Who will? Who sent you?" A fresh prickle of annoyance washed over her. She kicked him in the leg but, being barefoot, it probably hurt her more than it did him. "Enough stalling."

She kicked him again.

"Stop that."

She waved the gun in his face. "Do you think I won't shoot you? Do you think my partner isn't going to use all those horrid implements up there on you? You're going to be in terrible pain for a long time if you don't start talking."

The man let out a long sigh. His breath smelled like rotten meat. "Fine. I'll tell you everything. Who I am. Who sent me." He looked up and met her gaze. "And why."

Acid jutted out her chin. "Go on then."

"My name is..." he started, in a low voice. But as he continued, the volume fell away completely so she couldn't hear what he said.

"Speak up."

He mumbled something else she couldn't hear. The annoying bastard. He was messing with her. She leaned in, pressing the suppressor nozzle against his neck.

"I sorry," he wheezed. "My throat. It is dry. I feel faint. I cannot..."

Acid glanced about. Should she get him a glass of water? There were bottles in the fridge, but he was leaning against it. "Tell me. Now." She leaned in so she could hear him. "Name."

"Okay," he whispered, with hardly any breath behind the word. "My name is..." Acid leaned closer. "My name is—"

There was a flash of movement and her forehead and the bridge of her nose erupted in pain. Then she was on her arse, trying to make sense of what happened. An intense pressure filled her head and ears. A shadow stepped over her, the big man on his feet.

Shit.

He glared down at her and pulled his arms apart, snapping the cable ties with ease.

Shitting hell.

Her vision was hazy and awareness pinballing around the room. The gun was still in her hand. She raised it, but the man grabbed something beside him and flung it at her. There was a flash of gold and she felt a sharp pain in her shoulder. Someone yelled. It could have been her. Raising her forearm, she blocked a stool as it closed in on her. It bounced off her onto the floor, and as she scrambled over it she saw the big man running for the door. Pushing herself upright, she squeezed the trigger three times. Each of the rounds thudded into the wall to the right of the door as he yanked it open.

No!

She was a better shot than this. Much better.

She fired again, but there was a scalpel sticking out of her shoulder and it was throwing off her aim. The shot went wide once more. She screamed in frustration as he sprinted down the corridor and jumped over the handrail to the landing below.

"Shit! Spitfire!"

But he was already standing beside her, dressed now in a white vest top tucked into a pair of navy trousers. It took him all of one second to understand what had transpired. He glared at her like he wanted to kill her. "I don't bloody well believe this."

"I was..." she gasped, still trying to regain full alertness. "I didn't mean to... He just—"

"You stupid girl," he snapped. "Stay here and don't move until I get back. Do you hear me?"

She nodded, but he was already heading for the door. She watched as he grabbed his coat and sprinted down the corridor after the man.

"I'm sorry," she mouthed after him. "I'm so sorry."

CHAPTER 20

Spitfire burst out of the main door of the building and jumped the four steps down to street level, catching sight of Blondie as he turned the corner at the end of the block. He chased after him, cursing Acid with every step. Calling her every appalling name in his repertoire.

She wasn't ready for this. But he'd known that all along. Yet he'd been so perturbed with what else Caesar was asking him to do, he'd not appreciated how bad the idea of partnering with Acid on the actual hit was. The more he thought about it, every aspect of this mission was ridiculous. If they'd sent him to New York alone, Bakov would be dead by now. No question about it.

What was Caesar thinking?

Had he lost it?

He got to the end of the block and barged past a couple of guys loitering outside the pizza place on the corner. "Out of my way."

One of them yelled something after him, and for a split-second he considered turning back. He'd like nothing better right now than to beat the pathetic fucker to death with his bare hands. Or the butt of his pistol...

Buggering fuck!

Why hadn't he grabbed the pistol from Acid as he left the apartment just now? He would never fire it in a built-up area, that was against the code, but there were other uses for a heavy chunk of metal. It would at least lessen his handicap against the much larger man when he caught up with him.

If he caught up with him.

The mouthy prick on the corner didn't know how close he'd come as Spitfire ran down the next street. He still had Blondie in sight, but the giant brute was remarkably fast and he wasn't closing in on him as he'd hoped. Halfway down the street, the big man stopped and looked back at him before disappearing down the side of a Polish nail bar.

What the fuck?

As he got up to the building, Spitfire discovered the narrowest of alleyways running between it and the adjacent brownstone. The enormous goon must have crab-walked to the end, because it was barely wide enough for Spitfire to fit. Scraping his shoulders against the concrete, he raced along the passageway, coming out in a dark courtyard. He stopped and cast his attention around the space, bouncing up onto the balls of his feet as he did, ready to counter an attack. But except for a tabby cat sitting on an old rusty fire escape, the area was deserted.

He ran across the courtyard and down a second alleyway on the other side. If he let the prick get away a second time, he might as well hang up his cufflinks and tell Caesar he was done. Hell, if he let the prick get away a second time, Caesar would tell him he was done. Right before he had him eradicated for being such a useless bastard.

One thing Spitfire knew – if you wanted to excel in this life, you had to take responsibility for everything that happened to you. Once you accepted you were the problem, you could work on being the solution. Acid Vanilla might have fucked up tonight, but this was on him just as much. It was up to him to make it right.

Leaving the alleyway, he found himself back on West 81st Street, near their apartment. They'd come full circle, but he was still on Blondie's tail. He set off after the man, who was crossing the street at the end of the block. They ran in tandem past the grounds of the American Museum of Natural History. Floodlights illuminated the old building, but Spitfire had no time to appreciate it as Blondie veered left, down another alleyway, and vanished from sight.

Spitfire got there a few seconds later and slowed to a stop. This alley was a lot wider than the others and lit up by the windows of the hotel that backed onto it. A row of commercial dumpsters ran down one side and, as Spitfire squinted through the gloom, he saw it was a dead end. Blondie was still here.

Moving slow and steady, careful not to make a sound, he stepped into the alley. There were three dumpsters, with a gap of about three metres between each one. Enough space for someone as big as blondie to hide behind.

But that was the obvious option.

Playing along, keeping away from the light in case his shadow gave him away, Spitfire side-stepped towards the first dumpster. As he reached it, he crouched, ready to spring forward with a tasty uppercut. But peering around the side, there was no one there. He stayed low, shuffling over to the next dumpster, squeezing his fists tight and going through the same process of crouching in readiness. Same process, same result. No one was there. But he noticed a rusty metal bar leaning against the wall. He picked it up. It had a good weight to it, though was slender enough that he could hold it in a firm grip. The perfect weapon.

He rolled his shoulders back. There was only one dumpster

remaining. One place left to look. Except that wasn't true; because in the rigmarole of checking behind the first dumpster, he'd noticed a metal fire escape rising out from the shadows on the far side of the alleyway. He'd not lingered on it, lest he give the game away, but he could see it in his peripheral vision. Light from the hotel shone off the metal handrail where the paint had rusted, but the area beneath the first flight of steps was so dark it was a black abyss. That would be where he himself would hide if the shoe were on the other foot.

Resting the metal bar on his shoulder and with his biceps tensed, he counted to three in his head, then went for it. The metal bar clanged noisily against the side of the dumpster as he lunged at nothing, but he used the momentum to spin around.

"Let's have you!"

In the same fluid movement, he lashed out at the immense presence looming at him out of the darkness. The metal club connected with the side of the man's head and then....

Shit.

He'd expected the blow to do more damage. The force of the impact jarred the bar against Spitfire's wrist, but Blondie only staggered away and grinned. Spitfire swung again before something like a freight train hit him in the chest, propelling him backwards. He hit the hotel wall with a thud, winded but not down. Now, with more space between the two of them, he could make out the thick blond beard and black pinprick eyes of his adversary. And he was laughing at him. So much for a surprise attack.

Swinging the bar in a wide arc in front of him, Spitfire dummied to his left before circling to the right. He was heading for the open space of the alley, but a heavy fist slammed into his ribs, knocking him into the dumpster. Bouncing off the metal side, he carried on moving, though unsteady on his feet, and another fist to the back of the head floored him. He hit the ground hard as rough hands gripped his shoulders. There was a rather one-sided struggle before he was on his feet, with Blondie's huge forearm once more around his neck. Tightening his upper body, he slammed his elbow back into the man's kidneys, over and over. While the big man adjusted his hold on him, Spitfire dropped like he was a dead weight. As he fell, he banged his nose on the bone of the bastard's forearm, but the swiftness of the move freed him from the choke hold.

He staggered forward, putting more space between them as he gasped for air. Turning, he saw Blondie gnashing his teeth in frustration.

"Not as easy as it looks, is it?" he said, raising his fists and dropping into a crouching stance.

Blondie snarled. "I kill you."

"We'll see. But I certainly admire your resolve." He stepped back. There was no way he could win this blow for blow, but if he stayed low and worked the kidneys, he could wear the man down enough to get him in a sleeper hold.

The idiot grinned and shifted into a fight stance. "I kill you."

"You know, you sound like a broken record," Spitfire told him, as a renewed confidence washed over him. Blondie was light-footed and quick for his build, but Spitfire was faster. And he had more tricks up his sleeve.

The big man charged forward. Spitfire did the same. At the last moment, he twisted to one side and stamped down on the side of the bastard's leg.

Jesus.

It was like kicking at a brick wall. As he pushed down, the counterforce sent him airborne and he lost his footing. It was an error on his part, but he didn't have chance to chastise himself before the enormous man tackled him to the ground. Hitting the cold concrete, a deep shuddering pain rippled through his torso and down his limbs. Now Blondie was on top of him, his hands clutched around his throat. Spitfire tensed his neck muscles and clawed at the man's face. He had about five seconds before it was all over for him. Scrabbling around in the slush and dirt, his fingers touched something hard. The metal bar. Desperate, he tried rolling it into his grip, but he couldn't get to it. He was fading fast. He punched the man in his big bushy face, but it did nothing. He shoved his thumbs in his eyes, but he simply raised his head out of reach.

This was it.

This was how he died.

A black fog seeped across his vision. He knew it was going to happen one day. He didn't think it'd be like this.

Blondie roared in his face as he squeezed the life out of him, spittle and foam falling from his mouth.

Was this the last thing he was ever going to see?

A big ugly bastard drooling on him?

No. No way.

With his last ounce of life force, he smashed his fist into the centre of the man's face. The blow made a satisfying crunching noise, and he felt cartilage shift beneath his knuckles. Blondie cried out, his hands instinctively letting go of Spitfire to protect his face.

But it was too late for that.

Shifting his torso over to one side, Spitfire pushed off from the ground with one hand and reached for the metal bar with the other. He grabbed it, held it, was about to swing it when he saw a flash of blue lights reflected off the back of the alley and heard the high-pitched blip of a siren. He let go of the metal bar and looked back, sheltering his eyes from the glare of the headlights. Two dark silhouettes exited the vehicle.

"All right, break it up! Hey! Stop!"

Blondie was already on his feet and heading for the fire escape at the back of the alley.

"Police. Stop right there!"

Sucking in a lungful of air, Spitfire watched as the big man ran up to the metal stairwell and began to climb, hauling himself up with help from the rickety handrail.

"Freeze!"

The cops were agitated. One of them ran up to Spitfire and drew his gun.

"Stop or I'll shoot."

But Blondie wasn't stopping. He was already halfway up the fire escape. The cop fired his weapon, but the round ricocheted off the metal stairwell in a shower of sparks. Spitfire winced. Anyone with any experience would know there was no decent shot from where the man was standing. Blondie reached the top of the fire escape and peered over the railing. He met Spitfire's gaze for a moment before turning and clambering up onto the roof. There'd be no catching him now. The buildings in this part of the city were close together and of similar heights. He'd be halfway across town before he needed to come down from the rooftops.

The cop fired again, but it was out of frustration. He stared at the space where the fleeing man had been moments earlier before turning to Spitfire, gun still drawn.

"Let me see your hands," he shouted at him. "Now."

Spitfire did as he was told. "Thank god you guys arrived when you did," he gasped, his voice rising an octave as he slipped effortlessly into the role of Dr Charles Summers. "I was walking back to my hotel and that... that... man dragged me into this alley. I don't know what would have happened if you hadn't shown up."

The cop looked at his partner, who had now joined them. He nodded curtly, and the first cop lowered his piece. "Apologies, sir. Can't be too careful." He holstered the weapon.

"No, it's absolutely fine. Thank you. Can I...?" Spitfire held his hand out and the cop helped him to his feet. Up close, he was younger than expected.

His partner, who was older and angrier, walked up to Spitfire. He had sad eyes and a paunch. "You get a look at the guy?"

Spitfire paused. He knew where this was going, but he needed to play dumb if he wasn't to arouse suspicion. "Not really... I... He had blond hair and a beard. And he was huge!"

"Was he armed?"

"I don't think so," he replied, thanking his stars he hadn't grabbed the pistol after all.

"All right, sir. I need you to get in the car."

Buggering shit.

He looked at the younger cop, but he didn't return eye contact. Clearly, he was taking the older cop's lead.

"Really? Is that necessary?" he said. "I'm a little shaken up and I must get back to my apartment. I mean, you saw him as well as I did. I'm sure—"

The older cop stepped towards him, wagging a stubby finger in his face. "Sir, you need to get in the car. Now!"

Spitfire looked at the ground. "What's going to happen?"

"Once we get a full description from you, we'll canvass the area. See if we can find the man who attacked you."

Spitfire had noticed that the younger cop hadn't clipped his holster shut just now. If he spun around, he could grab it and take both cops out before they could say *Dunkin' Donuts*. He considered this for a moment, but remained staring at the ground. There was a hotel right next door.

"You do want us to catch him, right?" the older cop asked, gruffly rhetorical.

"Yes. Of course."

"Okay. So get in the car and we'll try to find that son of a bitch."

CHAPTER 21

After introducing themselves as Officer Ben Anderson (young, nervy) and Officer Brian Kowalski (older, brusque), they pushed Spitfire for a more thorough description of his attacker. Unfortunately for them, Dr Charles Summers was rather shaken up by the experience and couldn't remember very much.

"That's all you got? He had blond hair and was wearing a long coat?" Kowalski asked, in a classic Brooklyn accent to rival his classic New York cop name. "What colour was the coat?"

"I'm sorry, I don't remember. Dark, I think."

Kowalski twisted around in the passenger seat and stared at him. "Did he say anything to you?"

"Not really."

"He must have said something. He stole your wallet. Did he tell you to give it to him?"

"I can't remember."

Kowalski looked like he wanted to rip his throat out. "He take anything else? Your shirt, maybe?"

Spitfire looked down at the vest top he was wearing and

pulled his coat around himself. "It was hot in my room. I only came down to get some supplies..."

Kowalski didn't seem convinced, but he didn't pursue the matter.

"Was the man who attacked you holding a knife or a gun?" he asked, slowing his cadence. "Dr Summers, I'm trying to ascertain if this guy was carrying a weapon. Because if he was, this turns into a felony stop, and we need to catch the creep."

"It helps sometimes if you close your eyes," Anderson piped up. "You do that and the outside stimulus goes. You can concentrate better."

Spitfire glanced up in time to see Kowalski give the younger cop a stern look.

"What happens if we don't see anyone who fits his description?" Spitfire asked. He knew they didn't have a shot in hell of finding Blondie. If it was him, he'd have covered as much distance as possible across the rooftops, before moving to the lower ground close to his place of residence and staying in the shadows.

The man was a professional. Spitfire was certain. But that meant either he was a freelancer after the contract on Bakov – and was trying to get rid of the competition – or someone had specifically sent him to kill Spitfire and Acid. The problem was, neither of those possibilities made sense.

He turned to the window, making out like he was perusing the streets for his assailant, but with his mind on Acid. She was alone in the apartment, without a clue what was going on. He didn't think Blondie would return there tonight. But if he did, she was a sitting duck.

His hand flittered between each of his pockets, tapping each in turn. His heart sank as he pictured his phone and tracker on the nightstand in his room. He'd placed them down next to the wallet he'd supposedly had stolen.

"You see him?"

He looked back to Kowalski and shook his head. "No. I think he's gone. He was a big fellow. I believe we'd spot him if he was still in the area. Thank you for your time, officers. I appreciate the help. But it's getting late..." He trailed off, hoping Anderson might continue his thread and tell him he'd drop him on the next corner.

"These sons of bitches usually have an escape route planned out for such eventualities," Kowalski said. "He's probably back home, going through your wallet as we speak. It happens. We can't do anything about that."

"Of course. I understand. Thank you for your help."

He slapped his knees, the British signal for when something was over, and it was time to move on. Kowalski clocked it and frowned.

"We still need you to come down to the precinct and make a report, Doc."

Bloody buggering shit.

He held his hands up. "Are you sure? I don't want to make a fuss. You've both been so helpful, but I don't—"

"You're coming down to the precinct," Kowalski snapped. "I'm sure Mayor Bloomberg would be over the fucking moon if we didn't fill in a report. It'd help his CompStat figures no end. But it ain't happening. We've been driving around looking for this guy for the last half hour; you can take another twenty minutes out of your evening to file a report."

"I understand," Spitfire replied. "But I've told you everything I can think of already. I'm not sure I have anything to add."

Kowalski stared him out. Anderson shifted in his seat and looked as if he was about to say something, but didn't.

"You're coming to the precinct," the older cop told him. "Because what happens when you need a police report for your credit card company, huh? We let you go now and you'll be showing up first thing in the morning with a face like a saggy ass begging us to file a report. So, we do it now while the memory is still fresh. That okay?"

It was another rhetorical question. Spitfire nodded anyway. "Yes. Fine."

Spitfire had worried about how Acid was coping back at the apartment. But now at the precinct, sitting in a cold interview room and sipping an insipid cup of coffee Anderson had got for him, he was less worried and more irate.

This was on her. All of it. She was a bloody nuisance.

Kowalski asked him again what had happened, and he relayed the events as close to how he remembered telling them in the police car earlier. There were a few moments where Kowalski stopped writing and looked at him from under hooded eyelids, but Spitfire read his manner as exasperation rather than suspicion. Still, that didn't stop the bad-tempered old cop from going through every single aspect of the process by the book and keeping him there much longer than had been suggested in the car. Maybe he was a thorough kind of guy. Maybe he was just close to finishing his shift and wanted to run down the clock back at the precinct rather than out on the streets.

Once the report was complete, Spitfire signed it as Dr Charles Summers. He was given a number he could call in a few days to see if there had been any developments, but was told not to get his hopes up. Finally, Kowalski showed him to the door and told him, "Be careful out there." It was the sort of hackneyed thing a cop in a soap opera might say, and Kowalski probably didn't buy the sentiment any more than Spitfire did. But it was clear the old cop was done with the weird British doctor who didn't seem to want to help himself. And thank god for that.

Spitfire hadn't been inside a police station since he was eighteen, and he was eager to get the hell out of there.

The sun was coming up as he stepped out onto the street. It was a cold and frosty morning, but the icy chill in the air was refreshing after being cooped up in an interview room for the last two hours. As he walked down to the corner where a line of taxis were parked outside a hotel, he felt that same hollow feeling in his soul that he often got when he hadn't slept. Whether he'd be able to catch up on his sleep anytime soon was debatable. He had to find the damn mark and end this debacle once and for all. It should never have got to this point.

Once more, he found himself cursing Caesar for sending Acid Vanilla along for the ride. Blondie might have complicated matters, but it was her alone that had got him into this ridiculous mess. If it wasn't for her, Spitfire would have eradicated Bakov on the first day. He'd be back in Blighty with his feet up by now.

He crossed the street and yanked open the back door of the first taxi in line, telling the Hispanic driver the address as he climbed in. There was a lot to process and a lot still to do, but right now all he could think about was getting to the apartment, smoking a cigarette and taking a hot shower. It had been a long night.

CHAPTER 22

It took for the cab to pull up outside his building before Spitfire realised he didn't have any cash to pay the fare. After a lengthy exchange with the driver – who didn't appear to speak any English other than the words 'money' and 'you pay me' – he finally got the point across and, through a series of gestures and mimes, informed him he'd give him his watch for safe keeping while he ran up to the apartment to get his wallet.

Cursing the entire fucking world, he raced up the two flights of stairs and down the corridor, ready to run into the apartment, grab his wallet and head back down to pay the driver. Only, the blasted door was locked and he didn't have a key.

"Fucking pissing shitting hell!" He banged the bottom of his fist on the door, exorcising only a minor amount of the rage swirling in his chest and not caring if he splintered the wood in two. "Acid! Open the bloody door!"

She must have been sitting at the dining room table, because he only had to wait a second before he heard a key in the lock. Pushing against the door as it opened, he barged past her and headed for his room.

"Spitfire?!" she called after him. "Where the hell have you been? What's going on?"

He didn't answer as he strode into his room and grabbed his wallet. Turning around, he found the infuriating girl blocking his path. She was now wearing a pair of black jeans and a black hooded top but didn't look to have slept. Her hair was lank and her eyes wild.

"Are you all right?" she asked.

Holding his hand up to her face, he walked past her and out the door, slamming it behind him. The watch he'd given to the cab driver was worth a hell of a lot more than his paltry fare; if the fucker had driven away, he'd hunt him down and gut him. But he was still waiting as Spitfire ran down the steps to the street. He shoved a twenty through the open window and held his hand out for the watch. The driver hesitated for a moment before handing it over. Good choice, Spitfire thought, as he replaced the watch on his wrist and went back inside.

"Are you not speaking to me?" Acid asked as he entered the apartment. "I was worried sick. Where have you been?"

He'd planned to go straight to his bedroom, but he stopped and turned on her, leading with a sharp finger.

"Where have I been? Where have I bloody well been? Down at the fucking cop shop. That's where I've been. And what an absolute joy it was. So thank you for that."

Acid flapped her mouth. "You got arrested?"

"No. Of course not. I caught up with Blondie and we were having a bit of a wrestle when a couple of uniforms showed up. The big guy got away and I had to make out he'd mugged me. They made me file a bloody report. Like I was the damn victim."

He sniffed. Acid's face was unyielding, but he sensed the quiver of a smile starting at the corner of her mouth.

"Don't you fucking dare laugh," he told her, taking off his coat and flinging it over the back of the nearest chair. "This is your fault. If you hadn't been here, I'd have killed Bakov and collected my fee by now. But, no. I have to babysit some stupid kid who doesn't even know how to dress for the weather and then puts us both in danger. You've been nothing but a bloody liability from the moment we set off."

Acid's face dropped into a sharp scowl. "Piss off. You don't need to babysit me. I'm a grown woman. Maybe I haven't as much experience in the field as you, but I've got skills you haven't."

Spitfire scoffed. "Skills? Really? Jesus Christ. I don't know what Caesar was thinking."

"It's not fair to blame all this on me."

"Who should we blame then?" They were both yelling now and that wasn't good. He took a moment to settle himself. When he continued, his voice remained low. "I think it's best if I lead from now on."

"What!" She scrunched her nose up as if she couldn't believe what she'd heard. "You have been leading. And I let you. Because you're older and because I respect the chain of command, or whatever it's called."

He held his hands up. "Hey. Calm it down. I mean it. You're showing yourself up. Acting like a child." He wagged his finger in her face. "You brought that fucker to our door last night. We'd both be dead if I hadn't woken up. Then when we have him tied up, you let him escape. I mean, come on, please tell me – what would you do if you were me? Would you want to work alongside someone who was so clearly not ready for this sort of work? I don't get what Caesar sees in you, in all honesty."

He could tell his words hit her hard, but that had been his intention. She glared at him, fighting back tears.

"I know I've been reckless," she said. "But neither of us knew that bearded goon was going to show up in New York. You can't blame me for that."

"You do know we're going to have to move out of here now, don't you?" he asked, not waiting for a reply. "You've compromised our location. Caesar won't like that. It's more expense. More upheaval. This was supposed to be a straightforward job. It is a straightforward job – for a professional. But not one who has an annoying kid to look after at the same time."

Acid snapped her head away as if he'd whacked her. He almost wished he had. It would provide her with some justification for the tears now rolling down her face.

Screw it.

He was past caring.

He went to his room and grabbed a towel from the closet before heading for the bathroom and locking the door behind him. As he turned the shower on, he heard Acid at the door, telling him they should talk about it. But what was the point? What the bloody hell did they have to talk about? He'd meant what he said. She was nothing but a stupid girl. An insolent, idiotic, waste of fucking oxygen.

He stared at his reflection in the mirror. One of his cheeks was grazed and his ribs were a little bruised under his right arm. He raised his head. His face was so stiff with rage that he looked almost comical. He held onto the sides of the porcelain sink unit and sucked in a deep breath. This was all wrong. After his shower he'd call Caesar and let him know what had happened here tonight. All being well, he'd demand Acid gets the next flight out of here, leaving him to get the job done. Without her and all these ludicrous distractions, he could still turn this around. He got undressed and stepped into the shower.

CHAPTER 23

Twenty minutes later and Spitfire was sitting on the end of his bed, pink and steaming from the hot shower and with a towel around his waist. He had Caesar on the phone. They'd been talking for the past five minutes, and the boss was now doing that thing where he muttered to himself and you didn't know whether he was angry or just thinking.

Spitfire lowered the phone from his ear to check the time on the display. It was a few minutes after ten. Early afternoon in the UK. He'd already relayed to Caesar everything that had happened over the last twenty-four hours, not going as far as saying it was all Acid's fault but implying as much. As he returned the handset to his ear, Caesar was still muttering amidst a chorus of sighs and tuts.

"But you didn't give them anything?" he asked. "The police, I mean."

"No, of course not," Spitfire replied. "I remained in character and played dumb."

Caesar clicked his tongue. "And what about DNA and fingerprints?"

"They didn't take any."

"Are you sure?"

Spitfire instinctively sat up and stuck out his chin. Maybe his subconscious hoped the physicality would give his voice more gravitas when he answered. "Absolutely. I'm clean. As always. Don't worry."

"Good boy. No harm done then."

"Are you serious?" Spitfire turned to the door to check it was closed, and got up off the bed. "I can't work under these conditions. We've been here for two days and I want to kill her. I know she's got potential, but she needs more training and more experience on a local level before she's sent out in the field."

At this, Caesar made a growling noise and Spitfire hesitated. He was pushing it, speaking so boldly to the boss, but it needed saying.

"Look," he added. "It's no one's fault. I thought she was ready, too. But she's all over the place. Bring her home and let me finish this mission on my own."

The line went silent again. Pressing the phone between his shoulder and cheek, Spitfire removed his towel and dried himself while he waited. He had his foot up on the edge of the bed and was shoving the towel between his toes when Caesar spoke.

"No," was all he said.

"No? No, what?"

"Acid will stay with you. She's part of the mission. Just take her in hand, you old dog. You can do it. This is why I sent both of you on this job. If anyone can tame that feral minx, it's you."

"But that's a big part of it, boss." He stopped drying himself and placed his foot on the floor. "This other aspect of the assignment – making her fall for me – it's messing with my head. I need to focus on what I do best, Caesar."

"What you do best is having young ladies fall at your feet. Is that not true?"

Spitfire glanced at his naked form in the mirror. He couldn't help smiling. "You know what I mean. It's having a detrimental effect on the work."

Caesar went silent again. "Fine," he snapped. "But in that case, Spitfire, I need this job completed pronto. Plus proof for the client. Can you manage that at least?"

Spitfire swallowed. "I can certainly manage that, boss. Thank you. I know this is the right decision. Acid and I are too different. She'd never go for someone like me, anyway. Not to mention the fact she's so damn infuriating. We just need to—"

"Oi, cocky lad! I'm pissing well agreeing with you. I'll find some other way to break her in. But she is going to be a part of this organisation, so be careful what you say about her."

Spitfire raised his head high. "I understand. I didn't mean to speak out of turn."

There was a pause.

"It's all good. If Bakov meets a nasty accident in the next couple of days, we're all dandy. If you can eradicate this big blond fucker who's trying to mess things up for us, even better. Raaz is still working on her facial recognition software, but she's hopeful she can get a match. In the meantime, you can't stay in the apartment. It's been compromised."

"I know." Spitfire turned to face the full-length mirror. "I'll find us somewhere. It's my problem. I'll deal with it."

"No. I'll send you the number of a contact of mine in the city. He's got a few properties; he'll be able to help."

"Thank you. I'll sort it at once. Then I'll be straight out after the mark. I won't settle until I've eradicated him. No more games."

"Good boy. I hope, for all our sakes, the next time you call it'll be to confirm the hit."

"It will. And thank you for listening to my concerns."

"Oh, fuck off," Caesar scoffed. "You sound like a bloody wet blanket. Now go do your stuff, hot shot."

He hung up. Spitfire flung the phone on the bed and went to his closet, selecting his dark burgundy suit and a black shirt. Now back in elite assassin mode, he wanted to look his best. It was important. He hung the jacket and shirt on the closet door and placed the trousers on the bed. Selecting fresh underwear from his suitcase (white boxers and black socks, as always), he put them on before slipping into the trousers and a vest top and heading out to the kitchen. A cup of coffee would be wonderful. Then he'd finished getting dressed, call Caesar's contact and—

Bugger...

Acid was still sitting at the kitchen table. She didn't look up as he exited his bedroom and walked as far as the fridge. Her bottom lip was sticking out, giving her the look of a sulky child, but he got the sense it arose from genuine despondency rather than a pose for his benefit.

"How are you doing?" he asked.

She shrugged. "Dunno."

Normally this sort of pathetic navel-gazing bullshit would have riled him, but she looked so broken sitting there with her hair over her face and her sagged shoulders. He clasped his hands together, twisting the signet ring around his finger. What was he like at twenty? Probably more hot-headed and unpredictable than she was.

She'd learn. In time, she'd get it.

He tilted his head to one side as he watched her. Damn, she was attractive; even with a face like a slapped arse. Or maybe it was because of it. The stern eyes. The sharp pout. He was a bit of a sucker for surly women. He liked the challenge.

"Are you aware you fucked up?" he asked her, stepping closer.

She made a breathy tutting sound. The sort of sound a petulant child might make. It didn't do her any favours. "Yes. Of course I'm aware."

"And are you sorry?"

She looked at him. Her eyes were puffy and bloodshot. They searched his face as if looking for a tell that this was a trap. "Caesar said you should never apologise. For anything. It shows weakness. He said you should recognise the issue, then adapt and move on and—"

"Yes, yes, I know the drill. And he is correct. But as your... *colleague*... I need to know you take responsibility for what's happened. Then, maybe, we can both move on and adapt."

It wasn't like him to say any of this. Spitfire Creosote didn't do empathy or compassion. That's not to say he didn't consider other people's emotions, or that he was a psychopath (hell, it would be a lot easier if he was); just that over the years he'd learnt how to dampen those aspects of his personality. To excel in the killing business, you had to see the mark – whoever they might be – as less than human. Only by doing this could you free yourself from the moral or philosophical pitfalls that cause hesitation in the field. It was the same mindset that generals instilled in their soldiers so they could attack the enemy without going completely crazy. Maybe he'd explain it to Acid if he ever got the chance. He knew she was clever and hardworking; he'd seen that at Honeysuckle House. And he had enjoyed training her in the ways of the assassin. Caesar said he wanted Acid tamed, but maybe what he needed was for someone to take her under their wing. To train her on the job, teach her things she could only learn out in the field. Could he do that? He wasn't sure.

And she still hadn't answered him.

"Acid," he said. "Do you accept responsibility?"

She looked at him with a dull expression. "Yes. Who else's failure was it?"

"No. Not failure," he said, holding a finger up to emphasise his point. "That implies defeat. We're not there yet. This is simply a setback. I've just spoken to Caesar. He still wants you on the job. He still wants us to finish what we've started."

Her eyes brightened. "Really? He said that?" The relief that washed over her was palpable.

"Yes. Were you expecting him to call for your head?"

She shrugged. "Maybe. Yes."

"Well, he hasn't. Not yet. But I need you to pick yourself up. We've got work to do. Do you want a coffee?" He went to the machine and switched it on.

She smiled. "Please."

"Great. Make me one as well, will you?" He waved his hand dismissively at the machine as it whirred and clunked. "I've no idea how this blasted thing works. This can be your first step in redeeming yourself."

"Fair enough."

He winked at her and she looked away. Her cheeks were flushed. Ignoring how that made him feel, he turned and headed for his bedroom.

"Where are you going?" she called after him.

"I need to pack," he replied. "And so do you. As I said, we need to get out of here."

"Spitfire?"

At the doorway to his bedroom, he stopped and turned.

"Where will we go?" she asked.

"Don't worry about that. I've got it covered." He pointed to her, then the coffee machine. "Make some coffee. Then get packed. We've got one hour before we need to be gone. Leave the rest to me."

With that, he moved into his room and closed the door. As he caught sight of his reflection in the mirror he shook his head, but his eyes sparkled and he felt more buoyant than he had done in days.

It was true, Acid Vanilla was trouble. But didn't he like a little trouble? It certainly made life interesting. Now that he was no longer required to do any of that other nonsense Caesar had wanted him to do, they could concentrate on the task in hand.

He raised the bed frame and selected four handguns (two Walther PPKs and two Glock 19s), along with an assortment of push daggers, knives and six boxes of ammo. Lowering the bed, he placed the guns and ammo inside a canvas kit bag he'd brought with him for dirty laundry and placed this in his suitcase. Once done, he removed his shirt and suit jacket from the closet door and put these on. He decided against wearing a tie, but inspected himself in the mirror and was pleased with his appearance. He looked sharp and ready for business. The finishing touch to his outfit was a set of gold-plated Walther PPK-shaped cufflinks he'd had commissioned a few weeks earlier. It was the first time he'd worn them, and they looked perfect. He looked perfect. Mr Sensational.

He grinned at his reflection. It was a new day and playtime was over. It was time for action.

Time to do what Spitfire Creosote did best.

CHAPTER 24

Acid spun around in the centre of the loft apartment, trying to take it all in. It was the most amazing place she'd ever seen. The walls were the same raw brickwork as the outside of the building, but covered in enormous canvases that looked to be original artworks. Above them a massive skylight, made of just one piece of glass, took up most of the ceiling space. The other light in the apartment came from three modern chandeliers in steel and glass, positioned in a triangular formation above the open-plan living area. There was a kitchen zone, a lounge zone, and then a huge double bed over by the far wall next to another pane of glass that ran floor to ceiling and looked out over the street.

The bed was the first thing Acid had noticed when Spitfire let them in, and at the sight of it she'd felt a prickle of something that could have been nerves.

"There are another two bedrooms through here," Spitfire said, re-entering via the doorway on the other side of the room. "Plus a toilet and a separate bathroom. All looks spiffing."

Acid smirked, turning away so he wouldn't see. *Spiffing.* Who the hell said spiffing in 2003? She bit her lip and sniffed away the nervous energy rippling through her. It wasn't the time for humour or teasing. She might have made Spitfire a half-decent coffee back in the other place, but she was still a long way from redemption.

"It's amazing," she said. "I bet it was expensive."

Spitfire gave her a stern look. "It was. And we can't expect Annihilation to pay for it. So this comes out of both our fees."

She puffed out her cheeks. But fair enough. "I'll pay for it. Out of my fee."

"No. It's fine. That's not how I do things." He moved over to the large kitchen island and removed his jacket, placing it over one of the high-backed stools. "We'll still come out with a decent pay packet once we get the job done. *If* we ever get the damn job done."

Acid gave him a smile, which she hoped conveyed how sorry she was and that there'd be no more silliness on her part. She wasn't sure she managed it. A dark cloud of despair was rising over the cusp of her awareness. If the fat manatee of depression took over, she'd be even more useless than she had been up to now. But it couldn't happen. She had to stay away from the darkness. Keep her attention on what was important. Namely, finding the mark and properly redeeming herself. She'd make Caesar and Spitfire proud of her yet.

She joined Spitfire at the kitchen island, where he was sitting, deep in thought. His silver cigarette case and lighter were on the counter in front of him, alongside a steel ashtray. In his hand he held an unlit cigarette. He didn't look up as she dragged the nearest stool towards him.

"What's the plan?" she asked, slipping onto the stool.

Spitfire didn't look up. "We're close to the mark's hotel. Raaz said he hasn't checked out, so it doesn't appear as if he got spooked the other day, or even knew you were following him." He picked up the cigarette lighter and gestured to the bathroom.

"We'll freshen up and get back out there; stake the place out until he shows."

"Okay, great," she said. "Because I was thinking... what if we went up there and—"

"No!" Spitfire held up a hand to cut her off. "You leave the thinking to me from now on." He placed the cigarette between his lips and lit it with a grace that belied his tough demeanour. She watched as he exhaled a long breath of smoke.

"You know those things are bad for you." She cringed as soon as she'd said it. It was such a lame comment.

"I'll take my chances," he replied. "You'll probably see me off first, the way things are going."

Acid smiled, and now so did he. "I suppose I asked for that."

"Anyway, we've got to get going." He stubbed out the cigarette and got off the stool. "Do you want the first shower?"

She sat upright, fighting the impulse to suggest they get in together.

Jesus.

Where the hell was that coming from? He was a good-looking guy. She couldn't deny that. But he was classically handsome and not her type. Also, he was older than her and thought she was a stupid kid; he'd practically said as much. He'd laugh in her face if she suggested such a thing.

"Umm. I'll go first," she said. "If that's all right."

Spitfire winked. "Fine by me."

———

TWENTY MINUTES later and Acid was drying her hair in front of the mirror when there was a knock on the bathroom door. She turned the hair dryer off.

"Come in."

The towel she had wrapped around her covered most of her

chest and body but showed off a lot of leg. As Spitfire put his head around the side of the door, he eyed her up and down, a wry smile on his face. Feeling her cheeks flush, Acid turned back to the mirror, addressing his reflection.

"Sorry, I'll be out in a minute."

"Good. Because we're behind schedule now."

She nodded and lifted the dryer, ready to turn it on, before Spitfire held out a hand.

"Hey, be careful with that thing."

"What do you mean?"

"It's electric, and there's water all over the floor. The last thing I need is for you to bloody electrocute yourself."

She met his gaze. It was almost as if he cared about her. "I'll be careful."

"Oh yeah, I know that," he said, his voice dripping with sarcasm. "You're always careful."

He gave her another glance up and down and shook his head. "Two minutes. We need to get moving."

He left her and she finished drying her hair, then headed for the back bedroom (they'd agreed to take a room each and leave the bed in the main space for display purposes only). She got dressed in black jeans and a black turtleneck, and was applying some basic make-up when she looked up, startled, to see the mirror's reflection of Spitfire in the doorway. How long had he been watching her?

"Nearly done?" he asked.

She turned around. He was holding a bunch of papers in his hand. She saw a photo of Boris Bakov on top. He must have printed out the documents Raaz had sent over.

"You know that's out of order, bursting in on a lady when she's getting ready?"

"Is that so? Next time I'm with a lady I'll bear it in mind."

She flashed her eyes at him, playing at being shocked; and as he smirked back, energy fizzed in the air between them.

"Do you still have your tracker and phone?" he asked.

"They're both in the pocket of my leather jacket."

He raised his head. "But you'll wear the new red number I bought you?" He eyed her with a supercilious expression. She rolled her eyes.

"Yes. Fine. I'll wear it."

"Good. And make sure you keep both the phone and tracker on you at all times. Do you hear me? Especially if you plan on running off again. Which you aren't going to. Are you?"

She shook her head. "No."

"Good girl."

She turned back around. She hated it when he called her that. Is that all he saw when he looked at her?

"The shower's free, by the way," she said.

"I'll get one later. There's a basin in my room and I had a quick whore's bath while you were doing whatever you were doing in there."

She spun back around. "A what?"

"A whore's bath. You know – pits and crotch."

She wrinkled her nose. "That's not very nice."

"What isn't?"

"Calling it that."

He stuck out his bottom lip. "I suppose it is a tad uncouth. A hang-up from a past life, perhaps. But regardless, it means we can move things along. Now all I need is a bit of sustenance and we're ready to rock. I'm going to head out and pick up a coffee and some breakfast. Do you want anything?"

"No. I'm fine."

"You should eat."

"I'm not hungry." They stared at each other. White-hot

energy tingled down her spine and exploded in her pelvis. "But thanks for asking."

Spitfire nodded. "I'll be about twenty minutes. As soon as I get back we'll head out for the day. But it's cold and they've forecast more snow. So dress up warm this time."

"Yes. All right."

He left her to it. She waited until she heard the front door close before going through into the main space. Spitfire had left the papers he'd been looking at on the kitchen island. The mark's file. She picked up the top sheet, which showed his headshot and a list of his last known vital statistics. The man looking back at her was a lot younger than the real-life counterpart from outside the hotel, but he had the same sour expression, with a heavy brow and a square nose. She scanned the text below the photo, reminding herself he was an inch shorter than her and was using the alias, Letvin Gurkin.

"You're mine," she told the photo. "The second you step foot out of that hotel, I'm going to..."

She lowered the paper.

What if she didn't have to wait for him to leave?

She glanced back over her shoulder. The client wanted the hit to look like an accident. But accidents happened in hotel rooms all the time. People slipped in the shower. Closets fell on them. They electrocuted themselves with a hair dryer...

A smile formed, along with an idea. It might take more than a damp floor to kill someone; but what if they slipped whilst holding the electric dryer and fell into a bathtub full of water? That could happen. She'd be shocked if it hadn't been done. She glanced back at the photo. In it, Bakov had short hair, but in her mind's eye she saw him from yesterday with his long hair combed back from his face.

Perfect.

The bats were adamant. This was her chance to redress the

balance and show Spitfire what she could do. If she made the hit, there was no way he'd think of her as a silly girl. She'd be his equal. An elite assassin. Someone who the organisation could rely on. Who Caesar could rely on.

Do it! the bats told her.

This is your mark.

She returned to her room and got dressed, putting the red overcoat on over her leather jacket. It wasn't only a concession to Spitfire's instructions, it would come in handy for what she had planned.

A good girl, he'd called her.

Screw that.

She was a woman and a badass.

To further exemplify this, she marched into Spitfire's room and searched for the guns she knew he'd brought from the other place. Finding them in his suitcase under a pile of neatly folded and identical white boxer shorts, she lifted out a Glock. This was the first type of handgun Spitfire had taught her to use, and she felt an affinity with the brand. Checking the clip held its full complement of fifteen rounds, she grabbed a spare and placed it in the inside pocket of her jacket and stuffed the pistol down the back of her jeans. She felt every bit the deadly assassin as she did so. Then, with a bounce in her step and the bats screaming their encouragement, she tied the coat's belt tight around her waist and headed for the door.

CHAPTER 25

The man behind the reception desk smiled as he noticed Acid sauntering across the lobby. She sucked in her cheeks as she approached, putting even more energy into her hips and pout and stepping fully into the role she'd been constructing for herself on the walk over here. Her mannerisms might have been a little over the top, but she knew of people who acted this way and it helped get her into character. The new red coat helped, too.

"Good morning," the man sang as she stepped up to the desk. "My name is Santiago; how are you today?" Up close, she could see he wasn't much older than her. He was tall and slim, with dark colouring and perfect white teeth. Handsome, in a PG-13 kind of way.

"Good. Thank you. I wonder if you can help me," she said, swapping her Ws for Vs and Hs for Ks. "I am looking for someone very important to me."

She'd been practising her Russian accent on the way over; but doing it in real-time, to another person, she worried she was overdoing it. The words sounded harsh and had too much of a phlegmy edge. Regardless, she kept her cool, staring at the young man without blinking.

Santiago's demeanour didn't falter. "I'll certainly do what I can. Are they staying at the hotel?"

"Yes. It is my father," she said, relaxing her face. "Letvin Gurkin is his name."

Santiago lowered his gaze and began tapping at what she presumed was a computer below the countertop. He squinted as he read something, and then looked up. "Yes, we have a Mr Gurkin staying with us presently. He checked in two days ago."

"Excellent," Acid chimed. "Can you tell me what room number he is staying in, please?"

Santiago bared his teeth in a grimace. "I'm so sorry. I can't give out our guests' room numbers."

Her heart sank, but she remained in character. She raised her hand to her mouth. "Oh no! But I am his only daughter. I have come here today to surprise him. It is his birthday, you see. He and my mother are – how you say – estranged from one another. We have not seen each other in nearly three years."

"I'd love to help," he replied. "But I've not been working here long. I can't risk it."

Acid leaned over the counter, eyes furtively scanning the room on the other side of the reception desk. Tucked under a table in the corner was a rucksack with an old hardback book lying on top. She couldn't see the title, but she read the name Stella Adler written in gold leaf on the spine.

She pushed her shoulders back and returned her attention to Santiago.

"Of course. I understand. Only, I worry this is the last time I can see him before he goes back to Russia. Maybe forever." She dropped her face into a forlorn expression. "You see, I have been studying in California for the last few years. At UCLA." She raised her eyebrows and smiled, a more natural one this time.

Santiago's eyes widened. "Oh, cool. I'm hoping to move out West in a year or two. What's it like out there?"

As soon as the words came out of his mouth, she knew she had him.

"It's great. I love it a lot. I'm sure you will love it just as much. You're an actor, right?"

He placed his hand on his chest. "Erm, yes. How did you know?"

"Oh. I can just tell. You have excellent bone structure and presence. You'll be amazing." She was getting into the role now, extending her vowels, going for it with emphasis. *Boon stroocture. Preyseynce.*

Santiago looked to his left and then to his right. She guessed – hoped – he was checking in case any of his superiors were in earshot. "All right, I shouldn't be doing this," he whispered. "But screw it. I'm not going to be working here for much longer."

"Exactly! You're going to be movie star!"

"All right. Let's see." He peered at his computer. "Your father is staying in room 735."

"Thank you so very much." She grabbed his hand and shook it. She wasn't sure if it was the sort of thing a Russian woman would do, but she didn't care. She was genuinely excited at how well this had gone, and how quickly she'd thought on her feet. She knew she was clever and fast-witted, but sometimes overthinking tripped her up. Not today. And Santiago seemed to appreciate the gesture.

"I hope he likes the surprise," he told her.

"Oh. He will. Also, do you know if he is in his room?"

Santiago curled his lip, demonstrating he was thinking about it. He'd have to work on that if he was going to make it in Hollywood. Stella Adler would have sent him packing. "Mr Gurkin. Room 735. I've not seen much of him since he checked in, to be honest." He glanced at the computer screen again. "But

I can see he made an outside call thirty minutes ago and I don't recall seeing him since, so you should be in luck."

"You," Acid said, pointing at him, "are a total lifesaver."

"Happy to help," he said, offering her a sharp salute. "And the elevator is just over there." He pointed over her shoulder but she didn't turn around, having already scoped out the place as she walked in. She wasn't so green to fieldwork she didn't know to always check her entrances and exits. Much like an actor, she mused, as she thanked Santiago enthusiastically and hurried over to call the elevator.

As the steel doors sucked shut, she closed her eyes, relaxing the muscles across her chest and shoulders.

She'd done it.

She was on her way to Bakov's room.

But now came the hard part.

She reached under her coat and removed the Glock from the back of her jeans. It had a reassuring weight as she held it and racked the slide, putting a round in the chamber. There was no suppressor nozzle, but she only planned on using it as a last resort; or, worst-case scenario, she could use the handle as a blunt instrument. She placed the gun into her coat pocket and stepped back, watching the lights above the elevator door as they switched from level 3, to 4, to 5... Almost there.

She planned to get into Bakov's room, overpower him and get him in a sleeper hold. Once he was out cold, she'd drag him into the bathroom, strip him naked, run him a nice hot bath and then chuck the electric hair dryer into the tub with him. Most hotels of this ilk provided a dryer for their guests to use, and she hoped it would provide enough of a clear narrative to get a death-by-electrocution verdict. Caesar had told her that most luxury hotels did their best to cover it up if a guest died in suspicious circumstances. Many even had their own PR people, to help deal with the media. As long as the client knew the mark was dead and there were no links back to Russia, she'd be golden. Then she was free to spend the rest of the trip enjoying the sights and sounds of the best city in the world. The only problem she could foresee was that the hair dryer lead might not reach from the socket to the bathtub, but she'd deal with that if it came to it. She was good at thinking on her feet. When she was having a manic episode, as she was now (she only had to look at her eyes in the reflective wall of the elevator to know that), her thinking was truly innovative. Something would come to her.

The elevator shuddered to a stop on the seventh floor and the doors slid open with a ping. She stepped out onto the landing and walked through the open double doors opposite the elevator, coming out in the middle of a long corridor with doors spread out on either side. A plaque on the wall told her that rooms 701 to 719 were down to her left and 720 to 740 on her right. She was about to head right, towards room 735, when she noticed a maid's trolley outside one of the end rooms on the left.

She grinned. It was as if fate itself was smiling on her.

Rushing down there, she glanced into the open room and saw a small Latino woman changing the bed sheets. The woman didn't look up or notice Acid move around the other side of the trolley and hurried away with it.

As she got to the far end of the corridor, Acid could see the last room was 731, but then she turned the corner and came out on a small landing with two doors in front of her and one on each side. Bakov's room was the one on the right. From the layout, she presumed these rooms were suites. She brought the trolley to a stop outside 735 and did a quick summation, accounting for Bakov's below-average stature and the angle and scope of the fisheye lens in the door's peephole. Altering the location of the trolley a few inches, she moved up to the door, lowering herself so only the top of her head would be visible.

Once in position, she sucked in a deep breath. Her hand was in her pocket, gripping the handle of the Glock, her finger on the trigger. She wouldn't get caught out again.

She gave it three seconds and then, satisfied there was no one coming to attack her, knocked on the door. A shot of adrenaline rippled through her and she felt a pressure in her chest. She closed her eyes, calming herself as best she could.

You can do this.

Trust yourself.

A scuffling noise came from behind the door and then a man's voice. "Who is it?"

It sounded as if he was standing only a few inches away, the white wooden door with its ornate surroundings the only thing standing between them.

"Hola," Acid sang, in a generic Hispanic accent. "I clean your room?"

There was no response, so she bobbed her head for the peephole. He'd be looking out at her right now, checking for danger. Checking she wasn't an assassin coming to kill him.

"Please, I need to change towels, too. You open door. I give them."

"I don't need towels," he barked, in a heavy Russian accent. "Go away."

She tensed but maintained the act. "Please, señor. Is important. My manager says I have to do this. I come back and clean later, but I need to change towels now."

"I am leaving soon. I have meeting. Come back then."

A meeting? Shit.

All the more reason she had to do this now.

"I beg you, sir. I only want to pass you towels. It takes one minute. Less than one minute. I get into a lot of trouble if not."

There was another long pause. "Step back so I can see your face," Bakov snapped. "I cannot see you."

The request did little for her heart rate. "I am a maid," she said. "I work here in the hotel. Please, señor, I need to give you fresh towels." There was a stack of towels on the trolley behind her. If he looked out, he'd see them.

"I said show your face."

"Okay. Sure." She moved back half a step, enough he'd see most of her face but not the fact she was wearing this bloody red coat rather than a maid's uniform. "Here. You see?"

She stared at the peephole, smiling warmly so it would show in her eyes. With her Italian genes, she hoped she might pass for Mexican or Spanish. Most people would see through it, but perhaps not a Russian thug on his first trip to the West.

Wrapping her knuckles on the door, she tried again. "See me now? Yes? I have lovely fresh towels for you. All clean."

He wasn't buying it. She gripped the Glock handle tighter. If he was standing close to the door, a well-placed bullet might—

No.

That was stupid.

She didn't know if the round would even penetrate the wood. And even if she managed to get a kill shot, what then? The client was adamant it should look like an accident.

Shit! No!

She'd messed up. Again. Now the mark was onto them, and he'd be even more cautious. Harder to get to.

Shit, shit, shitting shit.

Spitfire would have returned to the new apartment by now and found her gone. He'd be furious.

He'd want to kill her.

He might actually kill her.

She was about to give in and slink away when she heard movement behind the door. "Señor?"

"All right. Wait there."

A shot of manic bat energy shook her body. She rocked back

onto her heels at the sound of a door chain being slid open and then a click as he released the lock. As the first sliver of light shone through from the room, she barged against the wood, slamming the door into Bakov. He cried out as she burst into the room and lunged at him, driving the bony part of her forearm into his nose. Up close he was even shorter than she'd realised, and the fact she had an inch or two on him buoyed her confidence. But he was thickset and had years of experience fighting for his life. He lashed out, punching her in the neck and twisting away as she grabbed for his shirt.

She needed to get behind him and her arm around his throat, but as the seconds ticked away her assurance waned. The element of surprise had been squandered, and Bakov was tougher than she'd given him credit. He shoved her away. She felt something hard against the backs of her legs. A glance down showed her it was a glass-topped coffee table, but in the split-second it took her to find that out, a sharp pain erupted in her head and the room rushed away from her. She lost all sense of direction as another sharp blow knocked her off her feet. She felt the air on her face, the lack of ground, and then a loud crash as she smashed through the glass tabletop. Small cubes of safety glass spiked into her back before hands gripped her collar and yanked her to her feet.

"Who are you?" Bakov snarled in her face. "Who sent you?"

She got a lightning-fast tour of the hotel suite as he swung her around. Holding onto her collar, he shoved her into the next room and smashed her back against the wall. The impact knocked her vision into focus.

"Piss off!" She karate-chopped him on both sides of his neck but he didn't let go. She tried again, chopping at his thick neck with all her strength. But she'd misjudged this. She realised that now.

"Was it Perchetka?" Bakov asked, grinding his cranium into

her forehead. Acid grasped his wrists as he twisted her collar, winding it tight around her throat.

"Who are you?" he spat. "Tell me. Or you die."

She didn't respond. She couldn't speak. But something told her she was going to die either way. She pushed off from the closet to throw him off balance, and they moved around the room, spinning in a mad, angry dance. The gun in her pocket banged against her hip. She pulled it out and swung the base of the handle at Bakov's head. She caught him above the eye and he released her before shoving her against the closet and smashing his fist into her stomach.

Shitting hell.

It was some punch. It felt as if her insides had been demolished. She dropped the gun as she fought for breath, and then Bakov was back with his hands around her throat. They tussled. Acid tried to get her thumbs into the pressure points between his thumb and forefinger but couldn't get purchase.

Bakov gnashed his teeth, cursing at her in Russian. She could see the gun lying on the floor a few feet away. It was gone. Useless. But then she had an idea.

Rallied by the thought, she dropped one hand into the inside pocket of her jacket before smashing the heel of the other into Bakov's angry face. It was a good blow, heavy and on target. Right on the bridge of his already bust-up nose. He let out a grunt; and as he released her, she reached around and slipped her hand into the back pocket of his jeans. Done. He hadn't noticed. Side-stepping around him, she caught him with a sharp elbow to the side of the face.

"Fuck you!" he yelled.

She made a dash for the door, but he swiped her feet away and she stumbled over. A stabbing pain tore through her abdomen as Bakov followed up with a kick to the ribs. She rolled over and felt something hard under her leg. The Glock.

She grabbed it and sat up, aiming at Bakov's head. Time slowed. He glared at her, at the pistol. She tensed her jaw as her finger tightened on the trigger. She couldn't kill him this way, but she had to get him to back off. If he jumped on her whilst she was in such a vulnerable position, it would be over. No fee. No redemption. No more Acid Vanilla. No more anything.

"Go to hell," she yelled, squeezing off a round. She'd aimed the shot above his head, but it was close enough to let him know she was serious. He turned and ran from the room, flinging a throw cushion at her as he passed the couch by the window. She got up and followed him through to the next room. He was yanking open the door as she got there and she fired again, splintering the door frame by his head. That did it. He was out of there, running down the corridor towards the emergency exit.

With a wry smile spreading across her face, she gave pursuit. Her plan hadn't worked out the way she'd intended. But she could still make this right. She had to. Her reputation depended on it.

Hell, her life depended on it.

CHAPTER 26

Spitfire stopped for more cigarettes on his way to breakfast. It was imperative he find Bakov and get this job boxed off today; but a short timeout, away from Acid, was just as important if he was going to succeed. One hour wouldn't make any difference to the mission and it would allow him time to reset and get his mind back on the job.

He smoked as he walked, travelling three blocks before he found a deli on the corner where he smoked another cigarette down to the bone whilst waiting for the attractive redhead behind the counter to make him a bacon and smoked cheese bagel and a strong black coffee. Once his food and drink were ready, he paid the girl (flirting with her long enough that he was satisfied he could take her home if he wanted to) and crossed the street to sit on an old bench overlooking the park.

The bagel was hot and tasty and hit the spot. Spitfire regulated his calorie consumption most of the time, eating mainly protein and few carbs. But whenever he was out in the field he allowed himself some leeway. He was being a naughty boy, after all; he might as well go the whole hog. As he finished his food and slurped down the last mouthful of coffee, he remembered something his old man used to say.

If you're gonna be a bear, Stevie, be a facking big grizzly bear.

He realised it was the sort of thing Caesar often came out with, and quickly brushed the thought away, along with whatever connotations were on the other side of it. Looking for a distraction, he pulled the packet of Marlborough Reds out of his pocket and flipped open the lid, tapping the bottom of the pack hard enough that a single cigarette rose from the crowd.

Placing it between his lips, he lit it and inhaled deeply. It was a nice day; cold, but the air was fresh and new. Across the street a middle-aged woman walked her dog in Central Park. It was one of those small, snuffling kinds of mutt. The sort favoured by camp men and rich, middle-aged women such as this one. Possibly the role of the dog in these relationships was substitute child, but why anyone would want a fake child, let alone an actual one, was beyond him. They were just so much hard work. You had to love them, care for them, have them rely on you. No. Not for him. Same with a partner. Even if he wasn't an elite assassin, there was no way he was cut out for family life.

Spitfire Creosote was a lone wolf. An alpha in the wilderness. He knew from experience that family and loved ones only got in the way. They could be hurt. Used as leverage. Then there was the flip side. If they weren't breaking your heart (or your nose), they were holding you back and manipulating you. Families were a perfect example of that old adage about crabs in a barrel. As soon as you tried to get away, or better yourself, someone would reach up and pull you back down into the pit of despair and averageness with the rest of them.

Finishing his cigarette, he flicked the stub into the gutter before getting to his feet and looking at his watch. He'd been gone forty-five minutes. Acid would be wondering where he was. He set off walking, but stopped before he got to the end of the block. She hadn't wanted a coffee, but maybe he'd get her one anyway. Only because she needed the pick-me-up. It was going to be a long day. He walked back to the deli and bought two more strong black coffees along with an apple Danish (he didn't know whether she liked them, but she'd need some sustenance) and headed back to the apartment.

As he walked, thoughts of her filled his head, but this time he made no effort to shoo them away. She was a pain in the arse and had proven herself to be ill-equipped for what was being asked of her, but it wasn't entirely her fault. Both he and Caesar had believed she was ready, but it was clear now she required more preparation and training before being sent out into the field. When they got back he'd have a word with the boss and let him know his thoughts. Acid had the right attitude, but her frenzied and chaotic nature needed channelling. So those attributes worked for her, not against her.

He smiled, recalling the look on her face when he'd got back to the apartment after being at the police station. She'd been angry, of course, but he'd noticed something else in her eyes when he'd burst through the door. Happiness. Relief. She was pleased to see him. He'd almost forgotten what that looked like. Usually when he showed up at someone's door, the person involved was most definitely not happy to see him. If they ever saw him at all.

The next intersection was busy with traffic, and he stopped to wait for the walk sign. He could see the mark's hotel up ahead. Raaz was certain he was still there, but time was ticking on. If Bakov was meeting with a handler from the CIA, it would be today or tomorrow. Once he was on their books, the situation became a lot trickier.

He crossed the street opposite the hotel. Should he set up a stake-out point now? He could call Acid and tell her to meet him there. He stopped and took a sip of his drink as he considered his options. The coffee was still hot but wasn't as pleasant as the first one he'd had. He wondered, in passing, if it had upset the cute redhead that he was buying an extra coffee for someone and she'd taken less care the second time. But that notion was wiped from his mind when he saw a man running out of the alleyway down the side of the hotel.

Bakov.

Bloody hell. Here we go.

Talk about luck. He looked around for a garbage can so he could toss the cups of coffee and give chase. He couldn't find one, and was about to leave them next to the building for some homeless person to find, when another figure appeared from out of the alleyway. A woman. She was wearing a long red coat, so it took a second for him to register who it was. When he realised, he flung the coffees angrily to the ground.

Acid fucking Vanilla.

That girl. She really was going to be the death of him.

He ran across the street after them, swerving around cars and holding his hand out to angry drivers as they leaned on their horns. Bakov was a hundred metres in front and looked to be running for his life. That meant Acid had most likely shown her hand and, unless they got to him now, he could be in the wind forever. Spitfire quickened his pace, running faster than he had done in a long time. Hot, bitter coffee rose into his mouth and he swallowed it down as he ran. Acid reflux. Never had there been a better bloody term for something. The woman kept on repeating like a bad case of heartburn. Forget about the two of them having some fun once this ended – right now all he could think about was ending her.

Winding around civilians, he raced onwards, following Bakov and Acid down the side of an immense red-brick building with garages at street level. It looked like a multi-level car lot, but as he got closer he saw it was the offices of the New York postal service. One of the garage doors was open and there was a row of parked delivery vans inside. He wondered whether he should commandeer one, but thought better of it. Fear had made Bakov fast, but he was closing the gap between them with every step. If he could reach him before he got to the park, he could push him into the fast-moving traffic that ran down the side of it.

Just like that.

It would all be over.

He caught up with Acid at the end of the next block. "What the bloody hell have you done?" he growled.

She jumped and gasped at the sound of his voice but didn't lose pace. "Spitfire! Don't worry. I've got it all under control."

It wasn't the response he'd been expecting. He almost crashed into a signpost, only veering around it at the last second.

"Is that so?" he hit back, as they got to another intersection and played a lethal game of Frogger over to the other side. "Well, forgive me if I don't share that sentiment, sweetheart. It looks to me like you've spooked the mark and allowed him to escape."

He craned his neck over the people on the street in front of him. Bakov was almost at the end of the last row of buildings before Central Park, but he still had to cross a busy divided highway.

Game on.

He could do this.

Putting every bit of energy that he had left into his legs, he raced down the next street, leaving Acid in his wake. Bakov was on the kerbside, head darting left and right as he waited for a gap in the traffic.

"Come on, old boy," Spitfire told himself. "One last push."

He was twenty seconds behind him. He pictured himself slamming into the back of the squat Russian thug, hearing the splat as he came into contact with a heavy truck. Spitfire would carry on running around the corner. He'd have left the scene before anyone even knew what had happened. Baring his teeth and ignoring the stabbing pain in his side, he pressed on. Ten seconds. It was happening. He'd done it. *Another one bites the—Fuck!*

There was a brief lull in the traffic and Bakov seized the opportunity, making a break for it across to the other side. Spitfire was only a few strides behind him, but as he got up to the kerb a bus zoomed past in front of him and he had to stop.

Bastard!

Pissing bastard bollocks!

As the bus continued on its journey, he saw Bakov vaulting over a low fence before disappearing into the depths of Central Park. Spitfire rocked back onto his heels, throwing his attention left and right down the bustling carriageway. If he made it across now, he could maybe still catch him.

He paused.

His heart fell into his belly.

"Oh my god," he spat, holding his fists up in front of his face. "I don't believe this. I don't bloody well believe this."

What would happen now? There was no way the mark would return to the hotel. Raaz could track him down eventually (there were things she could do with security cameras and closed-circuit television that boggled his mind), but it would take time. By then, Bakov would have met with his CIA handler and the job would be over. Spitfire's career, too, more than likely. Mad Dog Perchetka had influence over some of the more nefarious areas of the globe. Word would get out that Annihilation Pest Control couldn't finish the job. They'd be a laughing stock. Caesar would be apoplectic. And rightly so.

Shitting hell.

"Did he get away?"

He carried on staring ahead as Acid caught up with him. If

he looked down at her and she gave him the wrong kind of smile, he'd push her into the traffic instead.

"It looks that way," he muttered.

"Never mind.

Now he looked at her. Or rather, he glared. "Never mind? Never fucking mind? That was our big chance to take him out. It would have been perfect. And now he's gone. In the fucking breeze. And you talk like it doesn't matter. Are you completely mad?"

Acid tilted her head to one side. And there it was, the supercilious smirk that made him want to grab her face and shove it against something hard. The problem was, if he started he wouldn't be able to stop.

"You're a very stressed man, you know that?"

"You need to shut your fucking cake hole, love. Right now. I mean it. Otherwise I won't be responsible for my actions."

"I'm not totally stupid, you know."

"Aren't you?"

"What if I told you he's not getting away? What if I told you he's heading for a meeting right now and we can find out exactly where that is?"

Spitfire rubbed at his face. "Stop being cryptic. What are you talking about?"

She arched one eyebrow. The same way he sometimes did when he knew he held all the cards. He used to call it 'Doing a Roger', after the greatest Bond who ever graced a tuxedo. But he'd never told anyone that.

"I got into a scuffle with Bakov in his hotel room," she said. "Without him knowing, I slipped my tracker into the back pocket of his jeans. Get your phone out. Have a look. Those units are so tiny he won't have felt it…"

Spitfire yanked the phone from out of his pocket and had it flipped open before she finished talking. Opening up the GPS software, he saw the red dot moving through Central Park. As he zoomed in, he could pinpoint the mark's exact location.

"Wow. That's good thinking."

"I know."

The smile she gave him, and the look in her eyes, sent the blood rushing to all the wrong places. He rolled his shoulders back and pulled his attention away from her.

"Any sign of Blondie?" he asked.

"Not at the hotel. But that doesn't mean he isn't around. So let's get this done before he has a chance to scupper things."

Before he could respond, she ran off around the corner, displaying the determination and grace of a puma on the prowl.

Well, well...

He liked this version of Acid a lot more. Picking up his heels, he ran after her.

"There's a walk sign," she said, pointing down the block as he got up to her. "We can get across safely and give chase."

"My word, you have changed your tune."

She didn't stop running, but he saw a smile lifting the corners of her mouth. Then, as quickly as it had appeared, her face dropped into a sterner, harder countenance. "I just needed to get my head in the game," she said.

"So it seems." They got up to the crossing point. "I think we'll make an elite assassin out of you, after all, Acid Vanilla."

CHAPTER 27

Spitfire's system had barely recovered from chasing the mark across town before he was on the run again, racing through Central Park with Acid by his side. His throat was sore with dryness and his leg muscles burned from the exertion, but he kept on, matching Acid step for step. She wasn't even out of breath, and as he glanced down he saw her mouth was gripped in a harsh pout and her eyes were alert and intense. It was like she was a different person from the nervous try-too-hard who'd arrived in New York two days earlier. And yes, her methods might be a little unorthodox for his taste, but they were closer to getting the mark than they'd ever been.

This was the girl he'd met back at Honeysuckle House. This was the person, full of potential and fire, that Caesar had raved so much about. As they sprinted past an old couple walking their dog, he wondered if this was what she was like when she didn't have someone like him breathing down her neck. Was this his fault? Had he underestimated her? Either way, he couldn't help finding her incredibly sexy when she was this confident and eager to kill. He tried not to focus too much on that as he veered around a jogger coming the other way.

"Have you still got him on the radar?" Acid asked, as they tore along a wide walkway, splitting up around either side of two female rollerbladers.

Spitfire was holding the phone out in front of him, eyes flitting between the red dot on the screen and the path ahead. "Yes. He's not far away," he said, as their paths fell back in parallel with one another. "He looks to have slowed down. With any luck, we'll catch up with him around this next corner." He gestured ahead to where the pathway curved behind a group of thick shrubs.

"Do we have a plan for what happens when we catch up with him?" Acid asked.

"I thought you might have a plan. Seeing as you have the situation under control." He glanced over and she gave him a dirty look in response. "I'm not being sarcastic."

"Aren't you?"

"Maybe a little. But I am open to suggestions. We need to hit him now. Before we lose him again."

He swerved around a group of women pushing prams and had to race to catch up with Acid as she leaned into the corner.

"There he is," she said, already slowing as Spitfire reached her. "Over here." She grabbed his arm and pulled him behind the thick trunk of a huge American Elm. Bakov had his phone to his ear and was walking across the grass in front of a wooden building with a slanted roof that looked vaguely Japanese. As he passed beneath a canopy of bony trees, he looked back, his head moving erratically as he scanned the area. Like a perturbed owl.

Spitfire leaned back behind the tree.

"Did he see us?" Acid asked, doing the same.

"I don't think so." He risked another look. Bakov was standing in the same spot, deep in conversation with whoever was on the phone. Some CIA gimp, would be his guess. "Let's circle around and—"

As he looked back he realised Acid was leaning against him, still holding onto his arm. Their eyes met, and for a second he forgot all about Boris Bakov and Blondie.

"Sorry," she said, stepping back and letting go of him. But her eyes didn't leave his.

"It's fine." He shook his head to clear his thoughts. "Follow me. We can stick to the trees along this ridge."

He strode away from her, clenching and unclenching his fists to further regain his composure. This was not like him. Out in the field he fully stepped into the role of Spitfire Creosote. He was cold, calculating, cruel as hell. Sure, there might have been the odd pithy aside to whichever pathetic cretin he was about to send to hell, but it only added to the callousness of the act. Right now, he felt like he was losing himself.

Focus, old boy.

You've got one job.

He stayed in the shadows, zigzagging through the trees and not taking his eyes off the mark. Bakov still had the mobile phone pressed against his face, and was barking into the receiver as he walked along a winding path towards the weird gothic castle that overlooked the lake. Spitfire had visited Central Park many times over the years. The last time he was here, he'd met a contact at the foot of the castle. The top section facing out over the water had excellent tree cover and the rocky terrain below meant there was no foot traffic. It had been the perfect spot to purchase a selection of handguns without being seen. The perfect spot, too, for a turncoat Russian gangster to meet with a spook.

"Do you see the castle?" he whispered back to Acid. "My guess is he's meeting with his new handler on the other side, up near the lake. It's secluded there. If we double back on ourselves, we can approach from the other side and remain out of sight."

"Sounds good," she said, as they changed direction and

quickened their step. "But this has to look like an accident, remember? It's going to be tricky in front of some CIA prick."

"I know," he replied. "But let's see what happens."

The way Bakov was acting, Spitfire wondered now if this was simply a preliminary meeting. The fact it was so clandestine, too, suggested that Bakov's contact at the agency was holding the Russian at arm's length, assessing his value and validity before taking him to meet his bosses. They crossed over to the other side of the path and ran for the tree cover on the far side. From there, he could see the back of Bakov's head and the castle in front of him

"You were right," Acid whispered. "He's heading for the spot in front of the lake."

"Good. We can observe what happens from here. If it looks like the spook is going to take him somewhere, we'll have to think on our feet. But I'm almost certain he'll be leaving the meeting alone. Once he does, we'll hit him. If we have to make it look like a mugging gone wrong, so be it. It's an easy option and still believable. This is New York, after all. Either way, that fucker isn't leaving this park."

Acid stifled a giggle, but he now presumed it was excitement rather than her mocking him. Because something had shifted between them in the last hour. He'd felt it. He knew she'd felt it, too. For the first time since touching down at JFK, they were a team.

He was moving for the cover of a tree when Acid took a sharp intake of breath and grabbed his arm. "Spitfire," she whispered, pointing. "Over there."

He looked. "Ah... Shit."

Three small buildings stood at the top of an incline above the castle. Mostly they were obscured by shrubbery, but the bottom corner of the nearest building was visible, and standing there with his head and shoulders above the greenery was their old friend Blondie. He was watching Bakov.

"What are we going to do?" Acid whispered, but he shushed her. "Let me think."

He cast his attention around the area. Blondie was two hundred yards away from where Bakov was now waiting. He and Acid were closer, but they couldn't have him mess this up for them. Not again. They needed to take out Blondie without alerting the mark to their presence. Not a straightforward task. But if Blondie knew about the contract on Bakov, then he must also know it had to look like an accident.

"Spitfire," Acid tapped him on the shoulder. "We've got more company."

He looked at where she was pointing. A long-limbed man with neat side-parted hair and a black overcoat was walking down the path towards Bakov. It was a bright winter's day, so the sunglasses he wore weren't too out of place, but he couldn't have looked more like a spook if he'd tried. What was it with these people – were they stupid, or did they just consider themselves untouchable and didn't care?

Spitfire was suddenly aware of his chest rising and falling with each breath. A second went by. And another. He looked from Bakov to Blondie to the CIA guy and then back again. It felt as if he was standing in the middle of a tinderbox and one spark was all that was needed for it to go up.

Hold your nerve, old boy.

You've got this.

Or maybe not. Movement out of the corner of his eye alerted him that Blondie was up to something. As Spitfire craned his neck to get a better look, the big man lowered himself down on one knee and picked up a long-barrelled sniper rifle.

Bollocks.

Acid had seen it too, if the gasp of shock was any indication. The stupid bastard. If he shot Bakov now, the shit was going to hit the fan in so many ways Spitfire could hardly comprehend it. He had to do something.

Bakov had seen the spook walking towards him. He raised his hand to him, but the tall man patted the air in a sharp gesture, telling him to cool it. They were a few feet from each other when Blondie raised the sniper rifle to his shoulder and took aim.

Spitfire froze. It would take him four seconds to get up to the sniper nest. He might get there before Blondie fired, but it was unlikely. After that they lost the mark, the contract and Annihilation Pest Control's standing in the industry. The spook would likely make a run for it, but perhaps not before he took notice of whoever was involved in the killing of his asset. Spitfire suspected he was low down on the pecking order at the agency, but he was still a spook.

What to do?

What the bloody hell to— *Jesus Christ*!

A loud bang broke his thoughts in two and Blondie's shoulder erupted in a cloud of red. He fell against the side of the building and dropped the sniper rifle as Spitfire reeled, trying to make sense of what had happened. He couldn't hear anything except a loud ringing in his head. Turning, he saw Acid standing next to him with a pistol in her hand. Where the hell had she got that from?

A moment later all hell broke loose. He saw Blondie clutching his hand to his shoulder as he scrambled away into the undergrowth. He saw the gangly spook running sideways up the hill with a pistol in his hand, barking something into his sleeve. And he saw the mark running in the opposite direction down the side of the castle.

"Spitfire!" Acid grabbed his arm. "Bakov's getting away."

Yes. He could damn well see that. There was a split-second decision to be made. They could both go after Bakov; but with Blondie still in play, there was a risk he could come for them. Presently he was injured. Vulnerable. But he was still a big fucker and a tough catch. The spook had already fled the scene. He wouldn't be back.

He grabbed Acid by the shoulders and looked deep into her eyes. "Can you handle the mark? Tell me honestly."

She nodded. "Yes. A mugging-gone-wrong."

"Okay, do it. I'm going after Blondie." He was already running away from her when she called after him.

"Spitfire! Be careful."

He looked back over his shoulder. "I'm always careful," he said with a grin. "And you can do this. Now, go!"

CHAPTER 28

Even with a serving of hot metal in his shoulder, Blondie was fast. It amazed Spitfire how someone so huge could move with such agility and speed. But it was the main reason the annoying bastard was still breathing. Anyone else he'd have put in the ground by now.

Bugger.

Since splitting with Acid, he'd been pursuing his adversary in a wide arc in the hope he might catch up to him without being seen. But as Blondie reached one of the main roads that ran through the park, he looked back and their eyes met. He stopped running briefly; then threw his head back and appeared to bark at the sky before speeding across an extensive patch of grass and over another road.

Spitfire chased after him, almost getting skittled by some prick in a Ford Taurus who swerved to miss him as he ran across the road. It only spurred him on. When he was young and frustrated, his rage often tripped him up, but he'd got to the stage in his life now where he used his fury as fuel.

Blondie seemed to have picked up pace as he got closer to the edge of the park, but Spitfire was damned if he was going to let him out of his sight. The hope was he'd take a wrong turn at some point and end up down a blind alley. That's when Spitfire would pounce.

Summoning his strength, he pressed on, racing out of the park as Blondie's big, ugly head disappeared down the steps of the subway station on the opposite corner.

Spitfire slowed to a stop. "What the— Are you kidding me?" He ran to a nearby crosswalk and over to the other side.

He was going underground?

Seriously?

But it was a savvy move on Blondie's part and it told Spitfire the big man understood the assassin's code. In the same circumstances – recently shot and unsure of his injuries – Spitfire would have done the same thing. No one was getting hit while they stayed amongst civilians.

Spitfire got to the subway and grabbed the green railing that ran around the stairwell, swinging himself down the first flight of stairs and knocking a dirty old drunk out of the way. The man yelled something unintelligible after him, but he didn't stop, taking the next flight of stairs two at a time. As he got to the lower level he saw Blondie up in front, shuffling up behind a small Chinese woman to get through the barrier on her ticket. She turned around to stare at him and a look of penetrating rage creased her features. She said something before the big guy picked her up and carried her through the turnstile with him. Once on the other side, he shoved her against the wall and continued on his way. That was one way of doing it.

Spitfire weaved through the crowds after him, swiping himself through the turnstile and heading down a long, steep escalator. Blondie had taken the left-hand lane and so did he, shunting past those standing on the right as they both raced down to the lower level. The gap had now closed between them and Spitfire was only a few metres behind as they reached the bottom of the escalator, straight into a swarm of people. If he'd had a blade or a trusty push dagger about his person, he could have finished Blondie right there. A trip and a fumble. A blade up through the ribcage into the heart. In and out. It would incapacitate the big goon in seconds. He'd be dead in minutes. Long before that, Spitfire would have fled the scene unnoticed and jumped onto the next train to Successville. The saying – that there was safety in crowds – was also true for hired killers wanting to get the job done without being spotted.

Blondie turned and leered at Spitfire before barging his way through the crowd and into the left-hand tunnel for trains going uptown. Leaning into the corner, Spitfire followed him down the long passageway, surfing the moving sea of civilians. People bustled and shoved against him and, as he turned the corner, the atmosphere in the tunnel changed and the flow of the crowd speeded up amidst frantic chatter. There was a train waiting on the platform. A shrill beeping noise permeated the air, letting everyone know it was about to depart.

Spitfire stopped and rose onto the balls of his feet, looking over the rows of heads between him and the train. The big man was clambering into the nearest carriage. He was going to get away. Leading with his elbows, Spitfire shifted down to his left, heading for what looked to be a less crowded part of the platform. The train beeped again, meaning he had about three seconds before the doors slid shut and he lost his chance to finish this. Putting his head down, he barged his way towards the train, grabbing onto people and pushing them aside to propel himself along. In front of him the train doors were sliding shut. He leapt for the opening, knocking a pale young man with dyed black hair out of his way. The kid hissed at Spitfire, who jumped on board, banging his arm on the doors as they sucked shut and the beeping sounded again.

The carriage lurched as they set off, and he grabbed onto the nearest handrail, peering around to get eyes on his prey. He'd travelled laterally down the station, but he was sure they'd boarded the same carriage. The train was packed, but as he pulled himself up to his full height he saw Blondie standing in the space between the next set of doors. His face was twisted in a frown of concentration and his hand was under his shirt, poking at his shoulder. No doubt he was examining the damage Acid's bullet had done. His thick corduroy jacket was dark burgundy, so his injury wasn't noticeable. But even if he'd been bleeding out in a white gown, those around him would have most likely ignored him. This was the New York subway, after all, and Blondie was a scary-looking bastard at the best of times. Indeed, no one but Spitfire appeared to be watching as he brought a bloody finger out from under his collar and shoved it in his mouth.

In contrast, Spitfire was taking a more gentlemanly tact, apologising and smiling as he snaked his way around the standing passengers to get closer to his target.

"I do apologise. Can I just...? Am I okay to...? Thank you... Can I get through...? Great. Thanks."

There was certainly something to be said for having an upper-class British accent at times like this. Some passengers remained hard-faced and wouldn't budge as he passed by, but others stepped aside as if he were a visiting royal. When he was only a few feet from the doors he stopped. Blondie glared at him as if he'd seen a ghost. But then a wide grin split his chops and he let out a low, growling laugh.

That annoyed Spitfire. He'd counted on the hairy bastard being a little disturbed when he realised they were in the same carriage, but he seemed almost glad to see him. They stared at each other, both trying to convey via only their eyes and facial movements what they wanted to do to the other.

You're dead. You're going to die...

Fuck you. I kill you...

Spitfire couldn't do anything. Not here. Not on this train full of civilians. Nor Blondie, if indeed he was a real assassin. Which, from his inaction, appeared to be the case. Because the code was adamant. No one in the industry was to act in view of civilians or draw attention to their work. The elite echelons of the murder-for-hire business existed in the shadows. Everyone knew the rules and what happened to you if you broke them.

The train pulled into the next station and, as the doors opened, Spitfire readied himself to give chase. But Blondie didn't move. A selection of people got off, but only one middle-aged man wearing a puffy winter coat boarded; meaning the area in front of the doors suddenly became more spacious and Spitfire could move around until he was facing Blondie. If they stretched their arms out in front of them, their fingertips would touch.

Spitfire shot him a look of mock concern. "Are you all right, old boy?" he asked. "You look a bit worse for wear."

Blondie growled. "I am fine. Worry about yourself."

The train set off and Spitfire rode the movement, steadying himself with the handrail above his head as he engaged himself in a stare-out contest with the highest of stakes. He realised he was still angry that he hadn't killed this prick on that first day, but no matter, death was coming. Blondie had been living on borrowed time for too long. As soon as he left this train and headed somewhere secluded, Spitfire would strike. The man might be big and sprightly, but Spitfire had killed plenty of men bigger and sprightlier than him over the years. The bastard wouldn't get away from him again. All he needed was the right moment to pounce and he'd crucify this fucker. He'd jump on his back and ride him to the ground with a sleeper hold. With the right pressure on the carotid artery, brain cells die after only a minute. After four minutes, the entire person dies. He pictured himself riding the human bronco, sensing the big man's muscles going limp. He smiled, allowing his bloodlust to show on his face. Blondie leered back.

"Hi guys, hope you're all having a great day."

The sound of a nasal voice to his left broke Spitfire's concentration. Looking over, he saw a young guy with an acoustic guitar strapped across his torso. He had long, greasy hair and was wearing a dirty white t-shirt and the sort of jeans kids wore these days that made them look like they'd shit themselves.

"Don't worry," the kid went on, with a beatific smile on his face. "I'm not asking for money or anything like that. I just want to entertain you guys and provide a bit of joy on your journey today."

Spitfire's hand tightened on the handrail before he remembered something Acid had said to him on the plane. She'd been chirruping on and on about music and bands she liked. He'd only been half-listening, but he'd perked up when she talked about her hatred for what she called 'heartfelt bedwetter music.'

"I'm telling you, Spitfire, it's the worst. All those earnest wankers thinking being sensitive will get them laid. It's awful. You ask me, no matter where you go in life, whenever you're trying to have fun, there's always some prick who shows up with an acoustic guitar to ruin it."

He let his gaze drop for a moment as he smiled to himself. But the thought of Acid brought with it renewed worry (the fact that this was now accompanied by an out-of-tune rendition of *Roxanne* by The Police didn't help). Did he do the right thing by sending her after the mark? Should he have let Blondie escape and gone with her? He screwed up his eyes, trying to block his ears at the same time. He trusted her. She'd be okay.

He hoped she'd be okay.

He opened his eyes as the train slowed. The kid had finished his song and was pulling a blue velvet cloth cap from out of the back of his jeans, waving it meekly under the noses of the other passengers.

Not asking for money.

Yeah, right.

The train shuddered to a stop and the kid stepped in front of Spitfire. As the doors opened, Blondie flashed him a wide grin and alighted onto the platform.

"Afternoon, sir," the kid said, offering the cap up. "I don't suppose you can—"

He yelped as Spitfire grabbed the side of his head and pushed him out of the way.

"Not today, Sting," he snarled, bustling his way out of the carriage. The sign overhead told him they were at 103rd Street Station, Upper Manhattan. Glancing around, he saw Blondie running along the platform before he disappeared down a tunnel leading to the exit.

He was getting away.

He couldn't let him get away.

CHAPTER 29

Spitfire ran through the station, following Blondie up the fast lane of the escalator and then onto a wide concourse with shops on either side. They both slowed their pace, walking with keenness until they got up to the barrier. Here people were milling around, many with tense, angry faces. Some guy in blue overalls was tinkering with the ticket-reading machine on the turnstiles whilst a woman in uniform waved people through a single gateway on the far side. As the people from Spitfire's train joined the fray, the bottleneck worsened. He waited, his muscles raw with tension, while a uniformed man opened a larger gate in the centre of the barriers, normally used for disabled passengers. When it opened, the crowds rushed through. Spitfire saw Blondie over to his left and headed that way, shoving and pushing to get behind him as the wave of people reached the steps and carried him up to street level.

An icy chill spiked his skin when he got to the top. The temperature had dropped a few degrees since he'd been underground, but there was plenty of opportunity now to warm up as

Blondie broke free from the milling crowds and ran down the side of the park.

Spitfire set off after him. "Not a chance, sunshine."

He followed him across an intersection and down West 105th Street. Here Blondie got a second wind, putting distance between them as they ran along a tree-lined street with residential properties on either side. Spitfire had always prided himself on his athleticism and strength, but after chasing Bakov all morning and now this big fucker, he was feeling the strain.

How the hell was Blondie so resilient?

It could be steroids or some other performance-enhancing drug. It could also just be good genes. He certainly looked the part of an Aryan superman, albeit a rather scruffy one.

But Spitfire wasn't giving in. He still had him in his sights as they headed down the next street and the brownstones turned into builders' yards and warehouses. Unless his legs stopped working or his heart burst open, he would keep going. At the next intersection, Blondie raced across the road and was almost knocked over by a large truck. Spitfire saw a chance as the truck screeched to a halt and Blondie stopped running to bang his enormous fists on the vehicle's bonnet. Unsurprisingly, however, the driver remained in the cab until the giant brute ran off.

Damn it to hell.

Spitfire ran after him, veering around the back of the stationary vehicle. In doing so, he lost sight of his quarry, and by the time he'd reached the next corner, Blondie was nowhere in sight. A large building stood on the corner with scaffolding up its side. Next to this was a row of run-down houses before the street opened up. As Spitfire got closer, he saw a wide driveway and another building set back from the road. A brown UPS van was parked outside, but it didn't look to be a depot. It didn't look to be anything other than a dilapidated warehouse. Metal shutters, painted closed, covered most of the windows and there was a chain-link fence running around the perimeter. At the end of the driveway was an old security guard's shack joined onto the main building. The door was hanging open.

Blondie was inside. He had to be.

Driven by self-belief and an eager desire to show the bastard who he was dealing with, Spitfire strode towards the shack. Outside the door he stopped and pushed his attention into the room beyond. He couldn't hear anything, couldn't sense anyone's presence. Moving slowly, and with his instincts and muscles bristling with readiness, he entered the building.

Inside it looked like the Mary Celeste of industry. The room was covered in dust and cobwebs, but laid out like it would have been when it was still in use. There were desks and filing cabinets and even a yellowing fax machine in one corner. As he moved over to the door leading into the main body of the warehouse, he noticed a mug of furry green coffee on a desk and wondered if he might appropriate the mug as a makeshift cosh. But then he saw a long, thin piece of wood leaning against the wall in the corner. He reached for it and held it up. It was about a metre long with a metal hook on one side. It was most likely used to open the top windows in the warehouse when they could still open. It also made the perfect weapon.

As he opened the door to the main space, he was presented with a dark corridor. There was a light switch on the wall beside him, but he didn't touch it. Even if it worked, it would only alert Blondie to his presence. He walked with a light step to the end of the corridor, where another door was jammed open. The room beyond was pitch black, but as he stood in the doorway to let his eyes adjust, he saw chains hanging from the ceiling and huge packing crates stacked up against the wall in front of him.

He raised his makeshift weapon, holding it with two hands

over his shoulder as if playing baseball. The stance also guarded his torso with his left arm, and he had his elbow crooked, ready for a secondary attack. He narrowed his eyes, squinting into the gloom and ready to smack Blondie's skull into the bleachers. This was the main warehouse, and apart from the large shutters that faced the street, there didn't appear to be any exits. He held his breath, shifting his focus to his hearing. Except for the low hum of city noise coming in from outside, he heard nothing. But as he stepped into the space, he felt a shift in the atmosphere. Someone else was here. He sensed them.

"Well, here we are," he called out, his voice echoing in the cavernous room. "Just me and you. We really should stop meeting like this."

There was no point staying quiet. Blondie would have heard him come in, would have seen him in the doorway. He took another step forward, tense and ready. This was about instinct now. If he overthought it, or second-guessed himself, he would be a dead man. He exhaled and loosened his muscles.

React and move, old boy.

You hear something, you strike out.

Trust yourself.

He moved further into the space, twisting at the waist as he went, searching the darkness for a sign. He imagined himself clubbing the hooked end of his weapon into Blondie's face. If he could get an eye or fishhook him, it would be a bonus, but all he needed was a distraction, enough to disable the big bugger so that he could get him in his legendary chokehold. After that, it'd be game over.

A sound to his left spun him around. He lashed out with the hook, angry and perturbed when he found nothing but air. Turning, he swung again and this time connected with something too solid to be human, even one built like Blondie. As his weapon bounced off the packing crate, he jumped back into a fighting position. Placing his foot behind him, he felt something on the ground.

A boot?

Shit.

He struck out with the hook but was knocked off his swing by a blow to the head that sent fireworks exploding behind his eyes. It was as if he was floating in space, until a heavy blow between the shoulders knocked him to the dusty concrete below. He laid his hands on the cold ground, trying to push himself up. He was dizzy and disorientated. Scrabbling around on the floor, his fingers touched what he thought was his weapon, except he knocked it further away in the same movement. A searing pain shot through his skull as a hand grabbed his hair and yanked it back. He lashed out with his elbows, but the angle was too oblique and he was in no position to do any damage.

"Yes, my friend," a deep voice boomed in his ear. "Here we are, indeed."

"Go to hell," Spitfire rasped.

Blondie's laugh boomed in his head. His breath was rancid. Like he'd spewed up the contents of his stomach and then eaten it again.

"No, Mr Creosote," he said. "I don't think I will go to hell. That's where you're heading."

Spitfire spat and writhed, trying to free himself, but Blondie had a knee against his spine and his head yanked back so tight he could hardly speak. His neck couldn't be more exposed. He tensed, waiting for a blade to slice it open.

"Do it," he wheezed.

Blondie laughed. But released his grip on him. Spitfire lurched forward, gasping for air before a hand clutched the back of his skull in a death grip and slammed it downwards. Cool air wafted into Spitfire's eyes as he braced himself. A thought flashed into his mind. If he could shift his weight, he could use the big bastard's momentum against him. But then a blinding pain burst into his skull and it felt as if his entire head had splintered into dust. He thought of Bakov. He thought of Acid.

Then he no longer had any thoughts at all.

CHAPTER 30

The pain in his head was extreme, moving out from his sinuses to the nerves in his teeth. Even his eyeballs hurt. But blinking himself awake, Spitfire realised the bright spotlight a few feet in front of him might have something to do with that. As his awareness spread, he realised he was sitting on a hard wooden chair. He lunged forward, but his arms were tied behind his back. With hessian rope, if he had to guess. The fibres scratched his skin as he twisted his wrists against the knots.

"Spitfire Creosote," a voice boomed from behind the light. "I was beginning to worry I was too heavy-handed just now and you weren't going to wake up. That would have been a shame. It's no fun at all killing a vegetable. I should know. I've done it."

Laughter ensued. Spitfire lowered his head and took some deep breaths. There was no point trying to see through the stark light blinding him, and he needed to reserve his energy. With frantic fingers he worked on the rope, exploring the strands and bends, evaluating whether it would be easier to squeeze his hands free or work on the knots. But then he realised...

"Wait. You know me?" he asked, looking up.

Blondie moved the spotlight's tripod to one side and tilted the lamp to the floor to better illuminate the space.

"Of course I know you," he said, stepping forward. "You're the great Spitfire Creosote. The man they call Mr Sensational and The Flash Boy Assassin. The man rumoured to have made one hundred kills in his first five years in the industry. You took out José Curupira, the most feared man in Brazil."

Spitfire sniffed. The pain in his head was abating a little and he could focus on what was going on. More importantly, he could focus on what he needed to do to walk out of this place alive.

"You've done your research," he replied.

Blondie chuckled. "Actually, you're a bit of a hero of mine."

Spitfire took a moment to examine the big man's face. Up close, his skin was flushed but wrinkle-free. His eyes, too, although dark and cruel, were bright and alert. It was the beard that aged him.

"I can give you an autograph if you untie me," he said, unsurprised when he was met with more laughter.

"Always with the one-liner. You're a funny guy. Ha!"

"You know who I am," he said, folding his thumb over the heel of his palm and twisting it through a loop of rope. "But I'm rather in the dark as to who you are. Or what the hell you're doing here. Is there a contract out on me I don't know about?"

The big man rose to his full height. "I guess I can tell you. It makes no difference now."

He walked behind the spotlight to a low table and picked up something off the top of it. When he turned back around, Spitfire saw he was holding a Walther PPK in one hand and a Brausch silencer in the other.

"The classic Bond set-up," Blondie said, with a grin. "I knew you'd approve. Or not. Depends on how you look at it, huh?"

"Who are you?" Spitfire whispered.

The big goon tilted his head from side to side as if struggling over whether to tell him.

"My enemies call me Wilbur Das Biest," he said. "Wilbur The Beast to you non-German speakers. Or just The Beast."

"The Beast. How fitting. And what do your friends call you?"

"I don't have any friends." He screwed the silencer onto the end of the pistol. "There are no friends in this game, Spitfire. You know this. But I think this is true of all life. We come into the world alone, we die alone. Some people spend the interim period far too bothered by what other people think of them. But I never have."

"Who sent you?" He'd given up trying to work his hands free and was digging his fingernails into the loops and twists of the knot. It wasn't a rushed amateur job like he'd hoped. "Who wants me dead?"

"I'm rather new to the scene, as you're probably aware," The Beast replied, in no way of explanation. "Otherwise you and your cronies would have heard of me, I expect. But that would have ruined the entire plan."

"What plan?"

The Beast finished screwing in the silencer and pulled a chair out from under the table. He placed it down a few feet in front of Spitfire and sat.

"I was a freelancer for my first year in the industry," he went on. "Did some good work. Concise, clean kills. Mainly in Eastern Europe. But recently I've taken on a long-term contract – working for someone you may know. Artem 'Mad Dog' Perchetka." He leaned back and flicked up his eyebrows, as if he'd just dropped the biggest plot twist in history.

"Perchetka?" Spitfire's head was still throbbing and his energy levels were low, but he was certain that didn't make sense. "He hired us. He's the client."

"This is true. He hired you to be here. To carry out the hit on

Boris Bakov. And as far as the underworld and the industry are concerned, he *is* your client."

Spitfire screwed up his eyes. "Then why are you trying to stop us from eradicating Bakov? If Perchetka has changed his mind, he can cancel the contract. It happens."

"Of course Perchetka still wants Bakov dead! The fool is here in America to meet with the CIA. He must die before he shares any of our secrets. But when that pathetic coward escaped Russia and it became clear what he was planning to do, my boss had the most brilliant of plans. A perfect way of wiping out not just the traitor, but also his chief rivals. This way, he kills two birds with one stone. Or with one beast!" More raucous laughter erupted from the man's sizeable frame. It cut right through Spitfire's aching skull, but the pieces were now falling into place.

"So... what? You kill the mark instead of us and Perchetka kicks off? He tells anyone who'll listen that we messed up?"

"There we go! Mr Sensational! I knew you'd get there in the end. Not just a pretty face, as they say. Perchetka silences his deserter and discredits your organisation in the process. This entire mission was about setting you up to fail. He never wanted you to kill Bakov."

"But why?" Spitfire was so taken aback at hearing this, he'd forgotten about being tied up. He carried on trying to free himself as The Beast released another throaty chuckle.

"Think about it some more, my handsome friend. What if, for instance, Perchetka was setting up his own organisation of elite assassins? How do you think he might leverage this new project so it quickly becomes the go-to organisation for those wanting to spend the big bucks to get rid of the big targets? Easy, of course! By removing the competition. By making Annihilation Pest Control look like pathetic fools who can't carry out a simple hit."

Spitfire strained forward. "You think it'll be that easy? Caesar has great respect in the industry. Annihilation Pest Control is the best of the best. People know this. Our clients won't change allegiances because of one rotten job."

"Maybe not," The Beast replied, with a shrug. "But you know what these Russians are like. Their propaganda and disinformation methods are second to none. There's no smoke without fire, Mr Creosote. And Perchetka will ensure that this fire burns bright and across all continents. With two of his best operatives also dead, Beowulf Caesar will be finished. He'll have no other option but to step aside."

"I see."

"Oh? Did you think I was going to spare you?" The Beast raised the Walther PPK and scratched the silencer muzzle against his temple. "I'm afraid both you and the girl are going to die."

"No. Leave her," Spitfire told him. "She's young. She's no threat to you."

"Maybe not a threat. But she shot me." He slapped his hand against his shoulder. "It might only be a graze, but I can't let her live after that. It's better this way. The more men Caesar loses, the harder it will be for him to continue. And you have to admit, that girl is a real nuisance."

Spitfire sniffed. He tasted blood in his throat. "You rotten prick."

The Beast sneered. "You are upset by this? You like her? You are in love?"

"Don't be so bloody stupid."

"I get it. It is sad for me. As I say, you are a hero of mine. But then, hmm, it was also my idea to kill you. Oops."

His shoulders shook as he laughed silently to himself. It only made Spitfire more determined to get free and kill the fucker. What he wouldn't give to grab him by his fat head and thumb his piggy little eyes into his skull. After that, he'd slit his throat and watch him bleed out in pain and agony.

He strained at the ties.

He was going nowhere.

"Your deaths weren't part of the original plan," The Beast continued. "Perchetka knows the industry takes a negative view of anyone attacking operatives in the field. But I spoke to him just now whilst you were sneaking around outside. I convinced him otherwise. I explained that you and the girl have seen too much of me. Right now I am an outsider in the industry, with no prior links to Perchetka. People may suspect he was behind the plot to discredit your organisation, but they will have no proof. Soon the only thing anyone will care about is that Annihilation Pest Control is not the organisation they thought it to be. Once word gets around that the great Beowulf Caesar has failed his client – and on such a simple mission as this one – he will be a laughing stock from East Timor to El Salvador.

"The industry is fickle, as you know, and those in power want to know they are hiring the best. The private contracts will dry up. Along with the big fees. It can still bid for open contracts, but Annihilation Pest Control will lose its footing in the elite ranks. But don't worry, because Artem 'Mad Dog' Perchetka's glorious new organisation will be ready to step into the fold." He shrugged. "You don't need to worry about this, my friend. You won't be around to see any of it."

He stepped forward and aimed the pistol at Spitfire's head. The atmosphere in the room turned to lead and the temperature dropped a few degrees. Spitfire stared up into The Beast's face, searching for a tell. Something to let him know he was bluffing. That this was a power play. But his expression was resolute. Spitfire Creosote was about to die. The knowledge hit him like an anvil to the guts and he stopped struggling with the rope. It was over. He was done.

"I'm sorry it had to come to this," The Beast told him. "You were a great man, Spitfire. One of the best. But not anymore."

He closed his eyes. "Just do it," he whispered.

He'd thought a lot about dying when he first started in the industry. Indeed, after his first few kills, he'd had nights where he'd lie awake wondering what it would feel like to be at the dangerous end of a gun, knowing you were about to die.

Would it hurt?

Would you feel pain?

Would you regret your life decisions up to that point?

But he hadn't thought about dying for many years. It was a pointless exercise and dangerous if you flirted with such thoughts out in the field.

But now he had his answer.

He felt nothing.

In fact, all he experienced as The Beast rested the silencer muzzle against his forehead was a serene numbness. It wasn't pleasant, but it wasn't the abject fear he'd expected. Most of the people he'd killed had displayed varying degrees of terror or sadness – the ones he'd seen up close, at least – so he knew this wasn't normal. But maybe he'd stopped valuing human life somewhere down the line, and that included his own life as well.

He waited.

Why was he still alive?

He opened his eyes to see The Beast regarding him with his head tilted to one side. He looked almost disappointed. Perhaps he wanted to see more terror or sadness from him. If he really was a fan of his, he'd probably been rehearsing this moment for a while. Most likely, it wasn't going as he'd hoped.

At that moment Spitfire knew he had a chance. The pistol was still aimed at his head but The Beast had stepped back. Spitfire shifted his weight forward onto his feet and felt the momentum of the chair beneath him. The concrete floor of the warehouse was uneven. If he rocked back, he could propel himself towards the lamp and knock it over, plunging the space into darkness. From that position he'd have a fighting chance to free himself and get away.

He had one go at this. And it had to happen now.

The Beast tightened his grip on the gun. "Goodbye, Spitfire Creosote. It was an honour meeting you. And now it is my honour to take your life."

CHAPTER 31

An hour earlier, on the other side of town, Acid Vanilla was standing on the corner of 5th Avenue and East 81st Street, assessing her options. She'd observed Spitfire's instructions, having trailed the mark across Central Park, awaiting an opportunity to dispose of him using the mugging-gone-wrong narrative. Yet as they'd neared the edges of the park, she'd realised a better option would be to allow him to reach the main road then shove him in front of a speeding vehicle. That was the cleanest solution and would mean no comeback from the client.

So she'd hung back, sticking to the trees out of sight as Bakov reached the gates. This was her big chance to prove herself after all the shit she'd caused over the last few days. She couldn't screw up. But as Bakov reached the roadside, Acid's plan crumbled faster than a corrupt politician with a knife at his throat. In horror, she watched as he hailed a cab and jumped in the back seat.

Bollocks! Shit!

She burst out from her position. But by the time she reached the road, the car was gone. She glanced around, hoping to hail the next cab and give chase, but there was none in sight.

Noooo!

This can't be happening.

The mark had got away. Again. After stamping her feet and cursing herself, to expel the demons in her head, reason took hold and she remembered Bakov still had the tracker in his pocket. They could still do this. Spitfire could find the mark using his phone. And that also meant she could find Spitfire using hers.

Scrambling in her coat pocket, she pulled out the phone and flipped it open. She wondered for a moment whether she should just call him, but thought better of it. She needed time to compose herself and come up with a decent script before she confronted him with her failings. Besides, if he was engaged with seeing off Blondie, a call from her would be the last thing he needed. It was best if she went to him and explained herself face to face.

Opening the maps software, she saw Spitfire's red dot was uptown, not too far from their apartment. Most likely, he was on his way back there after completing his part of the mission. It only made her hate herself more, but if they were to find Bakov she had to face him. Rousing herself, focusing her attention on what she had to do rather than on her spiralling chaotic thoughts, she headed for the nearest subway station.

It took her twenty minutes to get to Columbus Avenue, and once back on street level she checked her phone again. For most of the train journey she'd been imagining Spitfire pacing up and down in the apartment, waiting for her to return, but as she opened her phone she saw the red dot at a location a few hundred metres away. Spinning around on the corner, she found her bearings and crossed over, hurrying along West 105th Street.

It took her three minutes to reach the abandoned warehouse. She stopped outside to calm herself and evaluate the situation. The building looked deserted, but she trusted Raaz's software. Spitfire had to be inside. Or his tracking device was. She headed down the side of the warehouse, to where the battered door of an old outbuilding was hanging open a few inches.

Once there, she stopped again and waited, listening. No sounds were coming from inside, but the bat chorus in her head was deafening – her heightened senses telling her something was wrong.

She hurried up the steps, sliding the Glock out of her pocket as she pushed at the door.

"Spitfire?" she whispered.

Stepping inside, she swung her aim around the room, finger poised on the trigger. The only light came in via a grimy window on the opposite side, and it looked to be an old office, with desks and filing cabinets. Another door, round the corner from the one she'd entered through, was also hanging open, but the space beyond was too dark to see anything. She side-stepped over there, leading with the Glock as she moved into the corridor on the other side of the door. The air smelt stale and there was a sharp chill as she paced down to the far side. Now she could see into the next room.

A glimmer of light speared up the wall directly in front of her, illuminating only a small section but enough for her to see it was a large warehouse space with a high ceiling; stacks of packing crates and thick chains hung from the rafters. Leaning her back against the wall of the corridor, she paused, allowing her hearing to take over. A voice came from deep within the room, but from this angle she didn't have a visual. It was a male voice, low and gruff. Now laughing. That didn't sound good. Her entire body was rigid with tension until she heard the unmistakable upper-class drawl.

Spitfire!

The relief came in an intense, physical sort of way. But her instincts told her he was in trouble. If the other person in the room was the big blond goon, he had the upper hand. She raised the Glock, resting the cool stainless-steel barrel against her cheek as she shuffled closer.

She could now see that the source of light came from a halogen spotlight sitting atop a tripod on the far side of the vast space. It was angled towards the ground but gave off enough light so she could see Blondie parading up and down. He had his back to her, waving his arms around as he spoke. He had a gun in one hand with a silencer nozzle, and as he stepped to one side, she saw Spitfire in the chair.

No...

He looked to be tied to the chair, but apart from a cut above his eye, she couldn't see any other injuries. His jacket was off, and his neatly combed hair was sticking up at all angles. He was alive. But for how long? What could she do? As she watched, the bastard pointed the gun at Spitfire's head and she thought her heart might explode.

Stay calm, she told herself, remembering what he'd taught her. About how important it was to stay loose in high-pressure situations. To not allow your emotions or thoughts to get the better of you.

Trust yourself, she heard him saying.

The bats were ready. She was too. But she only had seconds. Letting her instincts guide her, she whistled and stepped out from the corridor. As the big man spun around, she aimed at his head, but she wasn't counting on how fast he could move. He fired at the same time she did. The air moved centimetres from her face as a bullet whizzed past her. Dropping to her knees, she fired again. But he was already running behind a row of crates stacked high along the wall.

"Acid!" Spitfire yelled at her. "Move! He's coming for you!"

She ran into the middle of the room, twisting as she went, aiming the Glock at the crates. "Where?" she cried. "Come out, you bastard!"

Nerves got the better of her and she fired off a flurry of shots at the crates. Wood splintered into the air. But that was all.

"Where is he?" she yelled, keeping her aim high, waving the gun whilst side-stepping closer to Spitfire. The rows of crates ran down the wall opposite, but there were spaces in between some of them. She thought she saw him flitting from one to the other and shot into the gloom, but the bullet only pinged off the concrete wall and ricocheted off a beam above her head.

"Fucking hell! Die, you bastard!"

The pressure in her head grew stronger as the bats screamed for blood. They were going haywire. The chaos behind her eyes was taking over. It felt like she was floating. She had no control over what she was doing. She saw movement. She fired. She yelled out. She fired.

Somewhere she heard Spitfire calling her. Telling her to stay calm. Then, at the far side of the row of crates, the big man appeared, hand raised and gun pointed at her. He was using a silencer so the muzzle flash was reduced, but she heard the pop and felt the whoosh of the bullet. He might have hit her. But she didn't think so; he was moving and firing, so his aim was bad.

She shot again, but her vision was spiralling along with her moods and she had no idea where the round went. It certainly didn't stop the bastard. He was heading for the door.

"Stop," she shouted. "I'll kill you! I'll fucking kill you!"

The rage in her body was all-consuming, but even in this heightened state she knew she was projecting it back to herself just as much. She wanted to run after him, to destroy him, to rectify this dreadful mess she'd helped create. But her legs wouldn't allow it. They were frozen to the spot. She was paralysed with a mixture of confusion, chaos, and... fear?

Yes.

It *was* fear.

Fear of the big man, but fear of failing as well. Fear of death. Fear of life. Fear of never being able to be who she needed to be. All she could do was stand in situ and shoot after him and then at the empty doorway as he disappeared down the corridor. Full of righteous fury, she kept on pressing the trigger, firing until she'd emptied the entire magazine and the slide action locked. She yanked the spare out of her back pocket, but her hands were shaking and she couldn't load it. It was pointless anyway. He was gone.

"Shitting hell!" she yelled, throwing the spent pistol across the room. "Bastard!"

Her yells turned into a banshee screech of despair and anger. She stamped her feet, balling her fists up so tight her knuckles burned. She wanted to hit something. She wanted to die. This wasn't supposed to happen.

"Acid!" Spitfire called out. "He's getting away. Go after him. You can do this."

She shot him a look. "I can't," she spat.

As her system calmed, she walked over to him. Without a word, she moved around the back of the chair to untie the ropes around his wrists.

"Is Bakov dead?" he asked her.

She didn't answer.

"Acid?"

"No. He's not. Okay!? I lost him."

"What?" She released the rope and he pulled his hands around to the front to inspect his wrists. "What happened?"

"He jumped in a cab," she replied, shuffling around to face him as he got to his feet. "I was going to hail one too, but there weren't any. All being well, the tracker is still in his pocket, though, so we can find him."

"Bloody hell, Acid. You should have finished him off. And why come here?"

"I wanted to find you. It's a good job I did, isn't it?"

Spitfire got to his feet. "No, Acid, that's not how this works. We need the mark dead. That's our job. That's your job. Your only job." She stepped back as he thrust a finger in her face.

"I saved your life."

"I didn't need saving. I had it under control. Now the mark is in the wind and The Beast is still out there. Yes, we've got the tracker, but it's getting late. If Bakov has any sense, he'll move locations and change his clothes. Then what? We're worse off than we were three days ago. What a fucking joke. And I tell you something, Perchetka doesn't need The Beast to discredit the organisation. We're doing that on our own."

"What are you talking about?"

He shook his head. "It's a long story. For now all you need to know is that Blondie is called Wilbur Das Biest – The Beast – and he's been sent by the client to make sure we fail."

Acid curled her lip. "But why? I don't get it."

"Perchetka wants to discredit Caesar so his new organisation can take over as top dogs in the industry." He stepped closer, his voice rising as he continued. "So now we need to find the mark before The Beast does, and we need to kill them both. Which is a big ask, I'd say, at this stage in the game. But we had them. We had them right where we wanted them. If you hadn't... Argh, fuck!" He spun away from her and punched the air.

Acid swallowed back a whimper. She didn't know what to say. Her head was spinning and her insides felt like they were on fire. She opened her mouth, hoping the right words might find their way out, but Spitfire turned back before she could speak.

He glared at her with wide, angry eyes, stabbing the air with his finger as he spoke.

"Caesar is going to be bloody furious. Do you know that? And well he might be. I knew you were a wild card, Acid, and had some crazy ups and downs. But I believed, with a little encouragement and patience, you'd learn to hone that anarchic approach so it could be of value. Hell, we'd trained you well enough. But no. I was wrong. You're nothing but a crazy bitch and you're dangerous. But not to them." He pointed to the open doorway. "Oh no. Not to the people we're actually here to kill. But to yourself. To me."

She tensed, breathing rapidly through her nose as a tear rolled down her face. Despite this, she didn't take her eyes off his. She wanted to claw his face off. She wanted to scream.

"I was only trying to help. I thought if we—"

"No, Acid. Enough! I know I said it was important not to overthink things in the field, but pissing hell, a modicum of thought is required. Otherwise you're just a whirling dervish bouncing from one disaster to the next. That's not how I trained you. It's not what Caesar wants. I don't care what happens next. We need to— Oh, fucking hell! Don't be so stupid. Come back!"

But she wasn't listening to this any longer. She couldn't. And he couldn't tell her anything she didn't already know. With Spitfire yelling for her to turn around and stop acting like a stupid girl, she ran for the exit. She was going to find The Beast, or whatever he was called, and she was going to kill him. Or maybe he'd kill her. What the hell did it matter anymore? Spitfire didn't care. And neither did she.

CHAPTER 32

Spitfire had been harder on Acid than was needed. He knew that. But that didn't stop him from muttering angrily to himself as he slipped on his suit jacket, retrieved her pistol and left the warehouse. Out on the street, the frosty January air did little to assuage his frustration. If the stupid girl had done what she was supposed to, this would be over by now. The mark would be dead. Annihilation Pest Control would have fulfilled their part of the contract. All would be as it should be.

Of course, there was the distinct possibility Spitfire, too, would be dead. But that wasn't a certainty and in this business that's what you dealt with. Certainties. Facts. Anything else was just opinion.

He walked to the end of the block. There was no sign of The Beast, but he didn't expect him to have stuck around. On the corner he stopped and stretched his neck from side to side while casting an eye around the area. He hoped he might see Acid skulking down one of the intersecting streets. But no.

"Bloody stupid..."

He trailed off, unsure what was needed at the end of that

sentence. She'd acted rashly just now, but it had been brave of her to burst in on them with no thought for her own safety. And, he supposed, she had sort of saved his life. He might have had an escape plan, but there were plenty of variables that could have gone wrong.

He walked back to the apartment and stood outside, gazing up at the tall building. At one time it would have been some kind of depository, but in the last decade or so the façade had been sandblasted and the windows replaced. Add on the impressive green awning that projected out from the lobby and it was now a perfect example of Upper Manhattan sophistication. Not surprisingly, it was costing a small fortune to stay there, and this was another reason why they needed to eradicate Bakov. The fee. Perchetka might be planning to undermine and discredit Caesar, but he was still technically their client. If Spitfire got the hit, he'd have to pay up as agreed. It was an integral aspect of the industry code of ethics and there were terminal ramifications for those who didn't follow the code.

The thought of Perchetka and his devious plans spurred Spitfire into action. He entered the building and ran up all five flights of stairs to the penthouse. He unlocked the front door of the apartment and then, on the count of three, pushed it open whilst simultaneously sliding to the right of the doorframe. He froze, ready to act. But there was no gunshot. No one jumped out at him. He waited for another three-count before glancing around the side of the door. The space beyond was empty.

He stepped into the apartment and closed the door behind him. The place was silent and there were no lights on. He headed straight for Acid's room, glad to see her suitcase was still on the floor at the end of her bed. Kneeling beside it, he lifted the top items of clothing – two faded black t-shirts displaying bands he'd never heard of. The Cramps and The Dead Boys? They sounded awful. He returned the shirts and stood. Acid

Vanilla. She was still such an enigma to him. Part surly teenager, part highly trained killer. But there were other parts of her too, weren't there? The part that was witty and exciting and even sophisticated at times. The part of her that was chaotic and complex and confusing, but which also intrigued him the most.

Bloody hell.

He certainly had a lot of ideas about who she was, considering she meant nothing to him. His breath caught in his throat. This was bad. Not just bad, it was dangerous. You looked out for your colleagues, but not to the extent of jeopardising your own safety.

He left Acid's room and went through to his own. After stripping down to his underwear, he examined himself in the mirrored door of the closet. He had a cut on his forehead, but it had stopped bleeding and didn't look too bad. Other than that, he was golden. A lucky escape.

Jesus.

Luck? What he wouldn't give for some of that right now.

After showering, he dressed in his remaining clean suit (a bottle-green number from Chittleborough & Morgan on Savile Row), and then sat on the end of his bed for far too long, just staring into space. Whatever he thought about Acid, whatever he felt, it was pointless. It couldn't happen. It wouldn't. He grabbed up his phone and selected 'Home', calling the number as he walked through into the living area.

It was Caesar who answered. He'd been expecting Raaz.

"Is it done?" the boss growled. It sounded like he had a mouthful of food.

Spitfire swallowed. "Almost. There were a few eventualities we hadn't counted on."

A heavy sigh came down the line. "Go on then, enlighten me."

As succinctly yet comprehensibly as possible, Spitfire

relayed everything that had happened since they last spoke. He told him what he'd discovered about Perchetka, and that Wilbur Das Biest was new to the scene, which was why Raaz hadn't been able to get a positive ID. Finally – and careful with his words lest it sound like an excuse – he explained how he and Acid had been set up to fail so the organisation would be thrown into disrepute.

When he'd finished, there was another long silence. Spitfire waited, knowing better than to carry on speaking to fill the gaps.

"You should have finished off the mark on the first day," Caesar said. His voice was chilling in its calmness. "Why didn't that happen?"

Spitfire puffed out his cheeks. He'd been prepared to give the boss the full story, warts and all, every fuck-up and misstep. But now it came down to it, he couldn't do it. It would mean throwing Acid under the bus, and that wasn't the act of a gentleman.

"We were blindsided, boss. The Beast is a tough, mean bastard. Fast, too, for his size. We weren't factoring him into the plan."

"I want that fucker dead. And the mark. Do you hear me?"

Spitfire rubbed the back of his thumb across his brow, forgetting his wound. He winced, but in a way the pain felt good. It was cathartic. It focused him.

"Caesar, it's over. They're both in the wind. I'm sorry, but—"

"I want them both dead! Do you bloody well hear me?!"

Spitfire walked back into his room and stared at the two Walther PPKs and the remaining Glock he'd placed on the chest of drawers. "Yes, boss. Loud and clear. But I don't see how we move forward from here. The mark's location has changed. So my guess is he knows about the tracker. And with The Beast out there too..." He trailed off, realising how he sounded. Like a failure. Like someone who'd given up.

"Where's Acid?" Caesar asked.

"She's in the shower," he lied.

"As soon as she's done, get out there and get the job done. I don't want to see or hear from either of you until Bakov and this Beast prick are on slabs in the city morgue. Do you understand?"

"Caesar—"

"Do. You. Understand?"

"Yes."

"Good. I don't care what it takes. No more pissing around. No more acting like a couple of bleeding amateurs. You work for me, remember? You're supposed to be the elite, for Christ's sake."

"I know."

"So pissing well act like it then! Goodbye."

He hung up. Spitfire held the phone in his hand, fighting the urge to fling it against the wall.

Come on, old boy.

Cool, calm and collected...

"Fucking hell."

He stuffed one of the PPKs into the back of his suit trousers and made for the door. He needed to find Acid. He needed to come to terms with what Caesar had just told him. But most of all, right now, he needed a damn drink.

CHAPTER 33

Acid was sitting at the bar, sipping from a shot glass, when Spitfire walked into CBGB's thirty minutes later. She had her back to him, and he waited a moment before going over to her. She was still wearing the red coat he'd bought her, but after only two days it looked like something she'd found in the gutter. In contrast, her dark hair was lustrous and wavy. As he watched, she brushed it back over her shoulders and glanced along the bar, exposing the profile already imprinted on his mind. The full lips, pressed into an eternal pout, the long lashes caked in mascara, all centred by a strong but perfectly shaped nose.

Damn it.

She did things to him. He couldn't deny it.

She shifted in her seat and sat up straight as if she knew she was being watched.

"I thought I might find you here," he said, walking over to her.

She didn't look around. "Yeah, well. I wanted a drink."

"I know the feeling. Can I join you?" She stuck out her

bottom lip and shrugged. He took that as a yes. "What are you drinking?" he asked, sliding onto the stool next to hers.

Another shrug. "Some bourbon. I don't know what it's called."

"Sounds divine." He got the barman's attention and pointed to her glass, holding up two fingers; one for himself and another for her. Once settled, he looked around the room, trying not to sneer at the grotty décor and unpleasant odour. "This your sort of place, then?"

"I thought it was. But I don't know why I came back here. I suppose it's the only place I know. Although, now I realise I never knew it at all."

The barman slid two glasses in front of them and free-poured some decent-sized shots.

"Start me a tab," Spitfire told the barman, receiving a curt nod in reply as he sauntered away to serve someone else. He picked up his glass. "Well, cheers. I think it's going to be one of those nights."

Acid turned to look at him and he tilted his head to meet her gaze. Her eyes were bloodshot. Either she'd been crying or this wasn't her first drink. Probably it was a little of both.

"Did you speak to Caesar?" she asked.

He nodded. "He wasn't happy. But I only told him what he needed to know."

She leant back and scowled. "Did you say it was all my fault?"

"What would have been the point? Besides, it isn't all on you."

Acid snorted. "I'm not sure about that. But thanks."

A silence fell between them. They downed their drinks in unison, and with a flash of his wrist, Spitfire ordered two more. The bourbon was standard stuff, if not a little harsh on the throat. A few more and it wouldn't matter. He waited for the barman to top up their glasses and leave before saying what he needed to.

"Caesar still wants us to finish the job." He let the words land before continuing. "I told him it was over. That we have little chance of finding the mark before the agency puts him up in a safe house. But he was adamant we keep going. He wants The Beast eradicated too."

"He doesn't want much."

She sounded serious, but when he laughed so did she.

"It is over. Isn't it?" she added.

He picked up his glass. "I don't see how we go forward."

"No. I get it." She exhaled a deep sigh. "But this is on me, Spitfire. All of it. I'll tell Caesar as much. Then I'm going to tell him I'm through with this job. I'm not cut out for it. I thought I was. I wanted to be. But I'm not."

He didn't have the heart to tell her it didn't work like that. You didn't get to hand your notice in and leave with a good-luck card at the end of the month. You didn't get to walk away at all. It was like Keith Richards always said about being in the Stones – the only way you got to leave was in a coffin.

"Don't talk that way," he told her. "You're a good operative. You will be. Don't forget, you've only been doing this for eighteen months. I've been in the industry for ten years. It's a learning curve." He also didn't want to tell her she should never have been sent on this assignment. Or the real reason why Caesar wanted her here with him.

She sniffed. "Thanks. I think." She sipped her drink.

"Don't act so bloody defeated," he told her. "Hell, maybe we can still do this. If Bakov does have the tracker on him, there's a chance." He pulled out his flip phone. "Shit."

"What is it?"

He flung it on the counter. "The battery's dead."

Acid scoffed. "It's over, Spitfire. We're done."

"We've got a charger back at the apartment. We can go back and plug it in. There's always a possibility that..." He stopped himself as he noticed her sneer. "Yeah, what am I talking about? It's over. Bakov will have gone underground by now." He finished his drink. The bourbon tasted better.

"I was hoping you might tell me I was wrong," Acid said, turning to him and closing one eye. "But at least we're being honest with each other."

"There is that." He leaned his forearm on the bar top and shifted around on the stool so they were facing each other. He let his eyes linger on hers. Electricity danced in the air between them. "At least you got to visit New York."

She smirked. "Not exactly under the circumstances I'd dreamed of. But yes."

"Why do you love it so much? Is it just the music and culture?"

She narrowed her eyes at him, as if trying to work out what angle he was coming from. "On the surface, yes. I love what the original idea of punk was all about – personal expression, art, rebellion, railing against the mainstream, celebrating the underdog. Plus, my mum lived here for a few years, and she had so many great stories." She picked up her glass and gulped back most of her drink before releasing another long sigh. "But I think it goes deeper than just loving the culture. It was the place I'd always dreamed about visiting when I was little, and later, when I was put in Crest Hill, it became like a Mecca for me. An exciting colourful place, full of possibility and creative energy. The exact opposite of the life I had. If we're going deep, I might even say it became an externalised representation of my happiness and my dreams." She laughed, but stopped almost immediately. "So... yeah."

Spitfire leaned back. He knew she was smart – savvy, too, when she wasn't letting her chaotic nature get the better of her

– but up to this point he hadn't realised how thoughtful she was.

"That's kind of beautiful," he said. "And I get it. We do that, I think, those of us who've had a less-than-idyllic childhood. It's a means of escape. At least in our minds." He was pleased when she stuck out her bottom lip to show she was impressed. She wasn't the only one who could do profound, but he'd meant every word. It was good to talk this way with someone who understood. It was rare he got the chance.

"You had a rotten childhood?" she asked.

"You could say that. But I don't think about it. It happened to someone else."

"Who?" She flashed her eyes at him. "Who did it happen to?"

He wagged his finger at her. "Are you asking me my real name? Come on now, Acid. You know that's against the rules."

"I'll tell you mine." She leaned closer and he did the same.

"I don't want to know your name. Acid is good. It's a fine name."

"A fine name?" Her eyes darted to his lips. Only for a microsecond, but he was paid to notice these things.

He moved closer, letting his gaze drift down her body, back to her eyes, her lips. His breathing had speeded up. He sensed hers had, too. Heat rose in his body.

Shit.

Was this a good idea?

He didn't care. He was so far away from caring, it was untrue. Their faces were only an inch apart now. She opened her lips a fraction. But as she did, he pulled back. Reason, along with years of experience in the field, claimed him momentarily. As an elite assassin, you existed in the shadows. You didn't draw attention to yourself by jumping on someone in a bar. Once you were spotted, you were done. And The Beast was still out there.

Acid gasped, her expression falling as she looked at him. He thought he saw something about to die behind her eyes before he placed his hand on hers.

"Do you want to get out of here?" he said. "There's a bottle of bourbon back at the apartment. We can have another drink there. Or...?"

"Or what?" she asked, raising one eyebrow.

He grabbed her hand and helped her to her feet. "Come on. Let's go."

CHAPTER 34

After a short but expensive cab journey (expensive because Spitfire didn't have any notes less than a fifty and didn't want to wait for the change), he and Acid burst through the front door of their building riding a wave of lust, bourbon, and a shared desire to lose themselves in each other.

They stepped into the elevator, the doors barely closed before they flew at each other. Limbs and tongues wrapped around one another as they kissed passionately and without coming up for air all the way to the fifth floor. When the doors slid open, they hurried down the corridor, not letting go of one another, and – after some grappling with Acid's firm hold on him – Spitfire opened the front door. They fell through into the apartment in a breathy embrace that carried them over to the huge bed in the far corner where they made short work of tearing each other's clothes off. By the time he guided himself inside her, Spitfire was seized with the kind of lust and passion that felt animalistic and ethereal all at once. Their lithe bodies fit together perfectly, as if forged from the same piece of bronze.

Having grown up in a rough part of East London, Spitfire

had never been a particularly romantic or poetic man, yet he found himself with these strange new thoughts as they grappled and clawed at one another. Acid's naked body was how he'd imagined it, but so much better. Firm and athletic, yet soft and smooth in all the places that mattered. She was energetic and eager, but inexperienced enough that she let him take the lead. She came first. He made sure of that. A few seconds later he reached the point of no return and pulled out of her in time, sparing them both the trouble of further complications; they had enough of those to deal with. Panting and spent, he dropped to the bed beside her and they both lay there, catching their breath, staring at the ceiling.

Acid spoke first. Or rather, she made a whistling noise. "Whoa. That was... *gooood*."

"Good? Is that it?"

"Okay, it was amazing." She giggled. "Probably the best I've ever had."

He rolled over and looked at her with a smirk. "*Probably?*"

"Okay. Definitely." She rolled over too, propping herself up on her elbow.

He pulled a face. "All right, calm down, darling. You're coming on a bit strong there."

"Piss off." She raised her hand to slap him, but stopped as he jerked his head out of the way. She laughed. He laughed. For a few seconds nothing else mattered.

"Drink?" he asked, sitting up and sliding off the bed. He didn't make any move to get dressed. Why bother? He knew he looked good naked. He wanted her to watch him as he strutted over to the kitchen area. The conquering hero.

"Just a small one," she shouted after him.

"Hey!" He stopped and looked back over his shoulder.

"The drink, I mean. *Obviously*." The way she flicked her eyebrows at him sent a hot shiver of electricity down his back.

Shit.

What the bloody hell was going on?

He fixed them both a neat bourbon and brought the drinks back to bed. Acid had propped herself up against a pillow, but had made no move to cover herself either. He liked that, and not just because she was great to look at. She was just lying there, naked, smiling coquettishly at him as he climbed on the bed beside her. There were not many women he met who had the confidence and spirit to be so relaxed in front of him at this stage in the relationship.

Fuck me.

Relationship?

Careful, old boy. You're stepping into a bloody minefield.

"Here you go, madam." He handed her one of the glasses before gulping his own drink down in one.

"Thirsty?" she asked.

"Thirsty work."

She sipped her drink before reaching over and placing it on the bedside table. When she turned back, her cheeks were flushed. "Can we go again?"

"Jesus. I mean, yes, absolutely. But give me a few minutes, will you?"

She laughed. "Sorry, I forgot you were so old."

"Hey. Enough of that."

She smiled; the first genuine smile she'd ever given him. She looked different suddenly. Not younger, but lighter and less burdened. Happy could be another word for it, but that had too many connotations.

"Now you've ravished me, are you going to tell me your real name?" she asked.

He scowled. "Is that what this was all about? You wanted to get that out of me?"

"Yes, that's it. All part of my cunning plan. So come on, *Spitfire*, spill."

"I can't. It's not allowed. We're not supposed to discuss our pasts or give out our old names."

She tsked. "I'm pretty sure you're not supposed to put your penis inside your colleagues either. But don't worry, Caesar's HR department is rather substandard, I hear."

He shook his head. This woman. "Fine. My name is – *was* – Stephen Carter. How do you do?"

"Oooh, Stephen," she repeated, snuggling up against him. "Stephen Carter. I like it. Pleased to meet you. I'm Alice. Alice Vandella." She held her hand out.

This was a bad idea, he knew that. It felt weird. But he took her hand regardless and shook it.

"Charmed, Alice. But I still prefer Acid."

"Yeah, I know what you mean. So go on then, you might as well go the whole hog while we wait for little Stevie to get his strength back. What's your story?"

He laughed. "You're a bloody nightmare when you want to be, aren't you? I don't think I've ever met anyone like you. It's like you've got about six personalities."

"No. Only three," she said, but her voice had lost its giggly timbre. She rolled her shoulders back and smiled. "Please. Tell me about Stephen Carter. How did he end up as Spitfire Creosote? I'm interested."

He gazed into her eyes. They were so full of life. He could see a tiny version of himself reflected in her pupils.

"Well, as we established on the plane, I was a bit of a mod in my youth. I liked the clothes, the music, the hair, the imagery. The mod target that you see on everything from that time is taken from a Spitfire. That's where that part came from, I think. Plus, I was quite into war and the army when I was growing up and Spitfires were the best aircraft. I suppose, for me, they represented bravery and adventure."

"Sort of what I was saying about New York."

He nodded. "I think so."

"And what about Creosote? Where the hell did you get that from?"

He leaned back against the headboard. Now there was a question. He twisted the signet ring around his finger, wondering if he could – should – give her the full story.

"My old man was in the police when I was very young, but by the time my mum died he was making a living doing odd jobs around the neighbourhood. In the summer he did a lot of outdoor work, painting fences and the like. He always stank of creosote. Reeked of the stuff. It was what I could always smell on him when he was knocking ten shades of shit out of me. That and the seven or eight pints he'd downed after work." He relaxed his jaw, realising he was gripping his muscles there tighter than usual. "I chose the name because it reminds me of bravery and pain, of adventure and anger. I chose it because it spurred me on to be who I needed to be."

He looked away, worried if he saw any hint of compassion on Acid's face it might set him off. He chewed on the inside of his cheek as he stared into his empty glass.

"What happened to your mum?"

"I'll tell you some other time."

"What about your dad?"

When he looked over, she was sitting up with an expectant look on her face, as if hanging on his every word.

He cleared his throat. "I killed him."

"Whoa. That's rough."

He didn't know how he'd expected Acid to react to this revelation, but it wasn't with such concern. She reached up and touched his cheek and he held her hand there, snuggling into her touch. The compassion he had turned from a minute earlier now snaked a warm arm around his shoulders, and for the first time since he could remember, he welcomed it. Yearned for it. Acid must have noticed something too, because she leaned in and kissed him on the lips. Unlike the grappling, passionate kisses they'd pressed into each other's faces for the last hour, this one was soft and gentle and full of...

No!

He didn't want to think about that. He closed his eyes and let the moment wash over him.

"What happened?" Acid whispered as she pulled away.

He lowered her hand from his face but kept hold of it. "My father was a bad man. And a rotten drunk. He beat on my mother, then me once she was gone. Any money he made he spent on drink, women and the horses. He ended up owing a lot of money to a lot of dangerous people. One of them was Caesar. Caesar was just setting up the organisation when I met him. I was twenty-four, I'd just been thrown out of the army for gross insubordination – punching my commanding officer – and he came to the house looking for the old man."

"You were in the army?" Acid whispered. "I always wondered if that was the case."

He scowled. "Oh?"

"You have the discipline and the refinement." She smiled. "It was supposed to be a compliment."

"Right. I'm just a little new to you being nice, that's all."

She stuck out her bottom lip and flickered her lashes playfully. "Oh, come on. I'm always nice to you." She slid her hand over his chest, stroking at the hair between his pectoral muscles. "So Caesar asked you to kill your own father?"

"Pretty much. He was much more brutal back then. He was prepared to kill me in my old man's place, but said he'd spare my life if I killed him myself. Now I know it's part of his induction process. It's clever. He makes you demonstrate how ruthless you can be, whilst at the same time proving your loyalty to him."

Acid stiffened at this. "Yeah, I get it. I had to kill someone I'd been close to at Crest Hill. It was hard."

"Of course it was. Your first kill and it's someone you know; even if they are a total shit and you despise them with every cell in your body. It's a head fuck." He'd carried this story with him for over ten years and hadn't told another living soul. It felt good to say it out loud. "That night the old boy came home pissed out of his head, as usual, and started laying down the law, readying himself for a fight. But I stood up to him. I battered the shit out of him and then strangled him right there on the living room carpet. After that, I smashed up the house, opened drawers, that sort of thing. Then I called the police and told them I'd just got home to discover we'd had a break-in and my dear father had been attacked."

"Was it hard for you?"

"He was still my old man, you know? Caesar told me to put a record on loud, in case the neighbours heard anything. I chose my favourite album at the time. *The Gift* by The Jam. As I was squeezing the life out of him, *The Bitterest Pill* came on. I can't hear that song now without singing 'the bitterest kill' along to it in my head." He laughed, then stopped himself. "Caesar was impressed with my ingenuity. Two weeks later he picked me up in his big shiny Beamer and offered me a job. Now he trusted me, you see. Plus, he had something on me if I decided I didn't want the job. That's another of his little onboarding tricks. He's a clever boy is our boss."

He stared down at the ruby-encrusted signet ring on the middle finger of his right hand.

"That's your dad's ring, isn't it?" Acid said.

He nodded. "All I have left of him."

She reached over and held it between her thumb and forefinger. "It's pretty. Does it come off?"

He twisted it off and handed it to her. She turned it over in her hand and smiled before placing it back on his finger.

"Wow." She placed her palm over his. "Look how much bigger your hands are than mine. That's crazy."

Spitfire remained stuck in the past for a few moments longer before she tilted her head to make eye contact. Her cheeks were flushed, and the way she smiled at him made every bad memory crumble to dust. No one had ever been able to do that before, make him feel so present and so ready for the future. It was a little worrying, but not really.

"It's almost as big as my head," she went on, pressing his hand against her forehead. "You could pop my skull with one squeeze."

He laughed. "I'm not sure about that."

"Well, don't do it."

"I won't. If anything, I rather think you'll be the one finishing me off if it comes down to it."

She leaned back and her playfulness dropped away. "Never," she whispered, staring into his eyes with a seriousness he'd never seen before.

"All right, come here, you." He reached over and pulled her on top of him. They kissed, then she propped herself up on his chest, and for a fleeting second he saw something that could have been sadness in her face. "What is it?"

She shook her head. "Nothing. Everything's good."

"How did you know the ring belonged to my dad?" he asked.

"It looks old, so I knew it belonged to someone before you. More than likely a male relative. I also knew it was linked to bad memories. You fiddle with it when you're stressed."

"Do I?" He frowned. "Well, I'm impressed. Picking up on

those sorts of things is important for our work. And not everyone can do it."

She pressed her nose against his, the two of them giggling and grinning like Cheshire cats. What a strange turn-up for the books this was. Obviously Spitfire had imagined the two of them sleeping together. He'd imagined it often. But not like this. Never like this. He could tell she was falling for him, too. But what came next left a hollow feeling in his stomach. For now he ignored it. This moment was all they had. It was all that was important. They were both probably for the chop when they got back to London anyway.

"Are you okay?" Acid asked, placing her hand on his cheek.

The pressure must have shown on his face. He nodded, vanquishing his demons with a broad smile. "Absolutely."

"Good," she said, straddling his torso. "Because I think little Stevie is ready for his repeat performance."

She leaned forward and kissed him, before shuffling down his body and sliding him inside her. It felt good. It felt amazing. Nothing else mattered. Nothing else ever would.

CHAPTER 35

Most mornings, Spitfire went from being asleep to wide awake in less than a second. It was how he'd always been. One moment he'd be dead to the world and the next he'd be sitting bolt upright or leaping out of bed, ready for action. It was a useful trait for the early morning drills he'd endured as part of his army training, and just as valuable in his true vocation as a killer for hire. Yet this morning, he found himself waking in a much more carefree and dreamlike fashion. He stirred, aware of who he was and where he was, but without opening his eyes right away. The bed was soft and warm. As his awareness spread, he released a long, comforting sigh.

Acid. Wow.

They'd had sex four times in the end and must have passed out just before dawn, wrapped in a post-coital embrace, limbs and souls entwined.

It had been... wonderful.

And exciting. And passionate.

It had been rough, sensual, instinctive, even experimental in places. Spitfire's smile widened as he stretched out, feeling for her warm body beside him, eager to pull her close.

But she wasn't there.

He opened one eye, conscious now of movement over on the other side of the room. Rolling over, he was instantly alert, ready to confront whatever danger he was about to face.

"Ah, you're awake. Good."

Acid was pacing up and down in the middle of the room. Her hair was wet and combed back from her face in sharp, thick strands. She'd also done her make-up. Dark, smoky eyeshadow and an abundance of mascara complemented her exotic eyes, and coupled with blood-red lipstick she looked both sexy and savage. As ready for action as he usually felt at this time in the morning.

"What's going on?" His voice was croaky. "I was hoping we might make a morning of it too..."

Acid glared at him with wild eyes, but when he flung the cover off himself to show her how hopeful he was, her face softened.

"Later," she said, coming over to him. "Last night was incredible. And I want more of it. Lots more." She kneeled on the bed and kissed him forcefully before pulling away and staring deep into his eyes. "But we'll have plenty of time for that once we finish what we've been sent here for. Our work here isn't finished."

She pushed off the bed and walked back to the kitchen, picking something up off the island. She was wearing tight black jeans and a pair of black hobnail boots, similar to the ones he'd worn in the army. On top was a black and red mohair sweater, misshapen in places. The baggy sleeves hung down over her palms, so she had to yank the cuff back to show him what she'd retrieved from the kitchen island.

"What is it?" he asked.

She walked back over. "Your phone. I charged it up and it's still working." She grinned at him, her eyes flashing wide as if she expected him to leap out of bed and cheer. "The tracker, I mean. The GPS, or whatever it's called; it's still giving a signal. See the red dot? He's just moved over the river into Brooklyn, but he's been heading south for the past fifteen minutes. We need to move. We can still do this."

Spitfire swung his legs off the bed and raised his arms above his head. The muscles in his back and shoulders popped. "I don't know, Acid. It seems like a long shot. After everything that's gone down, I'm not hopeful. And now with the CIA involved..."

"It's all we've got." She snapped the phone away from him and carried on pacing. The expression 'cat on a hot tin roof' came to mind. In fact, he'd never seen the clichéd phrase so well personified. Because she wasn't just pacing, she was prowling. Like a caged animal, a wild untamed beast, penned in and desperate to escape.

He realised now what Caesar saw in her. Why he was prepared to take a chance on someone so young and inexperienced. She might be chaotic and undisciplined, but in the right frame of mind, under the right circumstances, she was ferocious in her determination.

"You really want to keep going?" he asked, locating his boxer shorts on the floor and slipping them on.

"This is our job. We can't go back to London without the hit. Caesar will have us both eradicated. You know that." She stopped and met his gaze. "Now more than ever, I want to live. Don't you?"

He lowered his chin but held her gaze. "I do."

"Okay, then. So get showered, get dressed, and let's do this." She waved the phone in the air. "This is him. I know it is."

"What about The Beast? Caesar wants him dead, too."

"Good. So do I. And if Bakov is still out there, then so is he. And now we know his plans. He wants the hit on Bakov as much as we do. So, we find Bakov, we use him as bait, and we get them both at once. Any way we can – accident, mugging-gone-wrong, professional hit; I don't care and I don't think Caesar will care either, now he knows the situation. We kill them, we get proof for Raaz, and then we come back to bed."

"I thought you wanted to see New York?"

She shrugged. "Meh, I've seen enough. There are other things I'd rather explore."

They stared at each other. Spitfire rubbed at his chin.

"It's a decent enough plan, but we don't know this is Bakov. He could have found the tracker and dumped it in a laundry cart or the back of a taxi. We could be chasing a red herring all over town."

"I know. But I can feel it. I know it's him. He's running scared, but my guess is he's set up another meeting with the spook at a new location. If the CIA thought of him as an asset, they'd have brought him in, found the tracker and destroyed it. But they haven't. I think Bakov is still trying to convince them he's got the information they want. Which is good for us. It means he's desperate. He'll take risks."

Spitfire was at a loss for words, but only because he didn't have anything to add. She appeared to have it all figured out.

"What happened?" he asked. "You've gone from being all down on yourself and wanting to give in, to... this. You're like a different person. I mean, I know I'm good in bed, but..."

She huffed. "It's hard to explain. I'll tell you all about it when we've more time. Just know my moods shift quite rapidly. A lot of the time I have this intensity driving me. When that's the case, I'm as good as I can be. I think fast, act fast, feel invincible. I don't need to eat or sleep." She was speaking without taking a breath. He could almost see the intensity bubbling inside of her.

Catching his stare, she looked away and smirked. "And the amazing sex probably had something to do with it."

He smirked right back, but the warm feeling fell away quickly as he considered the solemnity of their situation.

"You really want to do this?"

"Absolutely I do. It's what we came here for. We have to finish the job, Stephen. I know we—"

"Hey! That's enough of that." He walked over to where she was standing, aware his semi-nakedness lowered his status but not caring. He waved an authoritative finger. "Fine. I'm in. I like what you're saying. But if we're doing this, we do it by the book. I'm Spitfire Creosote. You're Acid Vanilla. We're both Annihilation Pest Control operatives. Whatever else is going on between us, we'll talk about later. But for now – until we get our mark – we act like professionals."

She nodded sharply. "Understood."

It looked as if she was about to salute, but she stopped herself. He turned and headed for the bathroom before a new smile could form.

Bloody hell.

The girl was amazing.

Cute, funny, sexy, clever. Scary as hell and a therapist's dream, but so captivating. He couldn't remember feeling this excited to know another person in his life. That was daunting in itself. But he'd meant what he'd said just now. If they had any chance of rectifying this mission, it was time to get their heads in the game and act like the elite killers they were supposed to be. Acid's determination and eagerness to succeed were infectious, and she was right about going back to HQ with their tails between their legs – it wouldn't be pretty.

Now more than ever, I want to live.

Her words echoed in his head as he showered and then dried himself. He felt the same. It was a nice feeling but tinged with danger. To be tied to someone in this life never ended well. Partners and loved ones could become cannon fodder. He would never hurt women or children to get his mark – Caesar wasn't keen on those tactics either – but there were those in the industry who wouldn't think twice about toppling a pawn to get to the king. The fact Acid was also an assassin changed things. But she was still someone else to concern himself with. Another life to worry about.

Shaking these thoughts away, he got dressed in a pair of grey wool trousers and a black turtleneck sweater. Inspecting himself in the mirror, he realised he couldn't look more Bond. No doubt there'd be some pithy comment coming his way when he stepped out of his room, but he found himself smiling at the thought of her joshing. He placed the remaining weaponry on top of a fresh towel and carried it through into the kitchen.

"Here we go, then," he said, lowering the towel on top of the island to show off the selection of guns and knives. "Choose your weapons. Ladies first."

Acid glanced at his attire but didn't say anything. Her mind, it seemed, was on other things. She pouted as she surveyed his offerings. "I'll take the Glock. Ooh, and this." She picked up the pistol and an old flick knife.

Spitfire hadn't seen one like it for years. In his opinion, a push dagger was a better choice, and he was about to tell her as much when he saw the delight on her face as she released the blade from the handle and swished it through the air. He took a push dagger for himself and a Walther PPK. He'd also brought through extra magazines. He handed two to Acid.

"Do we need this many rounds?" she asked.

"Probably not, but it pays to be prepared, darling." As soon as the word left his lips, he regretted it. He often called people darling, the way Caesar did. It was an affectation. Usually. Now the word had different implications that, although not unwarranted, were strange and new. Thankfully, Acid didn't pick up on it. She was too busy stuffing the extra clips and flick knife in the pockets of her jeans and sliding the pistol down into her waistband. When she was finished, she looked up at him.

"Ready?" he asked.

"Ready."

"Okay then. Time to go to work."

CHAPTER 36

Spitfire and Acid were more than colleagues now. They were lovers, yes (perhaps even more, he hadn't allowed himself to think that far); but just as important, they were a team. For the first time since they'd arrived in New York, he was filled with the confidence and drive he normally brought to a job. He and Acid were now on the same page. An elite unit. Tooled up and firing on all cylinders.

They left the apartment and headed for the nearest subway, catching the A train down to 42nd Street. The tracker still showed the red dot heading south through Brooklyn. The problem was, if they waited until Bakov reached his destination it might be too late. The Beast could beat them to it, or the spook they suspected Bakov was meeting could take him into custody for his protection.

They had to get ahead of the curve. Be at the location when he arrived.

Putting himself in the mark's position, Spitfire's best guess was that Bakov was heading down to the waterfront. If he was a deserting Russian gangster, knowing he had a contract on him, he'd want to meet the handler who could save his life somewhere out in the open, where he had a clear view in both directions. Somewhere like the boardwalk, or the beach, where there were fewer places for a would-be assassin to hide and where the possibility of a quick getaway existed.

He explained this theory to Acid as they headed through Times Square and down into the subway to wait for the next train to Ocean Parkway. As they stood on the platform, Spitfire leaned forward onto the balls of his feet and focused on his breathing. In and hold. Out and hold. As he was doing this, he noticed Acid peering up and down the platform.

"What are you looking for?" he asked. "He's not here. The tracker just placed him near Little Haiti."

"I know," she said, narrowing her eyes as she carried on looking. "I'm just wondering... Never mind, it's not important. Forget it."

He stepped back. "Are you sure you're okay?"

"Don't worry about me." She grinned. "We've got this. In a couple of hours, both of those pricks will be on steel slabs and Caesar will welcome us home with open arms."

He smiled. He wasn't sure about that, but he appreciated her optimism.

The train arrived and they stepped aboard before moving down into the carriage and sitting next to each other. No one on the train was speaking, so they didn't either, choosing to stare forward out of the window as they travelled through Midwood and Flatbush. At one point, just after the train had departed from Neck Road Station, Spitfire shifted in his seat and his hand touched hers on the armrest between them. He didn't flinch. Neither did she. But he didn't leave it there despite wanting to. This wasn't the time. For now, he was Spitfire Creosote. He didn't do emotions. He certainly didn't do relationships.

Once the train had pulled up at Parkway Station, they disembarked and walked at speed through the station and up to street level. It being January, and the air still icy, the streets were sparse of people. A few locals were going about their business, but no obvious tourists. They headed along Brighton Beach Avenue and took a left down West 1st Street, which brought them out in front of a small area of parkland. They crossed the street and stopped outside the park, scanning the area for the mark or the big blond prick who'd made their job so difficult up to now. Spitfire couldn't wait to take him out. He'd love to do it as slowly and painfully as possible, but any way would suffice at this point, just as long as they didn't draw attention to themselves in the process. The usual rules of engagement still applied. They might be going off-book, but it was important they remained in the shadows and completed their work away from the gaze of the authorities and the public at large.

Except for an old lady and her dog, the park was empty. Spitfire took the phone out of his pocket and flipped it open. The maps software was still on screen, showing the red dot was now only five hundred metres away from them. It had stopped moving.

"I was right," he said, nudging Acid and showing her. "He's down on the boardwalk, see? Near Luna Park."

"Ah, no way," she whispered, looking up from the phone screen in the direction of the actual location. "I always wanted to go there, ever since I watched *The Warriors*."

"Yeah. Good film."

She raised her eyebrows. "Wow. I half expected that reference to be met with indifference or ignorance. We have something in common, after all."

He tilted his head away. "Now, now, Acid. Mind on the job, please."

"Yes, sir!"

"I'm serious. Don't push it. We need to stay focused."

She sniffed. "Listen, *darling*. I'm ready to kill both of those sneaky bastards. Don't you worry about me. When I'm feeling like this, it's when I'm most powerful."

He regarded her, looking for a tell, but she meant every word. "Fair enough," he said.

They walked through the park and across the next avenue, before a ramp took them up onto the east side of the boardwalk. The red dot hadn't moved for at least five minutes. Bakov had stopped. He was waiting for someone. Now it all depended on who got to him first.

They moved along the wooden decking, Spitfire with his head down and walking at speed, and Acid keeping pace but skipping around him. Every so often she'd run up ahead and gaze out over the beach before looking back and giving him the most licentious of smiles. She looked magnificent, full of life and vitality. He should have told her to stop, to walk alongside him and act more professionally, but he didn't want to. Because maybe this was who she was when she had life by the balls. She certainly seemed assertive and in control of herself, unlike the overeager and nervy young thing she'd been at the start of the trip. Whether it was his influence or simply her relaxing into her skin, he wasn't sure. But he liked it. This was the Acid Vanilla he'd heard Caesar talk about. She was feisty and fierce and full of danger. Ready to get her hands dirty. Ready to do what was required of her. He'd seen hints of this same persona at Honeysuckle House when he'd first been tasked with training her. But now she was all grown up. She was a woman. And she was strong.

And he was shocked at how much that turned him on.

"Come on, old man," she called back, tilting her head to her shoulder and letting her hair dance in the chill wind coming in from the sea. "We're nearly there."

He quickened his step as she reached the edge of the funfair, where the wooden tracks of the famous Cyclone rollercoaster spiralled up into the sky. She stopped to wait for him, and was staring into the amusement park as he got up to her. He touched her shoulder, about to remind her of his plan – to get eyes on Bakov and then wait. He was fully prepared to take out a spook if it came to it, but his hope was The Beast would show up first and they could eradicate both targets before anyone knew they were there.

"Acid, we need to be careful now..."

She shrugged his hand off her shoulder with a sharp *shhh*. "Over there," she said. "By the Ferris wheel."

He looked at where she was pointing; to where a lone figure was standing in front of the big wheel, obscured slightly by a vintage carousel. He was wearing a sheepskin trapper hat with the ear flaps down and had a thick scarf wound around his nose and mouth, but it was him. The mark. Boris Bakov. His eyes darted around the place like an anxious meerkat on snake watch.

"I see him," Spitfire whispered, walking past her and scanning the wire fence that ran down the side of the park, looking for a way in. It being winter, the rides were closed and the main entrance was locked, but Bakov must have entered somehow. Halfway along he found a wheeled gate in the fencing, but when he tried to slide it open it wouldn't budge.

Shitting hell.

He stepped back. The fence was about eight feet high and the small holes in the mesh provided no footholds for climbing. The gate, however, had a thick metal pole running perpendicular across it and, with a bit of assistance, he reckoned they could climb it. He'd help Acid over from this side and then she could assist him once she was in the park.

He turned around, ready to explain his idea, but she was still staring into the park with a dark expression on her face.

"Spitfire, look," she whispered. "It's The Beast. He's here. We're too late."

CHAPTER 37

Acid grabbed the wire fence, watching helplessly through the mesh as events unfolded on the other side. The Beast had appeared from around the far side of the big wheel, striding purposefully through the amusement park. He was less dishevelled than the last time she'd seen him, dressed now in an orange beanie hat and a large fisherman's jacket. But he was no less intimidating. If anything, he looked even more threatening as he crept around the motionless children's rides on his way through the park.

"We need to stop him," she whispered. "He's going to get our hit."

From this position, she could see both men. Bakov, still glancing around him in a state of agitation, and the big man a few hundred feet away but approaching fast. From the way The Beast's attention was darting left and right, she deduced he hadn't yet got eyes on Bakov, but any second now he would pass alongside one of the larger carousels or the bumper cars and would get a clear view of him. After that, it was all over. She couldn't let that happen.

"Help me up," she said, looking back over her shoulder.

Spitfire hurried over to her. "I'll boost you over and then you help me up. Look, there." He pointed out an old broom leaning against the back of one of the rides. "You can shove the handle through the mesh and give me a foothold."

"Let's do it."

She grabbed onto the mesh as high as she could reach, bouncing on her toes ready to go. Spitfire moved alongside her and cupped his hands so she could step into them. As she did, he boosted her higher and she swung one leg and then the other over the top of the fence and dropped silently down on the other side.

As soon as her feet hit the ground, she spun around to check the situation. The Beast was skulking around the edge of a tall red-and-white helter skelter, closing in on Bakov with every step.

"Acid! Get the broom."

She could hear Spitfire calling her, but it sounded like he was speaking from another dimension, his voice all but drowned out by the discordant bat screams in her head. She looked from Bakov to The Beast.

There was no time.

Leaving Spitfire behind, and with the bats calling for blood, she ran into the park, approaching The Beast in a wide sweep. This way he wouldn't see her until it was too late. As she ran, she stripped off the red coat that was flapping behind her, leaving her dressed how she should have been from the start, in black jeans, black boots and her black leather jacket. Like a dark moth emerging from its ridiculous cocoon. The manic bat energy filled her with vigour and invulnerability as she homed in on The Beast's inner thigh. More specifically, where she knew his femoral artery to be. Her vision tunnelled on him, formed by an all-encompassing craving for revenge. Nothing else mattered. Nothing else was real. This man had made her look stupid. He'd hurt Spitfire. He'd threatened to put Caesar out of business.

She couldn't let him walk away from that.

Pulling the knife from her pocket, she flicked it open. She couldn't use the Glock or the mark would hear and they'd lose him. And she couldn't take the brute hand to hand. But she had ingenuity and the element of surprise on her side. She'd run at him, slice open the femoral artery in his upper thigh and be away before he had a chance to react. The shock would stop him in his tracks. He'd know he was bleeding out and would try to stem the bleed. When he was distracted, she'd run back and slice his throat open. Done.

Holding the knife down by her side and staying in The Beast's blind spot, she moved in for her first attack. The knife felt good in her grip. It had a decent weight and she liked that it was a flick knife. Old school. With New York as her backdrop, she was a Shark from West Side Story, one of The Warriors, a leather-clad demon ready to exact her vengeance on those who'd wronged her. She hunkered down, ready, as she got closer.

Do it, screamed the bats.

Kill, kill, kill.

With a grunt, she lunged at The Beast, leading with the sharp blade. She swiped it down the length of his huge inner thigh, but she'd misjudged the attack, or he'd moved at the last second – something happened – because she stumbled, and rather than slice his flesh open, she stabbed the blade into his leg.

"*Scheisse!*" he bellowed, jerking his body away. She tugged at the knife handle, but it was stuck in the bone. Pushing away from him, she deflected his arcing fist but a second one found its target.

Fuck.

It felt as if someone had smashed her around the face with a sledgehammer. The colours of Luna Park swirled together as she spun away. Fighting to focus, she swung out with her arms but found nothing except air. Another heavy blow smashed her in the chest. The ground disappeared for a second, before zooming up to meet her far too fast. With a heavy thud, she landed on her back. Everything stopped. She gasped for air but could barely get any. She tried again before her instincts told her to move. Now! Pushing herself up, she flipped away as a large boot stamped on the ground by her ear. She scrambled to her feet, staying low, keeping one hand on the ground as she regarded her enemy.

As The Beast righted himself from the stomp, their eyes met and for the first time she saw fear rather than hubris behind his dark, piggy eyes. She saw the knife handle sticking out of his thigh, right on her target. The blade was against the artery, stemming major blood loss; the moment he pulled it out, the clock would be ticking. It would take minutes for him to bleed out. He must have known this.

But that made him more dangerous.

Acid stayed low. As the Beast turned to face her, she leapt forward, her hand going for the knife handle, ready to yank it free. She wrapped her fingers around it, but a heavy blow between the shoulder blades sent her crashing to the ground. The concrete knocked the air out of her, but now the bats were in control. She flipped out of the way of another heavy boot.

"Fucking bitch!" The Beast snarled. "This is my fight. My time."

Acid jumped to her feet, shaking her limbs loose as she did and rolling her neck from side to side. "I don't think so. This is our hit. It always has been."

She ran at him, and as he reached out to grab her, she dummied to one side and slammed her elbow into the fleshy part of his lower back. He grunted. That was all. She leapt at him, trying to get her arm around his throat, but he swung around and slapped her out of the air and she stumbled into the side of a carousel. Her body was on fire and she knew she could take this prick, but the height difference was an issue. As he turned to her, she saw what she needed to do.

With a scream she ran at him, using wide, ungainly steps as if running through the tires on the obstacle course behind Honeysuckle House. The big man swayed at the hips, trying to predict which way she was going to go, his giant hands ready to grab her. He reached for her, but she swerved out of the way and stepped up onto the knife blade, propelling herself up his body. As he lifted his head to cry out, she snaked her right arm around his neck, clasping her hands together as she summoned every bit of strength and squeezed. The sharp bone in her right forearm pressed against The Beast's throat. He stumbled backwards, swinging around to get her off him whilst grabbing at the arm around his throat. But his fat fingers couldn't find purchase and Acid wasn't letting go. Every muscle in her body burned with determination as she constricted her grip.

"Die, you bastard," she snarled into his ear. "You piece of shit."

She leaned back out of range as he jerked his head to butt her off. He was fading. She could sense the life force leaving him. He walked backwards, hands scrabbling at the arm around his neck. It was useless. She squeezed tighter, a surge of vitality providing her with renewed strength. She had him. He was going down. Another five seconds and he'd...

Shit!

She thought he was done.

As he fell to his knees, he lurched forward and flung her off his back. She released the hold on him, falling awkwardly onto the concrete before something like a freight train slammed into her chest and knocked her to the ground. The world turned into a wash of colour as the pain swelled in her torso and into her brain.

Was this what a heart attack felt like?

Was she dying?

Shaking her head, she forced herself to focus. The bats screeched for her to get up. She had to get up. Right now. Before...

She heard laughter. A booming guffaw of derision. As her awareness improved, she looked up to see The Beast looming over her. He pointed the muzzle of a large handgun at her head.

"Funny, huh?" he said. "I think it is you who is going to die."

CHAPTER 38

Spitfire was twenty metres away, running across the park when he saw The Beast throw Acid over his head and pull the gun from his jacket. He stopped. At that moment, all the indignation and annoyance he'd carried over the fence with him unaided, dropped away.

He saw the mark.

He saw Acid in trouble.

He drew his weapon.

If he fired, Bakov would hear and flee to safety. They'd lose their last chance to complete the hit. But if he didn't shoot first, Acid was dead.

It would have been a tough decision – once – but he was already pulling the trigger.

He fired a flurry of shots, two in the chest to break the bastard's aim and one in the middle of his bushy moustache, right through the bottom of his T-zone. The shot took out his brain stem and disabled The Beast entirely, but as the force of the shots knocked him back, Spitfire squeezed off two final shots. One through each of the bastard's eyes. It was his signature move – showing off – but he drove each bullet home with sheer hatred as much as gunpowder. The prick had been seconds away from painting the nearest carousel with Acid's brain.

He couldn't stand for that.

She was his now.

His to protect.

As he got closer, The Beast crashed to his knees and fell face-first onto the concrete. He could still hear the gunshots echoing through the deserted funfair and as expected, when he looked over, Bakov was gone. Not what he wanted, but what else could he do? The noise from The Beast's kill shot would have spooked him just as much.

"Stephen!" Acid cried out. Her tone was jittery. "The mark..."

He knelt and held her hand, helped her to her feet. "He's gone. It's over."

"But we can't let... He's what we came here for... He was... Shit! I'm sorry. I'm so sorry." She grabbed hold of his neck, and he pulled her to him. They kissed. He tasted blood.

"Are you hurt?" he asked, stepping back to look.

"Not too bad." She rolled one shoulder and grimaced. "Bruised and battered, but alive."

"What were you thinking? After everything we'd talked about."

"I thought I could do it. I wanted to prove to you – and myself – that I had what it took. I've fucked up so much on this mission, I wanted to make it right. But I've damn well made it worse."

Spitfire pulled his phone out and checked the tracker.

"Anything?"

"No. He's in the wind."

"Bollocks. I'm sorry."

He took her head in his hands. "Listen to me. What's done is done. You tried."

She stared into his eyes, gave the slightest of nods. "Thank you."

He walked over to The Beast's fallen body. "Can you give me a hand rolling him over?" he asked her.

She joined him, and after a struggle they manoeuvred The Beast's sizeable bulk into position. Spitfire took a photo with the spy camera he carried for such purposes. It was proof, at least, that they'd done something useful since arriving in New York.

"Done," he said, turning to Acid. "Let's get back to the apartment and have a proper look at you."

Two hours later, Acid was sitting on the edge of the bed in her underwear whilst Spitfire knelt behind her, applying rubbing-alcohol to a nasty graze on her back with a ball of cotton wool. She was bruised down one side and there were more scrapes and grazes on her legs, but she'd been lucky. Another second and she'd have been dead.

"What do we do now?" she asked, sucking air sharply through her teeth as he pressed the cotton wool onto the wound. "About Bakov, I mean." She picked Spitfire's phone up off the bed where he'd placed it a few minutes earlier.

"Any joy?"

She turned it around to show him. The map software was still open from when he'd checked it but still showed no red dot. Bakov must have found the tracker and destroyed it. Acid flung the phone down.

"What a stupid, pathetic..."

"That's enough. No point beating yourself up."

"Is there anything we can do?" she asked.

"Not really. Once we've got you patched up I'll call Caesar.

I'll let him know we got The Beast, but in the process we lost the mark."

"*We* lost him?"

"I don't need to go into too much detail. Caesar will be angry, but at least we foiled Perchetka's plan. Wilbur Das Biest is dead. You're alive. I'm alive."

He lifted the used cotton wool ball and tossed it on the bed beside him, picking up a square of bandage padding and some surgical tape. Resting the bandage over the wound, he peeled off a strip of tape and bit it off the roll with his teeth.

"I just thought of something," Acid said, her voice rising slightly as he pressed the bandage down and applied the first piece of tape. "If Bakov talks to the CIA, is that such a bad thing? I know it's against the code to allow the authorities to get involved, but if he takes Perchetka down, the Russians are no longer a threat to the organisation."

Spitfire considered this as he applied another piece of tape. He didn't share Acid's positivity. If anything, her raising this point only added to his concerns. Bakov would have had a good look at her in the hotel. He could provide a decent description of her. If Caesar found out, Acid really would be for the chop. No question. Favourite or not.

"What do you think?" she asked.

"You might be right."

Her shoulders sagged. "It's not the point, though, is it? We failed. I failed."

Spitfire finished applying the dressing and kissed her neck. "You take what you can in this life, darling. The Beast is dead. Perchetka won't be able to fuck over the organisation the way he'd planned. Caesar can get ahead of this now and let the industry know what the Russians were planning. And when I speak with him, I'll make sure he knows we did all we could. Both of us. I imagine we'll forfeit our fee, but that's by and by."

Acid shook her head and laughed.

"I'm glad you find it funny. I rather like getting paid."

"It's not that," she said, twisting around to make eye contact. "What was it you said back in that warehouse? *That's not how this works, Acid. We need the mark dead. That's our job. Our only job.*" She'd put on a deep voice; not a bad impression of him, truth be told. "Yet you chose to save my life instead of going after Bakov."

He narrowed his eyes at her but couldn't help smiling. "Yes, well, it's the principle of the thing. I couldn't let that big oaf take out one of our own. Caesar wouldn't have liked that."

"And you?"

"No. I don't think I'd have liked that either."

She leaned in and kissed him. Her lips were soft and slightly swollen on one side. He kissed her back, but a niggling sensation deep inside his chest stopped him from relaxing into the moment.

Was this stupid?

Was it ever going to work between the two of them?

Caesar had wanted Acid to fall for him, but with the caveat that it was unreciprocated so he could break open her heart and make her cold and cynical about life and relationships. He got it. It was a harsh tactic, but it would have toughened the girl up emotionally. It would have worked. What neither he nor the boss had counted on, though, was Spitfire falling for her just as much.

The reason he'd always turned away from relationships in the past was that he knew another person couldn't fit into his world. He couldn't tell them what he did for a living. And if he did, they'd leave him in a second. But that wasn't the case anymore. Acid knew him, she knew what he did, she did the same. Was that better or worse? Would he always be wondering where she was and whether she was going to come back alive?

"What about us?" she asked, as if reading his mind. "What are we going to do about us?"

"What do you want to do?"

She looked away. "I don't know. I mean... I do know. But I don't want to say."

"Acid." He placed his hand under her chin and gently lifted her head so she was back looking into his eyes. "Whatever this is, I want to make it work. I don't know how we do it, or what it looks like. But I want to. I know that much."

She smiled. "Me too."

"We're going to have to be savvy about it, though. We need to consider how we sell Caesar on the idea. And how it works going forward."

"How do you think he'll react?"

Spitfire puffed his cheeks out. "Hell if I know," he said. "One step at a time, hey? I won't call him just yet. Why don't we go for a drink and let our hair down for a few hours? I think we deserve it."

She wrinkled up her nose. "What a fantastic idea. I know just the place."

Spitfire groaned. "CBGB's?"

"Last time I wasn't in the right frame of mind. I had no one to share it with. Now I do."

He reached up and brushed a hair out of her eyes. "Get dressed," he told her. "You owe me a drink, at least."

"I owe *you* one?"

"I've saved your life twice this week."

"I've saved yours once. And I let you have sex with me four times."

"*You* let *me*?"

She punched him on the arm. "Oh, you think it was the other way around? Pfft! Yeah, right."

Laughing, he got off the bed. He could sense where this was

going, but he did want a drink. As well as some fresh air. "I mean it. Get dressed," he told her, pointing down the corridor to her bedroom. "I'll give you five minutes, then I'm going without you."

She leapt up and gave him a sloppy salute. "Yes, sir."

He watched as she sauntered down the corridor, giving her hips and arse more of a wiggle than usual. Goddamn it, she was fiery. A true loose cannon. He didn't think he liked strong women, but one could always surprise oneself; it was what made life so fascinating.

Letting out a heavy sigh, he lowered himself back onto the bed. He still had that niggling uneasy feeling in his soul, but it would go in time. For now, all that mattered was that they were alive, they were together, and The Beast was dead.

CHAPTER 39

Despite everything that had gone wrong since they'd arrived in New York, all the problems she'd caused and all the mess she'd made, Acid had a spring in her step as they walked down Columbus Avenue. It was unclear how Caesar would react to the double whammy of news – that they'd not only let the mark get away but were now a couple – but she was prepared for whatever came next; even if Spitfire had fallen silent since they'd left the apartment and had a strange expression on his face every time she looked at him. She held her head up and breathed in the cool New York City air, letting the bat chorus fade into the background of her psyche. She was strong. She was invincible. She was whole.

"It's a nice day," she said, as they got to the intersection and took a left down 104th Street. And it was. The air was frosty but crisp. It made you feel glad to be alive.

"Are you not cold?" Spitfire asked, glancing at her up and down.

She grinned and leaned into him. "Don't start this again. Sorry, but I left that red monstrosity in Luna Park, didn't I?" She stuck out her bottom lip playfully. "The first thing you've bought me and I chucked it away. I promise I won't do that next time."

"Next time? You think there'll be more gifts?"

"I hope so. I know how much you get paid, remember?"

"Not when *you're* on a job with me."

He fell silent and his expression went dark once more. She watched him out of the corner of her eye, trying to get a read on him without making it obvious what she was doing.

"What is it?" she asked, when she couldn't bear it any longer. "Say what you want to say, Spitfire. Please."

He didn't answer her until they got to the end of the next block. Once there, he stopped and looked down at her.

"I was thinking about the future. That's all. How this would work. What we tell Caesar." He rubbed the back of his neck. "How do I let you go off on assignments knowing you might not come back? Can I do it? Can you? Or is there another way? I was wondering how you felt about—"

"Spitfire!" she hissed. "Look."

Time stopped as she stared across the street – at the stocky individual who'd just emerged from the door of a small pharmacist. He was wearing a black bomber jacket and a grey woollen hat, along with dark trousers and scuffed white pumps. He had a deep scowl on his face and a thick jawline. Boris Bakov. Unmistakeably.

"Shit," she whispered, bouncing up and down. "It's him."

"All right, Acid," Spitfire replied, holding onto her hand. "We need to consider our options here. The gods appear to be smiling on us, but we can't screw this up. We should split up. You take the next left and approach him from the rear. I'll take the street parallel to this one and overtake him. If we attack him from both sides, we've got more of a chance of—"

"He's getting away!" she gasped. "Come on!"

Spitfire said something else but she didn't hear. She was already heading across the road in pursuit of Bakov. He was walking fast as if he had somewhere important to be. He took a right at the corner and disappeared down the next street. Acid quickened her pace, keeping a distance between them in case he heard her footsteps. Spitfire was still calling after her, his voice rasping and hoarse, telling her to stop, to come back. But something else had taken over her. The bats were back, but it was more than them. It was an innate hunger to finish what she'd started. To get her mark. This pathetic thug, who'd given them such a runaround. He wasn't getting away from her this time. She'd rather die than allow that to happen.

She followed him into the next street before he turned right down West 103rd Street. Here he slowed a little and so did she. Glancing over her shoulder, she couldn't see Spitfire. Probably he was approaching on a different trajectory, cutting off the mark's choices for escape if he saw her and legged it.

But that wasn't going to happen.

She could see the green trees of Central Park at the end of the block. If that's where Bakov was heading, it made things trickier but not impossible. As he reached the end of the street, he stopped and looked back.

Bollocks!

She dived into a doorway. Every pulse point in her body was thumping. Her system bristled with nervous energy. She waited for as long as she dared before peering out from her hiding place. When she did, she saw Bakov scurrying down the steps of the subway station on the corner. He was getting away.

No, he damn well wasn't.

Grabbing the side of the building, she launched herself out onto the street, racing to the corner and down the steps of the subway station after him. As she reached the lower level she paused, going up on her tiptoes to see over the heads of the crowd. He was up in front, making his way through the barrier towards the platform. Weaving through the mass of bustling souls, she got up to the barrier and pulled the pass out of her jeans pocket. She swiped herself through and ran down the long flight of steps on the other side, casting her eyes over the platform below. It was full of people three or four rows deep in front of the tracks, five rows in some places. But no train waiting. As she got down to the platform she saw down to the left, just in front of the tunnel, fewer people were standing. And that was where Bakov was heading.

Without daring to breathe, she followed him, ducking behind a tall man in a trench coat when Bakov looked over his shoulder. Good. He hadn't seen her. He continued down to the far end, where he shuffled his way through the smattering of passengers and up to the yellow line on the edge of the platform.

The bats screamed. Acid stopped. She could feel the rumble of the train in her limbs and chest. She closed her eyes, sensing it was seconds away. If she got this wrong, it would be disastrous for her. But if she got it right...

She puffed out a long breath and waited.

One...

Two...

Three...

As she got to four she stepped forward. And as air shot out of the tunnel like gas from a gun, she barged into the mark then leapt backwards out of sight. All that was apparent to those standing around was Boris Bakov crying out before leaping in front of the train as it emerged from the darkness. There was a sickening smack, followed by a crunch and then a scream. The other passengers recoiled in a collective wave of horror as blood and body parts splattered across the platform.

"Oh god! No!" someone cried.

"Jesus Christ!"

As the news of what happened spread through the crowd, Acid sloped away to the bottom of the stairwell. It felt as if her heart was ready to burst, and she was pretty sure she was a hundred percent adrenaline at this point. But she'd done it. She glanced around her, eyes wide and unblinking. No one was looking at her. She waited another few seconds, then ran up the stairs to the exit.

She'd done it. She'd actually done it. She'd—

Shit!

A hand on her shoulder startled her and she spun around, raising her fist in readiness.

"Hey, it's me," Spitfire rasped, grabbing her by both shoulders. "What the fuck?"

His eyes were wide and flooded with colour and concern. He was the most beautiful man she'd ever met. She reached up, clutched his collar at the back of his neck and pulled him close enough to whisper in his ear.

"I got him. Bakov. He's dead."

Spitfire peered over her shoulder at the growing chaos. "Acid, this is bad. Someone could have seen you. There are so many civilians here."

She stepped back and scowled at him. "No one saw me. I swear. You told me yourself, crowds are useful."

"Yes, but security cameras aren't." He pointed up. "Look, there's one right above us."

"Maybe so." She grabbed his arm and pulled him to one side as two sombre-faced security guards hurried past them. "But there aren't any cameras where it happened."

Spitfire opened his mouth to respond, but she dragged him over to the barrier. She got through the turnstile first and waited for him, smiling gleefully as he joined her on the other side.

"I noticed it the last time we caught the subway," she continued. "There's a blind spot down at the far end, in front of the tunnel entrance. When I saw Bakov heading there, I knew I had him. No cameras. Everyone looking forward, waiting for the train. As far as anyone knows, he jumped. Once they realise who he is, and they ID the body found in Luna Park, it won't be a big stretch to assume they were connected – Bakov killed The Beast before realising he could never outrun his past and then killed himself. Something like that at least. The CIA will probably cover it up, anyway."

She headed up the stairs to street level. It was still a nice day. A great day. As Spitfire reached the top of the steps, she was waiting for him, leaning against a lamppost.

"Look at you," he said. "Like the cat who got the cream."

She winked. "The perfect hit, I'd say."

"Eventually."

"Meh. Semantics. We got our man. The right way. Shit, what about the photo? Proof of completion?"

Spitfire smirked. "Let me worry about that. City morgues aren't generally that hard to get into. Whether there are any distinguishing features on the poor bastard is another matter." He walked up to her. "I thought you'd decided Bakov talking to the CIA was a good thing."

"Come on, Spitfire. I know you were holding back before." She stared into his eyes. "We both know he got a good look at me. If I ended up on some agency list, that would be my career over before it started. My life, too, most probably."

He stared back at her. "You might be more perceptive than I've given you credit for, Ms Vanilla. And more resourceful. You'll be a top assassin. If that's what you want."

"Of course it is. Why do you say that?"

He lowered his head. "No reason."

"All right, then," she said. "Because Bakov had to die. It was the principle of it as much as anything else. We were sent here to carry out a hit. And we didn't stop until we'd finished the job. Because we're professionals. And that's what we do."

Spitfire smiled. "Yes, Acid. Yes, it bloody well is."

CHAPTER 40

Beowulf Caesar was reclining in the four-poster bed he'd had set up in the back room of his Soho HQ when there was a knock on the door.

"Who is it?"

There was a pause, and then Raaz's nasal West London drawl emanated through the wood. "Me. I've got your laptop, as requested, and Spitfire's on the line."

"Give me two minutes." He sighed and turned to the man lying beside him. "I'm afraid it's time for you to fuck off, dear boy. Duty calls and all that."

He watched as the lithe young thing climbed out of bed and got dressed. Once the show was over, Caesar sat up and swung his legs onto the thick shag-pile carpet. He was only wearing his dressing gown and he refastened it tight around his waist – a concession to Raaz – as he sauntered over to the door.

"You may enter," he told her as he opened it. She was carrying a silver tray, on which sat his laptop and a mobile phone. "Jesus, you could have warned me I needed a pair of shades."

She was wearing a luminous green tracksuit and had her

hair up in a matching headscarf. She ignored his comment and walked past him into the room.

"I set the emails up as you asked, and Spitfire is on line two. Once you're ready, you can... Oh, sorry!" She stopped as she saw the young man cowering in the corner.

"Don't worry about him," Caesar told her, before tutting and addressing the man. "You can take the mask off now."

Slowly, the young man peeled off the latex mask. It was one of those full, overhead types and a perfect likeness of Artem 'Mad Dog' Perchetka. He placed it on the side table and hurried from the room as Caesar shooed him away. After waiting a few seconds, he sat on the edge of the bed and beckoned Raaz to pass him the phone.

"Is he on?" he asked, getting a sharp nod in response. He leant back. "Spitfire, you saucy git! I hear you've got some rather wonderful news for me."

"That's right," came the reply. "Boris Bakov and Wilbur Das Biest have both been eradicated. I've already sent Raaz the proof." He paused, as if waiting for Caesar to say something. When he didn't, he continued. "Do you have a plan regarding Perchetka?"

Caesar picked up the mask. "Leave that rotten old sod to me. Been a bit of a struggle this one, hasn't it? But all's well that ends well."

"Absolutely..."

He sounded like he had more to say.

"Is there a problem?"

"No. Not as such. I was wondering if we might stay on here for a few more days. Acid has done well. She's a credit to you. I thought we could let her see the sights. It's her first time here and all that." He cleared his throat. "I'm just going to get some rest. It's been a tough week."

Caesar met Raaz's eye. She shook her head.

"Why not," he said. "We'll sort new flights for you both. You've earned it. Come in and see me when you get back."

He hung up and handed the phone back. Raaz curled her lip. "What are you going to do?"

"It's not for you to worry about. Now, let's get this over with. Get the Wacko-Jacko-obsessed prick on the line whilst I log in."

He grabbed the laptop and creaked it open to reveal two browser windows side by side. One was his secure email portal and the other was Annihilation Pest Control's primary bank account in the Cayman Islands. Raaz had already logged into both.

"It's ringing," she whispered, handing him the phone.

He took it and held it to his ear, scanning the two emails Raaz had drafted that morning.

"Mr Caesar," a gruff voice came on the line. "It is good to hear from you."

"Is it?" he bellowed. "Yes, I suspect it is. A surprise perhaps, also?"

Perchetka spluttered. "I don't know what you mean."

"No, of course not. Well, old boy. It's all done and dusted. We've fulfilled the contract at our end." The line went quiet. Then he heard a muffled discussion in Russian as if Perchetka had placed his hand over the microphone. "Are you still there?"

"I am here."

"Lovely stuff. Do you have a computer to hand?" He leaned over the laptop and used the mouse pad to send the first email. "I'm sending you proof of the hit now. I've got to say the poor bastard looks more like a bag of mince than a man, but you can just about make out that thick brow of his. Even a speeding subway train couldn't destroy it."

Perchetka sniffed. "I can see. So, it is done."

"That's right. And if you wouldn't mind releasing the fee whilst we're on the call together, we can box this off right now as a job well done. Another success story. Another happy client. *Da?*"

"I will send payment now," Perchetka replied. He didn't sound happy.

Good. The pitiable shag stick.

Caesar viewed the numbers in his bank account, all eight wonderful digits. He had to refresh the browser window once and then twice before a new amount appeared, showing Perchetka had sent payment.

"Perfect," he said. "It's arrived."

"Fine. We're done."

"Oh, not quite, old chap." Caesar returned to his emails and sent the second message Raaz had prepared. "You might want to take a peek at this next photo I'm sending over."

He opened the photo on his own screen. A close-up of Wilbur Das Biest with both his eyes shot out.

"Do you have it?"

Perchetka was quiet, but he could hear him breathing. "I have it," he replied.

"Good. Now, let this be an important learning point for you, sweetie. Don't fuck with me and my organisation. Ever! This is my world, Perchetka. My industry. You don't know who you're dealing with and, to be honest, you've embarrassed yourself. I'd suggest you lie low for a while."

"Fuck you."

"Not a chance. But I mean it. If I even hear about you planning something, I'll fucking crucify you. And that isn't an empty threat or even a euphemism. You do not mess with Beowulf Caesar or Annihilation Pest Control. Capeesh?" There was no answer. He handed Raaz the phone with a sneer. "Hang up on this wretched puss bag, will you?"

"Very good, boss," she said, doing as told and gathering the laptop and phone back onto the silver tray. "Do you need me to do anything else?"

"No. Leave me for now," he said, lying back on the bed.

As Raaz backed out of the room and shut the door, he let out a groan. Now he had some thinking to do. A decision to make. But his reputation and that of his organisation were still intact. There'd be other Perchetkas, of course, other pretenders to his crown, eager to take him down and destroy what he'd created. But let them come. He'd be ready for them.

This was Annihilation Pest Control.

The best assassin organisation in the business.

The best in the goddamn world.

CHAPTER 41

TWO WEEKS LATER...

Spitfire stood in front of the full-length mirror in his bedroom and checked himself. He was wearing his favourite navy suit, so dark it was almost black in some lights, coupled with a burgundy shirt and a mustard tie. He looked good. An ace face. He flicked out his shirt cuffs and adjusted his tie. He was ready. Outwardly, at least.

"Looking hot," Acid said, raising herself from the bed behind him. Their eyes met in the mirror. "Will you be long?"

"I don't know." He remained with his back to her, speaking to her reflection. "It's the first time I'll have seen him since we got back. I expect he'll want a full rundown of what happened. And then..."

"You'll tell him?"

He turned around. "I'll tell him."

"How do you think he'll take it?"

Spitfire sucked in a deep breath as he considered his response. The truth was, he didn't have a damn clue. If anything, he'd been putting off thinking about it. But he'd had plenty to distract himself with. After he'd got the photo of Bakov's remains, the plan had been to do some sightseeing, but they'd spent most of their remaining time in New York in bed. It was worth it. As was this last week, the two of them ensconced in Spitfire's bedroom, like John and Yoko if they'd had a very different message – chaos rather than peace. He'd only got dressed so he could go to the nearest shop for more supplies. Whisky, mainly. After only a few weeks, Acid's appetite for hard liquor seemed to be rivalled only by her voracious sexual appetite.

But he wasn't complaining. It was great.

She was great.

"It'll be fine," he told her. "I'll make him understand."

"Really?"

He smiled. He knew they could make it work. If they both knew the score and vowed never to let it get in the way. "Don't worry."

"Okay, cool." She ran her fingers through her hair, brushing it back from her face. "Then hurry back here. I'll be waiting for you."

He walked over to the bed. "I don't need telling."

She giggled and grabbed his face as he leaned down to kiss her. She was warm and soft, and he wished he could stay.

"I'll be back before you know it." He walked to the door.

"Stephen."

He hesitated. That had to stop. It wasn't on. Yet he couldn't help the shiver of hot energy that ran through him when she called him by his name. His real name.

"What is it?" he asked, turning back. Except he could tell from her face what she was about to say.

"I lo—"

"No!" He held a finger up to her. "Don't say it. Not until I've spoken to Caesar. We agreed." He turned around, but didn't leave right away. Dipping his head, he whispered back, "But I do too."

Then he grabbed his car keys and headed for the door.

"There you are, you old rogue. Good to see you," Caesar bellowed, as Spitfire entered his office. He stood up from his chair and gestured to the one on the other side of the desk. "Take a seat. Do you want a drink of anything? I've got a lovely bottle of Aussie gin kicking around somewhere that Hargreaves brought me back from his last job."

He pressed the buzzer on his desk to call Raaz, but Spitfire held his hand up. "Not for me. Thank you." He sat down and took his time to get comfy, crossing one leg over the other and resting his hand on his upper thigh. "Everything good?"

"Couldn't be better, now that we've shown up that rancid ball-sack Perchetka as the amateur he is. Great work over there. I know you had a few issues, but you got there in the end. I knew you would."

"It was Acid who got the hit. I can't take all the credit."

Caesar lowered his nose and peered at him as if looking over the top of an invisible pair of spectacles. "She did well."

"She did. She's going to be an excellent operative. She is already."

"Wonderful." He leaned back in his chair and rested his hands on his sizeable chest, steepling his fingers. "You both worked hard and didn't give up. I admire that."

"It's what we do."

"Exactly." He smiled and nodded. There was a pause. Spitfire tensed. Something was coming. These days he could read the boss like a book.

After a few more seconds, Caesar opened his mouth and held one finger up, like a bad actor signalling he'd remembered something. "I almost forgot. You were right to veto that silly idea

I had – about having Acid fall for you. I don't know what I was thinking. It was clever in theory, but it would have got too messy."

He carried on smiling, but his eyes told a different story. Spitfire looked down at his hands. He'd been inadvertently twisting the signet ring.

"I'd assumed she'd have fallen in love with you, and then when you shunned her it would break her heart. Just enough that it toughened her up. The way we need her to be." He sat forward in his chair. "So... if she was in love with you... and you were together... that's what I'd be asking you to do right now. Call things off. Break her heart." He stared without blinking as a cold emptiness speared Spitfire's chest and a heavy silence filled the air. It was crushing in its stillness. Then Caesar chuckled to himself and his tone was blithe once more. "But seeing as you didn't want to play, and it never happened, we don't have to worry about it. Do we?"

Spitfire held his gaze. "No."

"Is there a problem?"

"You know. Don't you?"

Caesar rolled his eyes. "Of course I pissing well know. I know everything. Especially about my operatives." He waved a fat finger at him. "You've had your fun, old boy. You've found out what's at the top of those pins, but now it's done. Over."

Spitfire swallowed. "What if we don't want that? What if we went forward as a couple? People have done it. Husband and wife teams exist in the industry. I know it's not what you wanted, but I think we could make it work..."

He trailed off. Caesar was batting his words away as if they were a bad smell. "I can't have it, Spitfire. I won't have it. It'll undermine other members of the organisation. We're a pack of lone wolves here at Annihilation Pest Control. You know that.

Families and relationships aren't for us. They complicate things."

A scrummage of thoughts and ideas flooded Spitfire's head. None of them gave him the response he needed. There wasn't one.

"Finish it," Caesar said. "Or you're done. Both of you. Do you understand?"

Spitfire nodded. Caesar wasn't referring to them collecting their unemployment papers.

He thought of Acid, waiting for him in bed. How would she take it? How would he? A passing thought came to him that maybe they could run away together, go into hiding away from Caesar and the industry.

But where would they go?

And what would they do once they got there

No.

He'd been stupid to think he could have a life with Acid. They'd been living in a fantasy world these last two weeks.

Being a part of Annihilation Pest Control was his entire life. He'd flirted with the idea of being Stephen Carter again, and had even enjoyed holidaying in his old persona, but that man was dead and gone.

He was Spitfire Creosote.

This life was all he knew.

He couldn't give it up. Not even for her.

And she'd be okay. Like Caesar said, this could be a good thing. She'd be devastated initially, but in time she'd recover and would be stronger for it. With her soul and heart hardened, she would become a top assassin. One of the best.

"Are you sure I can rely on you to do what's needed, old boy?" Caesar asked, raising his eyebrows questioningly.

Spitfire got to his feet. What was that thing pathetic people said? If you love someone, set them free. For the first time in his life, he understood what it meant.

"Yes, boss," he said, rolling his shoulders back. "Consider it done."

THE END

WANT MORE ACID?

GET YOUR FREE BOOK

Discover how Acid Vanilla transformed from a typical London teenager into the world's deadliest female assassin.

Get the Acid Vanilla Prequel Novel available FREE at:

www.matthewhattersley.com/mak

CAN YOU HELP?

Enjoyed this book? You can make a big difference

Honest reviews of my books help bring them to the attention of other readers. If you've enjoyed this book I would be very grateful if you could spend just five minutes leaving a review (it can be as short as you like) on the book's Amazon page.

ALSO BY MATTHEW HATTERSLEY

Have you read them all?

———

The Acid Vanilla series

The Watcher

Acid Vanilla is an elite assassin, struggling with her mental health. Spook Horowitz is a mild-mannered hacker who saw something she shouldn't. Acid needs a holiday. Spook needs Acid Vanilla to NOT be coming to kill her. But life rarely works out the way we want it to.

BUY IT HERE

Seven Bullets

Acid Vanilla was the deadliest assassin at Annihilation Pest Control. That was until she was tragically betrayed by her former colleagues. Now, fuelled by an insatiable desire for vengeance, Acid travels the globe to carry out her bloody retribution. After all, a girl needs a hobby...

BUY IT HERE

Making a Killer

How it all began. Discover Acid Vanilla's past, her meeting with Caesar and how she became the deadliest female assassin in the world.

FREE TO DOWNLOAD HERE

GET YOUR FREE BOOK

Discover how Acid Vanilla transformed from a typical London teenager into the world's deadliest female assassin.

Get the Acid Vanilla Prequel Novel:
Making a Killer available FREE at:

www.matthewhattersley.com/mak

ABOUT THE AUTHOR

Over the last twenty years Matthew Hattersley has toured Europe in rock n roll bands, trained as a professional actor and founded a theatre and media company. He's also had a lot of dead end jobs...

Now he writes high-octane pulp action thrillers and crime fiction.

He lives with his wife and daughter in Derbyshire, UK and doesn't feel that comfortable writing about himself in the third person.

COPYRIGHT

A Boom Boom Press ebook

First published in Great Britain in April 2023 by Boom Boom Press.

Ebook first published in 2023 by Boom Boom Press.

Copyright © Boom Boom Press 2015 - 2023

The moral right of Matthew Hattersley to be identified as the author of this work has been asserted by him in accordance with the copyright, Designs and Patents Act 1988.

All the characters in this book are fictitious, and any resemblance to actual persons living or dead is purely coincidental.

All rights reserved. No part of this publication may be reproduced, stored in a retrieval system or transmitted in any form or by any means, without the prior permission in writing of the publisher, nor to be otherwise circulated in any form of binding or cover other than that in which it is published without a similar condition, including this condition, being imposed on the subsequent purchaser.

Printed in Great Britain
by Amazon